KILLING AT THE CAT

A MYSTERY BY
CARLENE MILLER

KILLING AT THE CAT

A MYSTERY

BY CARLENE MILLER

NEW VICTORIA PUBLISHERS
NORWICH, VERMONT

Published by New Victoria Publishers, Inc., a feminist literary and cultural organization, PO Box 27, Norwich, VT 05055-0027

1   2   3   4   5   2002   2001   2000   1999   1998

Cover design Claudia McKay

Printed in Canada

Library of Congress Cataloging-in-Publication-Data
Miller, Carlene, 1935-
Killing at the Cat : a mystery / by Carlene Miller.
   p.   cm.
ISBN 0-934678-95-2
I.   Title.
PS3563.I3763K55   1998
813'.54--dc21   98-25229
                                                      CIP

For my parents who introduced me to mystery and detective novels,
for the friends who have stood with me—
and for all those marvelous teachers who do not yield.

CHAPTER ONE

The Cat slowly woke up to the night as I took command of my favorite stool at one end of the L-shaped bar. Resting my foot on the polished rail, I watched Alice and the other servers whom I counted as friends, remove chairs from table tops with silent speed. Hints of the evening menu drifted through the strands of blue beads separating the bar from the dining room, decorated in soft grays and imitation Greek. On a small raised wooden platform backing a dance floor, guitars, a set of drums, and a keyboard waited.

Hal, the early bartender, nodded to me as he finished checking his stock of clean glasses and supplies. His efficient movements belied his stocky build as he prepared my highball—bourbon with lemon-flavored Perrier and three large cubes of ice. He seemed more comfortable now that he was in his third month of mixing drinks in a lesbian bar. Marilyn Neff, the owner and his sister, had introduced him to the staff and regulars with, "He's my baby brother and needs a job bad enough to take one from his queer sister." At my raised eyebrows she had remarked to Hal, "Pay no attention to Lexy there. That look isn't because you're a man. It's because I said bad instead of badly. She taught English before she became a reporter."

I had bristled at the tinge of derision in her voice, but stifled a reaction, having learned early on that her ownership of The Cat included an umbrella teasing policy covering her regulars. From the moment she discovered I used to be a teacher, she nagged me for wasting myself writing feature fluff for a newspaper that talked down to women. I hadn't convinced her yet that I left the classroom for very good reasons. Maybe I hadn't convinced her because I hadn't convinced myself yet. My gut reasons were still too raw. Anyway, I intended to do battle with *The Ledger* from the inside.

The double front doors opened, accompanied by the rushing sounds of traffic from the busy city street. An imposing woman descended the three steps and crossed to the bar, the gloss of a Florida tan emphasizing her smooth cheeks and strong jawline, a simple gold chain around her neck and a few gold bracelets her only jewelry. Her long dark hair was gathered up stylishly. Half-seated, half-standing, one arm resting on the polished wood, she watched Hal pour her pink chablis. Then, sipping, she examined the empty dance area.

Her pain was tangible—her dark eyes lackluster, her smiles empty of warmth, an air of inner angry retreat effectively shielding her. Rita Burgess's partner had been dead nearly a year now, another young woman too early a victim of cancer. As I lifted my glass in greeting and received a curt nod, I wondered how long she would continue to grieve so deeply she couldn't get on with life. Then we both turned our heads as two hetero couples entered noisily and sought out a corner table.

"Tourists," Hal sneered through nearly closed lips.

"And the freaks are on display," I said.

"You're no freak, Lexy." His gruff tone betrayed his discomfort.

"Not many other straight men would agree with you."

Not certain how to answer that Hal turned back to chopping slices of lemon and wedges of lime.

I looked again at the foursome, then turned back to stare at my reflection in the mirror. I have the same swimmer's build, strong shoulders, square face and long jawline as my Uncle Kurt. Even his grin—or so all my relatives say. But it is having his thick auburn hair that means the most to me. My mother's twin, he died early in the Vietnam War before I was old enough to really remember him. I grew up with his pre-army, teenage pictures all around the house, snapshots of him combing his hair in imitation of Elvis. One picture even has his head turned to show off his ducktail.

My first defiant act as a teenager was to go to a barber, snapshots in hand. When I came home without my waves of long hair, my mother stared in horror, then clasped me to her, crying. I knew the tears were for her twin. I still sport the same basic cut—without the ducktail.

I suspected Hal was right about the foursome; they certainly looked like they thought they were slumming in a lesbian bar. I watched their reflections in the bar mirror, their eyes following two girls in boots, levis and checkered shirts, who selected a table near the dance floor and called to Hal for beers. One of the men ran the tip of his tongue along the inside of his upper lip. The woman next to him kept sucking in her cheek. The other couple pretended indifference but kept the girls in their line of vision.

"Damn them!" I shrugged my shoulders angrily as Hal's quick look told me I had spoken out loud. I hated the feeling of being on exhibit. I felt it sometimes even from straight friends who did their best to keep my gender preference from clouding their attitudes toward me. The anger melted into

8

self-reproach as I remembered the comment of a fellow teacher. "Sometimes, Lexy, you wear your lesbianism on your sleeve. That triangle ring ought to be enough."

Marilyn Neff strode in from the hallway that led past restrooms, her office, and a supply room to an emergency exit door. She was taller and less stocky than her brother. Tight black leggings were nearly hidden by a loose fitting rose tunic with wide sleeves dropping below the elbows. Short gray-blond hair still glistened from a recent shower.

A trace of New York remained in her speech despite a move to Florida when she was much younger. I guessed her to be on the young side of fifty but, like all others with good sense, seldom challenged her with personal questions. She was called 'Admiral' behind her back though I suspect she knew and liked it. She did run The Cat with a strong hand, keeping it a safe and attractive place for what she called 'uptown lesbian trade,' those willing to pay enough for drinks to cover a good band, or to order expensive meals in the dining room. Rumor had it that she also owned a smaller bar off Highway 17/92 that catered to a lesbian leather clientele.

She came over to the bar and said, "Hal, I've set the push bar on the side door so it will open for the plumber. A Friday night is no time for a stopped-up toilet. We need all three working."

"Think that's a good idea? We had those skinheads back there last week."

Marilyn frowned. "The cops warned them off. And I don't want a work-man coming through the front. Hey, Lexy, no big story to cover?" She was sniping again and didn't expect an answer as she took a stool next to me, waving to the woman at the other end of the bar. "We've got to get Rita a woman. It's time she let the dead go."

"In her own time, Marilyn."

"So what about you? Aren't you tired of quick fixes?"

My laugh was stilted. "You run the bar. I'll run me." Marilyn turned and watched a server carry a tray of drinks to the foursome. "I've seen that woman in here before. And not with a man."

I turned. "Which one?"

"The fake blonde too old for that cutesy dress. Probably been sampling the other side and thinks it's gutsy to bring her husband here. Keep an eye on them, Hal. I'm in no mood for trouble." She stomped off toward the kitchen.

Hal watched her go. "Hope she takes it easy on the help."

"Problems?" I asked.

"Not really. It's just that she's been in a mood lately that makes her what our grandmother used to call waspish."

9

The cowgirl duo called out, "Hit us again, Hal." I watched him fill two frosted mugs and slide them toward a waiting server. Suddenly there was a familiar pressure on my shoulder. Lips brushed my cheek and I inhaled the light scent of orange bath gel. Jodi Fleming settled onto a stool next to me, trim and neat in expensive tan slacks and an antique-white shirt with its sleeves rolled up to the elbows, yellow and white-gold bracelets on each of her forearms.

Even though it had been a year since we last shared a bed, she still stirred me. I couldn't look at her without remembering the exciting arch of her body under mine, the playful whispering in my ear. She swept her fingers through her ash-blonde curls in a familiar gesture.

"Still into bourbon, Lex? I'm into vodka sours, two olives." She had raised her voice for Hal's benefit. Without looking our way, he lifted a jar of olives, the kind stuffed with almonds. Her quick appreciative laugh was a sound I used to love to smother with my mouth.

They say that dreams, seemingly hours in length, take only a few minutes of actual sleep time. A wide-awake flashback can occur in a matter of seconds. In the time it took Hal to prepare Jodi's drink, I relived our meeting that first time.

It was the summer after I had quit teaching and was sampling lesbian spaces—sometimes with a group, sometimes on a date, sometimes alone. I had been most at ease at The Cat, and by the end of the summer had settled in as a regular. But as fall approached I began to feel an uneasiness, a discomfort. I knew it was a sense of guilt at not returning to the classroom and went into a sort of hibernation, avoiding friends and locales. After three weeks, Marilyn had called and demanded my presence or she would consider me a woman overboard and dump life preservers on my doorstep.

I had arrived well into the evening on a busy Saturday. Even my usual seat at the bar was taken. As I stood on the bottom step surveying the room, I felt myself captured in someone's gaze. In the darkness of the dance area, slashed by moving lights. I could tell only that she maneuvered her dance partner to keep me in view.

I tried to break eye contact with her, but couldn't. Insolently she tongued her companion's ear and trailed her hand from shoulder blade to thigh.

At that moment, Marilyn appeared and dragged me off to a table just vacated. I chose a chair so I could sit with my back to the dance floor and tried to concentrate on Marilyn's gruff, good-natured lecture.

Then came the finger slipped under the back of my collar and the sultry voice in my ear. "Your turn, Red."

I snapped my head around and we nearly touched lips. "No one calls me that."

"Then give me a name." I clenched my teeth to resist her feline magnetism, but lost the struggle. "Lexy." It was difficult keeping the inner quaver from my voice.

"Come dance with me, Lexy. I'm Jodi."

Taking the hand she offered and rising from the table, I heard the scrape of Marilyn's chair and a muttered, "Oh, shit."

At the conclusion of our last dance, she had said, with casual certainty, "It's time to go. I'll follow you to your place. I intend to have you in your own bed."

Several hours later I had awakened to the dim grayness of early dawn seeping into my bedroom, startled at the serenity of Jodi's naked form in bed next to me. In fact, the night had not been serene. Unusually aggressive, I had clasped and grappled, driven on by an acquiescence and yielding she had in no way indicated at The Cat. Sprawled as she was, I could see the triangle of fair hair. As I remembered the down like softness against my face, a moan escaped my throat and I closed my eyes, but my lids flew up at the feather touch of fingers on my lips.

Jodi's smile then was cryptically thin and brief, her words passionlessly spoken. "Where do you hurt, Lex? Here?" I parted my lips for her fingers but her hand lowered to grasp my throat gently. "Here?" Then the fingers twirled about my breast and plucked at the rising hardness. "Maybe here. No." With torturing slowness she moved to cup the mound between my legs. "I think here. Do you agree…Red?"

I had no breath with which to reply. Nor to object when, with surprising speed and strength, she seized me under my arms and nearly lifted me to my knees. Then with bruising grips, she clutched my thighs and positioned me over her face. I had not known such words and cries could be torn from me.

My awareness returned sharply back to The Cat as Jodi plucked an olive from her glass saying, "I think I'll be into these for awhile."

Her being into things is what had finally dampened our relationship. One moment she was into learning to read tarot cards, the next, it was coaching T-ball. Two months of almost nonstop volunteerism at a woman's crisis center was followed by dozens of never finished cross-stitch patterns. And at the height of each passion everything else was relegated deep into the background—including a parade of jobs and, ultimately, me. I chose to retreat before I became part of that list she was once committed to. When she finally noticed my absence, it surprised more than saddened her.

Now Jodi said, "Alone on a Friday night, Lex? Or are you waiting for

11

someone?" There was a bit of taunting in her tone.

"Maybe I'm waiting." I finished my drink and swirled the ice cubes in my glass catching Hal's attention for another.

Jodi's face became uncharacteristically contemplative. "She'll come along. You're too good a person not to luck out eventually. Now and then I'm sorry it won't be me."

"But just once in awhile," I countered.

The seriousness evaporated. "I don't change, Lexy. Can't. Heard what my latest is?"

At the slow shake of my head, she answered, "Karate."

"Karate!" Marilyn had reappeared. She turned sideways to Jodi, bent her knees and struck a stiff-arm pose. "Take you on any time, tough woman."

"Don't listen to her." Hal placed a fresh drink before me. "Must be twenty-five, thirty years since we took those classes, Sis."

"You thought it would make you attractive to Ann Pau!" she explained to Jodi and me. "And I started going to gay bars and some of those butches scared me."

"Not as much as the whole business scared Mom when that cop friend of Dad's told them about seeing you go into one," Hal said over his shoulder as he moved on to prepare more drink orders.

Marilyn snorted. "But wasn't Dad something! Don't know where a bricklayer like him got his open mind." In a lower voice she added, "He told old Hank to mind his own business then sat on the front stoop and waited for me to come home. When he first started talking, I could hardly hear him 'cause my heart was pounding so damn loud at having been found out. But then I think I must have listened to him with my mouth hanging open." She surveyed the room. "He told me that if girls were what I wanted, fine. Just be choosy and not try to depend on bars to find them. Course that was easier said than done. Part of why I try to run a decent place here."

Jodi and I exchanged knowing glances. I was sure her thoughts were skimming the past as mine had moments before. Jodi asked, "Where'd you get the name for this place?"

Marilyn sighed. "My first true love. She was dangerously attractive. Swore too loud. Drank too much. Drove too fast. When the glow faded a little and I dared to caution her, she just said, 'I'm as sure-footed as a cat. Never slip, slide, or fall.'"

"What happened to you two?" I asked.

"Oh, I took Hal with me to a drive-in one night. Still had them in those days. Recognized her car and went over at intermission. She was making out

12

with some hippie chick. Broke my heart. One of a bunch to do that, of course." I couldn't miss the brittle tone. "Still, first love is first love. So..." Marilyn's voice broke off then as she noted the hurried entrance of an attractive, slender woman dressed in a stylish deep purple suit, her blonde, fashionably permed curls dangling coquettishly over her face. Marilyn moved quickly to meet her at the bottom of the steps. They seemed to be having words with each other though I couldn't hear what it was about above the din of the bar. The woman reached to put a hand on Marilyn's arm, but the older woman stepped back from the contact. With a jerk of her head and an abrupt turn, Marilyn led the way past us and down the hallway, presumably to her office beyond the restrooms.

I glanced at Hal who was removing Jodi's glass and wiping the moisture from the counter. He just shrugged an 'I don't know' and moved away, but not before I saw the hard cast to his face. Not for the first time I thought he looked older than his sister, rather than younger.

As she slid off the stool, Jodi commented, "That's the most personal talk I've ever heard from the Admiral. Nice to see her lay all that stuffy efficiency aside for a minute."

I shook my head, only half amused by her tone. "Efficiency isn't all bad, Jodi." She stroked my throat with a single finger, but the softness of her brown eyes had already faded and I could see that the pupils were set for prowling. I was forgotten before she completed her turn, but I watched her as she wandered off to chat with the band as it began sound checks.

As the evening progressed, I stayed at my corner of the bar, sipping my second drink slowly, watching others drink and dance and converse. The band followed its usual pattern of three fast, then three slow. I declined the occasional invitation to join the crowd on the parquet dance floor. This was one of those nights when I placed myself in the midst of noise and motion despite feeling silent and secluded within myself.

At one point I noticed that Rita had left. We both would be going home to empty apartments, but at least mine wasn't haunted by a remembered presence in the same way. I noticed, too, that Marilyn was back, circulating between lounge and dining areas. I didn't see the purple-suit woman.

While I was trying to decide about a third drink, I heard an irritated "Excuse me!" from Jodi. I swiveled on my stool and saw her shouldering her way between the couple Marilyn had commented on earlier. The fake blonde was either arguing or pleading. As she went down the hall toward the restrooms, the man returned to their table, spoke to the other couple, and they gathered their things to leave. Next, I turned to see Jodi tap a petite Hispanic woman on the shoulder and lead her out onto the dance floor.

13

I decided on that third drink, planning to dilute it later with a solid meal. Hal had been joined by his co-bartender Melody, a large woman with easy, graceful movements.

As she flipped down a napkin for my drink, she said, "Time we were seeing you with someone, Lexy."

"Already heard that from the Admiral, Melody." I was careful not to shorten her name, something she never permitted. She even insisted on calling Hal, Harold.

Her eyes noted Jodi on the dance floor. "That one's gone, you know, and by your own choice. You need to let go all the way."

I frowned. She gave a musical laugh which went with her name, as did her choice of partner who played the clarinet and was much in demand for local musicals and jazz groups.

As she drew draft beers for the waiting server, she continued, "Admiral is a real whirlwind tonight. Who's she mad at?"

"I don't know. Hal—" At her look I switched to, "Harold said she's been in a tough mood lately."

I talked with Melody, Hal and others as the place got busier. I liked watching the interplay—couples veiled in intimacy or shrouded in tension. Women clustered at combined tables, joking and gossiping. Individuals observing or seeking. And I liked the varied voices warming the air-conditioned coldness whenever the band took a break. I especially liked the staccato sounds of the two bartenders at work, the play of ice with glass…

In a moment of unusual quiet, there was a heavy thud from the hallway. A concerned Hal went to investigate. He came back to report that he had been checking out the alley because he found some empty bottle containers overturned. To Marilyn he said, "I closed the exit door so it can't be opened from the outside. If no one hears him knocking, your plumber will just have to come through the front; if he ever comes."

Alice, picking up a tray of drinks, gave a guttural laugh and shook her head toward the dance floor. "The plumber better get here soon." Expertly she hoisted a large tray and moved past Marilyn who was giving her brother a sardonic half-smile.

"We don't have it as easy as you men in the pissing department," Marilyn said. "Hand me the phone book. That plumber should have been here by now. I'm going to call the emergency number and tell them to get someone the hell over here."

Just then I saw Jodi climbing the steps to the front door with her right hand, bracelets clustered about her wrist, casually tucked into a back pocket of her dance partner's jeans. I couldn't stop the twinge in my groin. Ice

14

clunked against my teeth as I drained my glass and then tapped it on the bar for Melody's attention.

Firmly Marilyn said, "Go have dinner, Lexy."

I jerked back my head and narrowed my eyes, but she deliberately avoided looking at me. I took a deep breath and released it slowly with a hiss, controlling a temper I very seldom lost. It drew a ghost of a smile from Melody, but Marilyn had already moved off to the telephone. I slid from the stool, bumping into the male plumber who must have come in past Jodi and her date. A server led him to the restroom, first making certain the area was clear of patrons while I wove my way through tables and people toward the dining room. Seeing Marilyn, I told her of the workman's arrival. Before leaving to supervise him, she strong-armed me into joining a couple of former friends Jodi and I had sometimes doubled with on weekend excursions to arts-and-crafts fairs.

She commanded, "Make nice. Good friends are good friends no matter who's not with whom. How's that for fancy English, 'Teach'?"

I ended up enjoying dinner and the light chatter. I passed on dessert, however, and wandered back out to the bar to say my good nights.

Marilyn was writing the plumber a check as he openly gawked at the fluid tableau of females. She had to wave the check in front of him to divert his attention. He stuttered a thank you, scribbled 'paid' on the bill and gathered the supplies at his feet while staring at the dancers. Marilyn asked a server to get more rolls of toilet paper from the supply room.

"I'll do it. Need a bit of a break." Melody sidled out from behind the bar.

I decided to take a similar break before leaving and followed her down the hall. As I pushed inward on the swinging door of the restroom, Melody reached for the knob of the door to the supply room. I held the swinging door open for a figure to exit and was surprised to see a slim girl in sleek leather pants and leather vest of a wide mesh through which I glimpsed splashes of tattoos. About to enter a stall, I froze at a falsetto shriek. I rushed out of the restroom only to be bounced against the door by a speeding Hal who then steadied a stumbling, gagging Melody. I stepped in front of them.

Sprawled awkwardly in the dim confines of the supply room was the woman in the purple suit, with her torso twisted to face upwards and staring at me with vacant eyes. As I registered how terribly still she was, how bloodlessly pale her skin was and how oddly her head was angled, I remembered how determinedly she had approached Marilyn earlier in the evening. I also remembered the Admiral's obvious displeasure.

Pushing past me, Hal hurriedly bent down to check her pulse, then

15

snapped, "Oh my god! Melody, see if there's a doctor in the house. Go on! Quickly! Quietly! You, Lexy, get Marilyn and for godsake, don't let anyone come down the hall!"

As I hurried to obey him, my insides curdled. I knew in an instant that this was going to involve more than a doctor. Much more.

CHAPTER TWO

The silence of The Cat was unnatural, relieved only by the low murmur of curious and agitated voices issuing from the dining room where Marilyn had gathered the entire staff. I sat alone at the bar, Hal and Mclody at a nearby table, leaning with their elbows on the table, their chins on their hands, as we all waited for the police.

I was unaware of Marilyn's return from the dining room until she squeezed my shoulder. "You could have gone with the others, Lexy."

"I called the paper, Marilyn."

"What!" She tightened her grip and I actually winced in pain. She lowered her voice. "You're picking now to become a real reporter?"

I frowned at her reflection in the bar mirror. "I am a real reporter. I've been divided between Features and News for months." I kept my voice low as well. "I called the night dispatcher and got lucky. It was Roger Lowe. He's...a brother. Agreed to let me be reporter-on-the-scene. I guess it's a busy night over there and it's better if I make the report, considering it happened at The Cat." I turned and looked at her directly but received no reaction. I continued, "We can keep most of it off the record that way, you see. For instance, who is that woman back there?"

I could read behind her eyes that she was adjusting her relationship to me. She answered, "You know the line I have to walk if I want to stay in business." She stared hard without blinking, "I don't need the publicity."

"Come on, Marilyn. Don't you know that's why I called the paper? Being a reporter doesn't stop me being Lexy at the same time. I'll do right by The Cat. I'll be fair."

Her hand was still on my shoulder. She slid it to the back of my neck and this time the squeeze was gentle. We were friends again. Then she jerked her head at the sound of sirens. "This isn't going to be like a school board or city council meeting, Lexy."

I wondered at her air of detached calm. It had been the same earlier when, after consulting with Hal and the summoned doctor, she had closed

17

off the hallway. Then, with a sharp wave she halted the band in mid-song and stepped onto the low platform. There had been sudden silence and total attention in the lounge although intermittent clatter continued from the dining room beyond.

In a steady but strangely emotionless voice, she had announced that there had been a bad accident near the restroom and she was going to have to call the police. The silence had then thickened with tension. Being out enough to come to a lesbian bar wasn't the same as being open with the police. Marilyn had added, "If you want to leave money on the tables covering what you've had, it would be appreciated. Now hurry, please."

There had been immediate comprehension. Hal emitted an old-fashioned "Wow!" accompanied by a blunter "Shit!" from Melody. Marilyn had repeated the same message in the dining room before calling the police.

Even now, hearing the thud of car doors outside, I didn't know whether to label it guts or insanity. Two uniformed policemen rushed in and Marilyn took them to the supply room. One quickly returned, opened the front door and called out, "Tell them we need a detective and all the trimmings. Then check the side alley. Watch your step."

He walked back toward the bar area and I thought I caught a flicker of recognition in his eyes as he looked at me. He picked up on the sounds from the dining room and detoured that way. Merely glancing in, he returned to us noting the money on the tables he passed.

"Where is everyone?"

He directed the question to Hal who rubbed the back of his neck and said, "Gone."

"And who's responsible for that?"

"Me." Marilyn stood framed in the light from the hallway. "People sitting at the bar heard me call you and the next thing I knew the place was empty."

They stared at each other antagonistically for a moment. Then the policeman looked out over the lounge area again. "And they just all happened to leave you money to cover their bills…" The sarcasm was heavy.

"I serve nice people."

He pushed his cap back a little. "Don't you mean nice fags." He spoke the last two words in a sneering tone.

"The term is lesbians. Fag is a derogatory term for a male homosexual." I cut in, not looking at him as I spoke, and so saw Melody mouth a "Be careful, Lexy."

The policeman stepped closer to me, the recognition stronger in his eyes. "You're a reporter. Right? *The Ledger*. Name's Hyatt…yeah. You

18

asked me questions last month over that hassle at the abortion clinic. Might know you'd be here in a place like this."

I glared, but Marilyn hurried between us. She asked permission to have the staff clear tables in the dining room, but I was sure her intent was to separate me and the man in blue. I slipped from the stool and walked to the hallway entrance. Ignoring a warning from Melody to stay put, I got to the door of Marilyn's office before the other policeman backed out of the supply room and ordered my retreat. I reluctantly joined Hal and Melody at their table while he stretched a yellow crime-scene tape across the entrance, about head high.

"What were you doing, Lexy?" Melody's cheeks were splotchy and red but there was still a whiteness about her mouth.

"Never did get to tend to business in the restroom." I knew that sounded flip but I wasn't going to admit to what I was really trying to do. I couldn't remember whether or not I had seen a purse when the woman entered or near her in the supply room. Figured it was worth checking for one in Marilyn's office since the Admiral obviously wasn't offering me an identification. I pointed my thumb over my shoulder. "Who is…was she, Hal?"

He gave me the steady, wide-eyed look students always used when preparing to lie. Before he could answer, a rush of people entered the front door and clattered down the steps. Most carried equipment and all had ID badges clipped to pockets or dangling. They passed our table without a glance and ducked under the yellow tape to follow the policeman waiting there.

A policeman ordered Hal, Melody and me to join the others in the dining room. I looked through the strands of beads but, since I couldn't see down the hallway, I finally let myself be tugged by Melody to a table. Our only knowledge of the activities beyond the beaded entrance was occasional noise and changing voices.

Finally there was the clinking sound of beads thrust aside as a brown-haired man around forty with an athletic build and clean-cut look strode toward us. The casual suit over a sport shirt made me wonder if he had been out on a date. What could have been a pleasant face was intentionally bland for us. I almost smiled at the orange spiral notebook he carried in his right hand. Three just like it were in my car and a dozen more at home. The man paused to scan the room and then spoke to a woman who had entered after him, motioning her toward the silently watching staff. She nodded and moved to them as the man turned his attention back to Hal, Melody and me.

The detective introduced himself as Sergeant Glen Ziegler and asked each of us to identify ourselves, checking what we said against information in his notebook probably collected from the first police on the scene. Or from Marilyn. He politely asked Hal to follow him back out into the lounge.

I watched the female detective move through the tables of staff asking questions and jotting down notes. She wore a dark green skirt with a lighter green, loose-cut jacket. The dangling earrings and strands of necklaces looked out of place on the job. I thought the same when watching televised women's professional golf and tennis tournaments. I always imagined I could hear some agent or relative saying, "Wear jewelry so you look feminine. You don't want people thinking you're one of those dyke jocks." I supposed it was the same for women on the police force.

Melody, beginning to seem more herself, let out an impatient sigh. I asked, "What do you think?"

"I don't know. I don't know anything. I didn't know that woman and I don't know why Marilyn took her in the back and then left her there." The spots of color had faded from her cheeks and her mouth was more relaxed. "Do you think she had a heart attack?"

I shrugged noncommittally. "If so, there's the question of what she was doing in the supply room."

"True. That place is little more than a large walk-in closet." After a few seconds of silence she tapped me on the wrist. "Lexy, go easy on being gay when they talk to you."

"I'm tired of that, Melody." I lightened the retort with, "And it's kind of obvious considering where we are."

"That's not what I mean and you know it." The old Melody's easy air of control had returned. "But if we don't push it at them, maybe they won't push at us about it so hard. And that might be a help to Marilyn...to The Cat." She tilted her head at me firmly requesting acquiescence.

"All right. I'll try." But I couldn't keep from adding, "if they let me. They're probably hoping they've got a butch/femme lover's quarrel turned murder here."

Immediately I regretted putting the thought I didn't know I had into words. I could tell it bothered Melody too, by the way she shifted uncomfortably and started smoothing her hair.

Soon a policeman came to escort Melody to the lounge and I sat alone resorting to making notes on a napkin. I had seen no signs of how the woman had died. No blood, no weapon. And Hal had immediately put a finger to her carotid artery checking for signs of life. But detectives and crime-scene personnel certainly didn't swoop in like this on death by natural causes or accident.

More than two hours had passed between her arrival and Melody finding her dead. Meanwhile dozens of people had been up and down that hallway. And for a time the back door had been propped open. Had Marilyn expected the woman to remain in her office or to leave? Did she go to the supply room on her own or was she forced there without anyone seeing? Was she killed on purpose? Accidentally?

I had been gripping my pen as though the pressure would help me think. I relaxed and flexed my fingers. I had to know more, even if I didn't include it in my article. I had to know who that woman was. What she was to Marilyn? Why had she come to The Cat tonight?

I was more than ready for my interview when I was ushered back to the lounge area. I wanted it over with so I could get on with my own investigating. The Cat was one of the few certainties of my life right now and I didn't like that being threatened. I tried to cloak my impatience as Ziegler divided his attention between me and his notebook while he asked basic questions. Then he zeroed in on my eyes when he asked, "Did you know the victim?"

There was a slight tightening of his jaw when I responded, "Victim? Of what?"

"The woman found dead in the back room—did you know her?" His voice had a sharp edge.

I answered back sharply. "No. Who was she?"

He ignored the question. "Ever seen her in here before?"

"No."

He continued, "Marilyn Neff ever talk about her?"

I countered that one with, "How could I know that if I don't know who she is?"

His jaw tightened a bit more. "No games, Miss Hyatt, please. I've got a woman dead. I need to find out how. Perhaps why. If necessary, who."

"You're saying she was murdered." I made it a statement.

"The coroner will tell me that. I just like to have all my ducks in a row before someone tells me which one to aim at." A nearly imperceptible flash in his dark eyes told me that he, too, was a by-the-seat-of-your-pants person who resented the pedantic barriers of authority.

I said, "I'd like to know those things, too."

"For *The Ledger*?"

"I am a reporter."

"And what else?"

I shoved back from the table, the chair legs squeaking on the floor. He made a conciliatory gesture but I remained away from the table. I was aware of Marilyn, Hal and Melody watching from a table near the dance floor but I didn't look their way.

21

After a staring contest, he lowered his eyes and began a series of quick questions and rapid notations. I admitted seeing the woman arrive and Marilyn lead her down the hallway. He asked me the time. Had I seen Marilyn return? Did I see the woman any time after I saw Marilyn back in the bar and lounge? Did I hear the noise Hal went to check on? Time of that? Why did Melody go to the supply room? Did I notice anyone going too often or for too long to the restrooms? I kept my responses short and delivered them in a near monotone.

Then he switched to questions about The Cat. Remembering Melody's admonition and partially agreeing with her, I tried to deliver information succinctly but without antagonism. I even tried to educate him a bit. "This is a unique place. The Admiral, Marilyn, has created a quality place with a sense of neighborhood for us. A lot of professional women come here. And young people—some secure as lesbians, some struggling to be. And a lot of couples as deeply committed to each other as any happily married straight pair."

That made him uncomfortable, but at least he didn't make a crude remark. "Whether you believe it or not," he said, "I don't put down your lifestyle. Don't understand it…but I don't put it down. And I know that a lot of cops do. But as you know, a death in a gay bar will get more than its share of media coverage. In your own paper, too, I imagine."

Since I couldn't deny that, I said nothing.

He changed subjects. "What did you do to irritate Patrolman Romero?"

"It's more a matter of what he did to irritate me."

Ziegler's bland expression slipped a little as the corners of his mouth twitched toward a smile. "Okay…" He gestured with his hand for me to go on.

I felt myself lift my head and thrust out my chin in what Jodi had always called my take-on-the-world look. "I was covering the abortion protests at the Woman's Care Clinic last month after the judge's no-man's-land ruling. Your Patrolman Romero wasn't making much of an effort to keep protesters out of that fifty-foot, free-movement zone for people entering the clinic." I ran my fingers along the edge of the table. "I simply reminded him of his official duty."

Surprisingly, the detective's lips widened into an open smile. "Very politely, I'm sure."

I matched his smile, relaxing a little under what had become a pleasant gaze. "I might have been what an old journalism teacher used to describe as 'unwisely nettlesome.'" I sobered immediately. "But his response was something about no judge's ruling counting more than the sanctity of unborn life. He's lucky I didn't identify him in my article as the author of those words."

"Why didn't you?"

I sighed, "Because he has as much right to his views as the women going into the clinic. He just doesn't understand that he has no right to impose his views on them. Or voice them while he's on duty in that uniform."

Ziegler fluttered the pages of his notebook. "There are more pertinent issues on hand here at the moment." He got up, the bland expression back in place. "Maybe we could compare views on abortion at another time…"

Though I knew it wasn't a serious offer, I grinned, "Why, Detective, have you forgotten you are talking to a gay woman?"

"Any man or woman can talk." The brusqueness of his words was belied by the flush that spread over his stiffened face and the tension of his shoulders as he strode away. Without looking back he added, "You can leave now."

I stayed where I was watching The Cat slowly empty of staff and police. I assumed that the body had been removed while I was in the dining room. Roger Lowe had been right about there being too many more newsworthy events for a death at a bar to stir immediate shock waves. And then there was the matter of the advertising influence of the Central Florida tourist industries. No Jules Verne octopus (or was it squid?) sent out more tentacles of control. Mustn't frighten off the tourists.

Eventually, only Ziegler and the woman officer remained, along with Marilyn, Hal and me. I noted that all the money had been removed from the tables and that Hal, standing and talking with Marilyn, had a bank deposit bag under his arm.

Hal spoke to Ziegler who nodded. Ducking under the crime-scene tape, accompanied by an officer, Hal went to stow the money in the safe in Marilyn's office, then on his way back quickly flipped off switches, reducing The Cat to the dimness of night lighting. Then he nodded at a comment from Ziegler and went out the front door after brief waves to both Marilyn and me.

Marilyn joined me as I got up and stretched back muscles stiff from the tension and sitting too long. Her voice was huskier than usual. "Looks like a cop is following Hal home. Don't know if that's courtesy or snooping. I said no thank you to Ziegler's offer to follow you and me home. Told him we were going out for coffee and woman-to-woman talk. Right?"

"Right," I agreed. I knew what kind of talk I wanted but wondered just what she intended.

"I don't think he liked it much," she added. "And I don't think he liked me saying that one and a half tough lesbians could take care of themselves."

"My saying..." I corrected automatically. "And I'm tougher than you think I am."

That earned me the sardonic smile. "No, you're not, Lexy. Half of you may be the tough reporter you've suddenly decided to be. The other half is the sensitive English teacher you wish you still were." I frowned at her emphasis on the last few words. My frown deepened as she continued, "When you get yourself all blended together again, no Jodi or anyone like her will be able to tangle you up. Say 'Aye, aye, Admiral' and let's get going."

She ignored my hiss and bustled us up the steps and out onto the street. Ziegler made sure the door was secure and asked questions about the alarm system. His partner got in their car as he followed Marilyn and me to the corner of the building and watched us get in our cars in the side parking lot. Before we closed our doors, Marilyn called out, "Feathers."

I saluted understanding. Turning the key in the ignition, I was startled by the raw power of Melissa Etheridge's voice and guitar rushing from the rear speakers. I pulled out onto the street alert to the vagaries of late Friday night traffic and willingly awash in the galvanic music.

CHAPTER THREE

I drove with the window down. The winter had been unusually mild even for central Florida and the late February night air was cool but had no bite to it. The waning crescent moon had yet to rise and the stars were wondrously bright.

At intersections Marilyn sailed through on yellow caution lights forcing me to stop on red, a technique Melody had remarked on after once following her to a restaurant supply warehouse. She had said, "I think the Admiral is either playing I-can-get-there-first or watch-the-spy-lose-the-tail." Now, as victim, I decided that she was playing another one of her power games. In one of our early morning, after-sex conversations, Jodi and I had practiced amateur psychoanalysis and concluded that much of Marilyn's flamboyancy was a defense mechanism, a camouflage for insecurities.

Jodi… Why did I let her roam my mind at will? Even when we became a pair, we knew it wasn't a forever thing. Neither of us gave up her apartment. We scattered our possessions between them. We fell into each other's beds never thinking of either one as ours.

I felt the familiar quiver and my thigh muscles contracted. Involuntarily I pressed harder on the gas pedal, remembering Jodi's face floating above mine, her scant, tight-lipped smile revealing her pleasure at the deep-throated sounds her adept fingers drew from me. Was she drawing them now from the enticing Latina she had so easily acquired for the evening?

The lyrics of Melissa's 'Bring Me Some Water' tore at my struggle for physical numbness, and I ejected the tape so ferociously that it leaped to the floor, skittering toward the passenger door as I turned hard into the parking lot of a large shopping mall. Halfway up the north side of the lot, a single building spilled softer than normal artificial light from large plate-glass windows. A huge neon feather of yellow-green appeared to float above the roof; miniature versions framed the heavy glass entrance door.

Marilyn's maroon sedan was parked slightly askew in the first row of white-lined slots. I found an empty space a row back and eased my smaller car in between two expensive vans. I stretched to retrieve the Etheridge tape, embarrassed at my lack of self-control, then exited the car.

Approaching the cafe slowly, I gazed at the brilliant Big Dipper etched in the dark northeast sky, thinking that the huge, but delicate, neon feather looked as though it could have drifted down from the bowl. My eyes traced the handle to the sparkling end star, pleased as always to remember from some long ago astronomy class, its name, Alkaid, meaning 'little chief.'

The cafe was about half full and I quickly spotted Marilyn in a side window booth. I tilted my head toward that area as the hostess came near me. She nodded and extended a menu which I waved away. I slid into the center of the light gold, padded bench seat and rested my arms on the imitation wood-grain table top. Within a few seconds a waitress in a rich olive-green tunic stood awaiting our order.

Marilyn ordered a glass of white zinfandel while I chose mocha cappuccino. We agreed to share a plate of cheese and fruit. Soon returning, the waitress settled our drinks and slid the attractively arranged plate to the center of the table. She placed two smaller plates before us topped with apple-green napkins. Having yet to speak to each other, Marilyn and I sipped our drinks, then reached for the colorful food.

Finally I spoke. "We're not here for the food and drink. So, who was she?"

She took another sip of her wine, appearing to roll it around on her tongue before swallowing. "Darla Pollard."

"Go on."

Her eyes, a thin blue, looked directly into mine. "Am I talking to Lexy or the reporter?"

"Both. You've been jabbing at me to take charge of my life. Well, I am. Accept it. Now, what have I heard you say dozens of times? Hoist sail or stay in port."

She crunched a slice of apple, dabbed at her mouth with the napkin, then responded. "She runs…ran an independent insurance agency. Specialized in coverage for bars, privately-owned restaurants, the like."

When she didn't add anything, I said, "Damn it, Marilyn. What are we here for?"

Her eyes narrowed, measuring me. "All right. I smell things in the wind that worry me. I want that brain of yours on my side. I know you're quick to see things and don't judge or condemn. Always thought you ought to speed that last part up a little. Now I'm glad you don't." She popped the rest of the apple slice into her mouth and chewed. Then she said, "I don't know how Darla died. Don't know why she was in that supply room. But obvi-

26

ously the police think someone killed her."

I knew my words were harsh. "And that would be a problem for you?"

Focusing somewhere past my shoulder, she said, "Anything that happens at The Cat becomes my problem…"

I hissed loudly through my teeth and began to slide from the booth. "You finish the food, Marilyn. And pay for it."

"Sit down, Lexy."

My tactic had worked. I sat back down. She drew in a long, slow breath, then said quickly, "I met her when I bought that bar, Leather Fever, on the highway east of town three years ago. She held a policy on it."

"And…?"

She answered promptly and bluntly. "And we became lovers. She was around thirty-five and I was in the mood for someone a bit younger and livelier. Trouble was she was lively with more than me." That patented sardonic smile again. "I like variety, Lexy, but one woman at a time." She drained her glass. "What was it Jodi was explaining to me once? Karma? Seems to be my karma to fall for women who cheat on me."

I picked up my cappuccino and held it in both hands, enjoying the warmth of the clear glass mug. Maybe trying to dilute the chill spreading through me. "I never saw you with her, Marilyn." I added thoughtfully, "Never saw you with anyone."

"Running bars, I have always thought it best to keep my own involvements out of them." She gave me a teasing smile. "Besides, makes it easier to manage all the raging hormones going on in my places. Like you lately."

I held up a hand to stop her. "No changing the subject. I assume you two broke up. When?"

"About a year ago. Sex with her was good and I hated giving it up but, tough as I am, I didn't like all the directions she swung in."

"Meaning?"

Marilyn sucked in her lower lip. "There were two or three leather dykes she let take care of her now and then. I could have turned my back on that for awhile longer maybe…but not the teenage thing."

"A baby dyke? Your Darla covered ground."

I got a stern Admiral glare. "She's not 'my Darla.' Twice I saw her with what looked like a teenager in the car. All I really saw of the girl was a head of that crinkly dark and light hair they think is attractive. Then I saw them early one evening when I was on my way to The Cat, walking around the downtown lake with the fountain. Didn't really think anything of it until I mentioned seeing them and Darla got damn huffy. Claimed the girl was part-time help and just needed to talk boyfriend problems." She cocked her head at me. "You know how far people get trying to lie to me, Lexy."

And I did know. Even when I had tried what I considered diplomatic fibbing, Marilyn would lower her chin, raise her eyebrows and simply wait for the truth. Even when she didn't get the truth, it was generally cease and desist on the lying.

Marilyn continued, "Adding what I thought I was hearing to what I knew and had seen with the leather ladies, I decided it was time for me to back out…again."

I tried to fill the ensuing silence with a lightness I didn't feel. "So we are both drifting on the waters."

"We don't sail the same boats, Kid. Hell, I'm the only sailor at this table. I do know about drifting and waiting for a breeze to catch. But you are a hiker…and you've been trying to hike on while still looking over your shoulder at where you've been. Stop that, Lexy. And don't go hissing at me. I've got other things on my mind tonight."

"Which you're taking your own sweet time telling me about."

Marilyn sighed loudly. "I'm not really stalling. I hate that Darla is dead. I may have ended our affair some time back, but there was a closeness once." She leaned toward me. "Lexy, however Darla died, I am in no way involved. But…but I do feel responsible that she was there tonight."

My interest quickened. "Did you invite her…arrange to meet with her?"

"No." This time Marilyn's sigh was more exasperated. "For a few weeks she's been calling me and wanting me to meet with her. Said she had a problem she wanted to talk over with me. I wouldn't have any of it. Told her to find someone else." She rapped the table with both her fists making her plate jump. "I wanted no part of her. Maybe because of the teenage thing. You know how I am on that. Kids need older women for role models—not lovers. She showed up tonight to force me into listening to her and whatever the problem was."

"Did you?"

She unclenched her fists and lifted her hands in a gesture of helplessness. "I never had the chance. She was agitated and anxious so I put her in my office, gave her a drink to calm her down and told her to stay put. Said I'd be back as soon as I could." She put an elbow on the table and rubbed her forehead. "So I never listened…and now she's dead."

I reached across the table and touched her arm. "Maybe the problem followed her into The Cat."

She snapped her head back. "I've been thinking so much about how I'm affected, I never thought of that. But I'm no fool. You know the cops will be happy to come down hard on us no matter how or why Darla died. It will

28

be just the death that counts. And where it happened." She heaved herself back against the seat. "And someone is bound to have seen us when she came in and will think we were arguing when I was just irritated at her for barging in like that. The cops will hear about it."

"Tell it like that. Just tell the truth."

"And neglecting to mention that we were lovers once won't matter a damn bit, will it?" Her tone was corrosive. I mentally recoiled, which she sensed. "Sorry, Lexy, you know it's me I'm mad at."

"Aye, Admiral. Just what is it you want from me?"

The light blue of her eyes was unreadable as she appraised me before saying, "Okay. I watched you and that Detective Ziegler. He seemed to accept you better than the rest of us. Except for one point when something got your dander up." I didn't open my mouth to enlighten her and she went on, "As a reporter, you have a legitimate right to ask questions. So…ask them. Be The Cat's inside man…woman." She tilted her head in a questioning manner. I appreciated the fact that she had said The Cat instead of 'my.'

I nibbled a strawberry down to the tiny green stem. "I'm going to push for this story, Marilyn. But if I get it, I'll do it right. I don't want to cover up things in the article. So be square with me."

"Have I ever not been?"

"No." I responded. But I thought to myself that neither had she ever found an ex-lover dead in her own establishment. I hoped my smile wasn't as weak as I felt it to be so I said with more optimism than I felt, "I may not be a sailor, Admiral, but pipe me aboard."

The waitress reappeared. We both requested regular coffee and then settled in to empty the plate of its delicate slices of fruit and bright wedges of cheese now nicely at room temperature.

Later, sitting in my car and watching Marilyn exit the parking lot, I wondered if she had been fully open with me. Although I couldn't be certain, I felt that enough time had elapsed between her taking Darla to her office and then reappearing in the lounge for some talking to have taken place.

I reached into the backseat for an orange notebook which had a pen clipped to it. By shifting slightly, I was able to catch the cold, blue-white glow from a nearby streetlight. I transferred my napkin notes, a list of everyone I knew to be in the vicinity of the bar right before and after I had noted the arrival of Darla Pollard, putting checkmarks by the names of those I remembered going down the hallway toward the restrooms. I squinted my eyes nearly closed as I always did when trying to visualize a scene, and added descriptions of the man and woman of the 'tourist' group Jodi had brushed by on her way through. To be accurate, I concluded the list with the plumber.

Closing the notebook and looking out the windshield, I saw the neon feathers extinguished and realized mine was the only car in the lot except for employee vehicles on the side of the restaurant. Automatically, I drew the seatbelt across me and locked the door. Twenty minutes later I pulled into a reserved parking slot in front of my apartment, one of eight single-story dwellings in a relatively safe neighborhood. Still, I looked around before unlocking the car door and lifting myself from the low seat.

Before I could close my door, I heard the metallic sounds of another car door opening. A glance over my left shoulder showed me a figure rising from a car in the row of spaces nearer the street. Having reported on enough muggings recently to understand the constant need for caution, I held myself ready to leap back into my car.

A quietly firm voice penetrated the moistening night air and soothed my shallow breathing. "It's Detective Ziegler, Miss Hyatt."

Masking my concern with bravado, I slammed my car door, twirled my keys noisily before dropping them in a pocket and said, "Running up the overtime, Detective?"

I couldn't read his face in the moonless dark, but his tone was even, unruffled. "Don't punch a clock. But I'm on my own time right now anyway. Do my best thinking in my car, so I thought I'd combine that with making sure you got home safely."

I found that hard to believe but said nothing. He crooked his right arm and placed it atop the roof of my car while I backed against the front side. I plucked a long pine needle cluster from the crevice beneath the windshield wipers and began braiding it.

Eventually he spoke again. "Anything come of the girl…the woman talk I ought to know about?" He must have noted the clenching of my jaw despite the darkness. "Lighten up, Miss Hyatt. I'm not the enemy."

I sensed the truth of that. "Sorry, Detective. It hasn't been a very normal night."

"For me, either. Most of the deaths I get called out on are shootings or knifings related to robbery, arguments, alcohol and drugs. Violence has become too normal."

My fingers slowly worked the pine needles. "I'd think there was violence in any death. Even one as quiet-looking as that poor woman's." I shuddered, remembering. "She looked almost relaxed. But there was absolutely nothing in her eyes. I couldn't even tell what color they were. Just that they

30

were horribly open."

"Know anything about her...hear anything?"

I regretted my momentary ease with him and parried the question with, "Not as much as you already learned from Marilyn, I'm sure. Maybe we could exchange information. You first. How did she die?"

Ziegler's half-smile seemed to indicate acceptance of a stand-off for the moment. He shifted away from the car and I thought he was preparing to leave. Instead, he watched the late night street traffic. "Off the record? You know we haven't even reached her next of kin with the news yet."

"I was only going to file a preliminary report tonight."

"I haven't received the coroner's report, but from my initial inspection, the contusions on her neck, I'd say suffocation. Beyond that, I have no evidence yet. Not bare hands." He fell into a long silence.

Finally I said, "Something else...?"

He spoke without turning toward me. "What's it like being gay?"

I stiffened and stayed silent, knowing that anger would constrict my voice if I didn't first relax my throat. I lifted my chin and stretched my neck, then let everything ease back into place and said, "Got a problem, Detective?"

The sarcasm, coarser than I meant, jerked his head around. "No! Of course n—" He stopped in mid-word. "Another time, Miss Hyatt. At the next information exchange."

I realized his anger as he plodded toward his car and felt vaguely displeased with myself. I tossed the braided needles and yanked my keys from my pocket and went to my apartment door. After I entered and flipped on a light, I heard his car start and pull out toward the street.

Normally I took morning showers, but the night's events had disrupted all routines. I stripped in the bedroom and walked naked to the bathroom. Opening the opaque shower door attached to the bone-colored tub, I pulled out the single knob slowly until the water temperature was almost hotter than I could stand. With my back to the spray, I enjoyed the dissolving tension. A tiny step back and the water pounded on my neck and the top of my shoulders, descending in rivulets down my arms and over my breasts. Since I had forgotten to turn on the exhaust fan, the small bathroom filled with steam; when I stepped from the tub enclosure, I breathed in deeply as though it would cleanse my insides. A few swipes of an old bath towel did little to dry me but the oversize white terrycloth robe I shrugged into completed the task.

I fell on top of my rumpled sheets still in the robe. Making the bed had never been part of my routine. I blamed the last cup of coffee for my alertness. Of course I couldn't easily fall asleep. I had seen a dead woman, been questioned by the police, and had worrisome thoughts about the involvement of friends and acquaintances. I wanted this chance to prove my substance as a reporter. The Admiral wanted me to play detective. And the real detective had just crossed a privacy line, making my hackles go up. And none of it blotted out the image of Jodi going off to casually bed someone else. Like Poe's lover of the lost Lenore, I needed my own nepenthe, a consuming method of forgetfulness. I shifted on the bed and pummeled the pillow. Neither reporting nor detecting was going to do it. Just as the image of Marilyn angrily stepping away from Darla Pollard's touch was imprinted in my mind's eye, so was the unusually curt, hurried manner with which Jodi had parted the couple blocking her escape from the hallway.

I pounded the pillow like a frustrated child, then pushed myself up and out of bed. If not a cure perhaps I could find escape in roughing out a preliminary report to hand in to Roger in the morning. For professional and personal reasons I had to make this story mine. At my small desk in the front room, I glared at the laptop computer that had yet to prove itself user-friendly and inserted a disk.

CHAPTER FOUR

I surveyed the clinical geometry of the main working room of *The Ledger*, an orderly arrangement of cubicles with shoulder high walls. Three outer walls were white, broken only by an occasional plaque and the leafy green stalks of large potted plants rising from pastel colored, ceramic containers. The fourth wall was solid glass beyond which were the semi-open offices of editors. My first reaction to the room was to consider it a gameboard constructed for an obsessive-compulsive child, but the riotous diversity within the cubicles was better suited to a manic personality. I heard the low hum and hollow clack of computer keys, and the squeaks of chairs.

When I had imagined being a reporter, it had been always been set in the first half of the twentieth century, in one of those disheveled, cacophonous city rooms of major newspapers peopled with employees shamelessly arrogant in their competition. Rooms dominated by wood and dulled by cigarette smoke, by furious attacks on typewriter keys and raucous, demanding voices. This room before me had no character.

The few people at work in the cubicles took no notice as I approached the glass wall. I stepped on the pressure mat and the glass doors parted soundlessly, but the movement caught the attention of Joe Worthington, the local news editor. His desk chair groaned as he tilted back precariously. His "What brings you in this fine morning, Lexy?" told me he had yet to review the night's police reports.

I slumped onto the edge of a straight chair at the side of his desk. "Here, my report on a death last night. I wanted to check it against what's come in from the police stations."

Worthington bit the eraser of his pencil and peered calculatingly over his glasses. Before he could speak, a runner in faded jeans, dirty sneakers, but a neat striped shirt, breezed through the doors almost before they were fully open and slapped down a stack of continuous computer sheets. His shoes squeaked on the tile floor as he left without a word.

Worthington shifted the stack to the center of the desk and began reading them. He turned the folds into a growing stack behind the original, creating the effect of a paper slinky. As he read he muttered, "Collision at I-4 exit and Colonial...armed robbery on Orange Blossom Trail...teenagers brought in after rolling car on Vineland...vandalism at vacant strip mall...suspected child abuse...domestic violence." A few pages into the stack he stopped muttering and threw me a hard glance, pursed his lips, then read phrases out loud. "Woman found dead in supply room of The Cat...unknown causes...identification pending notification..." I held his gaze unflinchingly when he returned it to me. His voice carefully emotionless, he said, "Familiar with the place, Lexy?"

I wasted no time on subterfuge. "I was there. It's all in my preliminary report."

Instantly he was alert. He brought up something on his computer screen. "Says here you caught the call." He glanced at my empty hands. "Where's the copy? Already computer filed?"

"This is a tad tricky, Joe." I seldom used his given name and I saw my use of it register in his eyes. "Can we talk off the record for a bit?"

"Those aren't words a good reporter is supposed to know when talking to an editor." But he tilted his head in a half-way consent.

I ran three fingers along the desk edge. "I was in The Cat last night as a customer. I was actually one of the first to come across the body. I called Roger before the police got there and told him I'd cover whatever there was to cover. "

"Which is?"

"Not much yet." I handed him my disk.

"Let's have a read." He quickly inserted it into his computer and brought up the file. "'On Friday night at a popular neighborhood bar and restaurant'—neighborhood? Nice discreet touch there, Lexy. '—a woman was found dead in a supply room by a patron and staff members. Cause of death is yet unknown pending further police investigation, identification of the victim and notification of next of kin.' Victim implies something more, good. But you have to name the restaurant and indicate that it will be closed for at least a few days until the investigation is complete."

"I don't see why at this point. The police won't identify a cause of death! But even I can tell from the way they taped off the scene that the doctor who looked at her must have found it suspicious!" I didn't mention Ziegler's confidential confirmation of that fact. "No one has said the word 'murder,' but all the technicians were on scene and those of us still there were thoroughly questioned." I sat up straighter. "I want to pursue this one, Joe. I have been paying my dues with features and city council meetings and misdemeanors long enough. And I'm part of the community affected by this. The bar is my main hang-out. These are people I know."

He tilted back again. "I won't argue with that. I'll even admit that you've got a nose for smelling out stuff, Lexy. But I haven't seen any drive yet and we have to name the restaurant."

I stretched out my legs, frowning as I noted that I had put on brown loafers with gray slacks. I said forcefully, "Okay. Give me this story and I'll show you the drive you haven't seen."

Worthington worked a thumbnail between two front teeth and out again. "You're in luck. With no elections in progress, there won't be some right-wing politician pandering to his voting base by attacking the 'degenerate' homosexuals. Our basketball team is making a run at the championship. The flooding in those ritzy new subdivisions is getting a lot of coverage. And teenage vandalism is a biggie…" He leaned forward and slapped the desk, "But you keep me up to date."

Thrilled, but restrained about it in front of him, I stood up. "Will do."

I maneuvered through the maze of cubicles toward a corner one and then waited patiently at the opening, staring at the straight back and the steel-wool head of hair blocking my view of a computer screen. Barbara MacFadden had been dubbed the Iron Maiden long before I arrived at the paper. The name was double-edged. One edge reflected her rigid body posture and commanding voice. Office scuttlebutt maintained that she was in her seventies and had been a teenage WAC at the end of World War II, first stationed in Japan then in Germany. Supposedly she was involved from the beginning in the information gathering and dispersement aspects of the military. In fact, the other edge to her Iron Maiden persona was the belief that no piece of information was safe from her acquisition or retrieval. Either seeing my reflection in the screen or sensing me, she turned around in a single abrupt movement saying, "Yes, Miss Hyatt?"

I spoke quietly. "Would it be possible for you to retrieve any information we might have on Darla Pollard? She was an independent insurance agent specializing in businesses, restaurants, that sort of thing. I want to know of any client cases or problems that may have surfaced in the news or courts."

"Of course it is possible." The voice was like stone. "Is it required for an article you are writing?"

I stuttered, "Ah…well…ah, it's connected with a breaking news story I've been assigned."

She made me feel like an awkward adolescent caught planning a misdeed. I had a suspicion she made everyone feel that way.

With scarcely any inflection, she said, "The term 'breaking' has been adopted by the television industry. Employ the word 'developing'."

I nodded my understanding as she reached for a piece of scrap paper which I knew she had reclaimed from reporters' trash cans. I gave her the name again and said a 'thank you' to her back as she returned to her computer.

Outside the building, I gazed at the gathering of clouds in the west. Though not always a sign of eventual rain, the darkening clouds were backed by a dull ache in my right shoulder. That shoulder had once powered softballs from left field to the shortstop in time for her to gun out runners at home plate. Being known as a bookworm in high school and an English major in college, I had had to prove myself capable on a ball field time and again. A distant rumble of thunder and a quickening of wind broke my reverie. A growl in my stomach, felt rather than heard, reminded me that I had skipped breakfast. A few minutes later I pulled into a convenience store, purchased a sausage-dog and a pint of milk and sat in the car to consume them. In front of me was a pay phone with its dangling book. Soon I was tossing my waste paper into a can and checking the yellow pages under insurance. I found what I wanted and jotted down the address of the Pollard Agency.

I located Pollard's workplace in a strip mall flanked by a hair salon and a shoe store. As there were no parking places in front, I had to take one much farther down the row of businesses. I reached for the door handle, but stopped when I saw Jodi approaching from the other direction. Frozen in place, I watched her enter the Pollard Agency. Dispassionately I collected my notebook, uncapped the pen and recorded the activity and time. But my stomach did not respond to the order for calm detachment, and the sausage and milk churned. What was she doing there? Why was it even open? Realizing I'd reach no answers in the car, I opened the door, pushing it wide with my foot.

A moment more and I stood before the large window, the interior of the business partially obscured by decoratively printed information. Still, I could see Jodi speaking animatedly with a young woman who reminded me of the cheerleader types of my high-school days: fluffed-up, lightened brown hair, lipstick-exaggerated mouth, too much eye makeup, high breasts. Not yet sure what I would say, I entered the office. Jodi's only movement was to turn her head toward me, her eyes registering both surprise and displeasure. The other woman moved swiftly to her secretary's chair behind a large desk cluttered with small business equipment and supplies.

Her voice when she spoke was irritatingly high, but I didn't know whether it was natural or from stress. She asked, "How may I help you?" To Jodi she said, "I'll get those forms for you in a moment." The twist of Jodi's mouth told me what she thought of that pretense, but she took a seat and stared out the window.

I asked, "Is Ms. Pollard in?"

"She seldom comes in on Saturdays. The office isn't really open. I've just come in to catch up on some paperwork." Her eyes kept darting to Jodi involuntarily. I could only assume that she had yet to hear of her boss' death and gladly accepted that it wasn't my place to tell her.

I thanked her and apologized for the bother which she barely recognized. Retreating out the door, I avoided glancing at Jodi but felt her eyes follow me as I passed the window. Instead of getting into my car I leaned against the driver side door, one hand tracing the side-view mirror and waited.

Soon they both came out and the young woman locked the agency door as she talked rapidly with much gesturing for a minute longer. Jodi lounged against the window with indolent grace, listening silently. I knew that pose well. Then she put her hand on the agitated woman's elbow and turned her toward her car, walking her the few steps to the curb. Jodi held the car door for her and appeared to be speaking, but I saw her head lift as she spotted me. She watched the car until it was out on the street, stared a few seconds, then walked towards me.

Her eyes, a fawn brown, were wide open, as true a storm warning as the dark underbellies of the clouds massing overhead. She stayed up on the curb and pinged the two-hour-only parking meter sign with a thumbnail before speaking, "Are you following me, Lexy?"

I answered in the same manufactured manner, "Just cataloguing your conquests. Going to write a how-to book."

She stepped from the curb and I hated my awareness of her nearness. My breath quickened as she straightened my collar, her fingers fluttering over the base of my throat. She said, "Seriously, Lexy, what's going on?"

"I wanted to see Darla Pollard on business."

Did I detect her eyes narrow before she looked down at the sidewalk? "Oh. I was just there to see Chrissy."

Of course her name was Chrissy. "Someone special? Sorry. None of my business."

"No problem. I was just mending fences. You know me. I say maybe and other people hear something more definite than I mean. She left some calls on my answering machine last night. Seems to think I had stood her up." She gave me the smile that used to draw me into her arms. "You know that's not my style." The storm warning had faded from her eyes.

"I'm out of touch with your style, Jodi." I removed my hand from the side mirror and was surprised at the stiffness of my fingers from gripping it. "You really don't know Darla Pollard?"

"No, should I? Never been in that place before. Chrissy just gave me an address and directions." Her eyes sparkled impishly. "Just wanted to smooth things over. Need a date tonight. Who is this Darla Pollard you just want to do business with?"

"I'm afraid it's who was. She was sweet Chrissy's boss. She was last night's woman in the purple suit trying to talk to the Admiral." I strained to catch a reaction in Jodi's expression. "She was the woman I found dead in the supply room."

"What!" The astonishment, the shock seemed real.

"Actually Melody, Hal and I found her." I went on to relate briefly the events, the police questioning, even a carefully edited version of the meeting with Marilyn in Feathers. I closed with a reference to Worthington okaying my covering the story for *The Ledger*.

"Why didn't you tell Chrissy her boss was dead?" Was the bite in her voice tension or anger?

"Not my place," I said. "Not with it being investigated by the police. Doesn't look like it was of natural causes. There's a couple of detectives on the case who'll get around to her soon enough. You know the bit about next-of-kin having to be notified first."

Jodi touched the smooth contours of the mirror probably still warm from my hand. "Hm, different sort of story for you to cover, isn't it, Lex? I thought you covered city administration and human interest. Branching out?"

Her presumption irritated me. "It is human interest, Jodi, not just some suspicious death. I was there. That makes it my story to cover."

She matched my irritation. "And what about The Cat? And Marilyn when you sensationalize this unnatural death at the local 'unnatural' dyke bar? What's that going to do to any of us?"

I softened my tone. "I'm not going to sensationalize anything! I care about The Cat. I'm Marilyn's friend. That's exactly why I pushed to cover developments in this case. If it turns out to be a gay bashing, that's one thing, if it's from within our own community, that's quite another. Don't you think I'm quite aware of the extreme sensitivity here. Besides, right now even I'm a suspect."

"That's crazy!"

"No more crazy than you being one as well."

Her ivory skin tightened over her cheekbones and she uttered a single word through compressed lips. "Explain."

"It was a busy night, peak hour. Lots of suspects. And you…like lots of others…went to the restroom while Pollard was waiting back in Marilyn's office. Or already dead in the supply room. Did you see or hear anything?"

Her eyes widened to storm warnings again. "I never went to the restroom!"

I locked eyes with her but I was the one to blink and break contact. Glancing up at another rumble of thunder, I said, "I saw you coming back. You had to get past the man and woman arguing…"

"No. You saw me changing my mind and turning around. That bad-blonde-dye-job was obviously on her way for a cry and I didn't want to get closed in with her." She paused, but I said nothing. "More questions?"

I gave her a wry smile and a slow shake of my head. "No."

Jodi looked down at my feet. "Then maybe you'll let me ask one. Who dressed you this morning? Brown with gray. Thought I taught you better."

We laughed together just as large drops of rain began to strike. With an off-hand "Bye," she sprinted down the sidewalk. I watched after her until a raindrop hit my forehead and dribbled into an eye. Seconds after I was seated behind the wheel, the clouds emptied their reservoir in typical Florida fashion.

Deciding to wait out what I knew would be a rain of short duration, I gathered up pen and notebook again. The few notations I made had big question marks after them. Meanwhile the deluge washed spring pollen from my windows. More cars entered the strip mall but no one exited until the rain ceased as abruptly as it had begun and brilliant sunlight flashed between separating clouds. As I backed out and started forward, water cascaded over the windshield and I had to turn on the wipers. Then inching forward to allow another driver to back out, I noticed a figure peering in the window of The Pollard Agency. Recognizing Ziegler's partner, the woman detective who had accompanied him last night, I pulled into the vacated spot. She was more casually attired in a light brown pantsuit, but the same clip-on earrings brushed her cheeks as she shaded her eyes against the glare and peered in the window. When she turned, I got a look at an oval face, with wide-set eyes and a thin mouth, framed by a cap of hair curling from the crown and only slightly darker than her suit. Her square build made her look shorter than she was. The nose of my car was only five or six feet from her and the idling of the motor drew her attention. I rolled down my window and said, "It's closed. Chrissy left."

She came down off the curb. "Christine Shoemaker?"

"Assuming that's Chrissy's full name," I responded. "Left about fifteen, twenty minutes ago."

"And you are Ms…?" She leaned towards my window, narrowing her eyes from the glare of sunlight off some car, and I saw that they were an alluring golden brown.

"Hyatt…Lexy." I applied the very slight emphasis to my first name that one gay woman often uses when testing the possibility of another. "But I rather imagine you have it in that notebook hiding in your pocket." I turned off the motor, reaching out to tap the wide, bulging pocket of her jacket. Then I placed my little finger beneath the laminated picture ID that was clipped to the smaller high pocket, lifting it slightly. "Detective Roberta Exline," I read. I withdrew my finger slowly, letting the card drop. "Bobbie?"

Her lips appeared fuller when they parted in a miniature smile. "Robbie." Within a breath, however, she returned to her detective mode. "What are you doing here?"

I answered with a question of my own, nodding to the passenger seat. "Wouldn't you like to get out of the glare?"

She struggled briefly with that, then walked decisively around the back and got in, giving me time to decide not to mention Jodi. She withdrew her notebook and waited for my answer to her original question.

"I'm sure you know I'm a reporter. I'm doing a little background check on Darla Pollard." I realized immediately the mistake I had made.

"How did you know where to check? The victim's stepfather and half-sister weren't notified until this morning."

Water had dripped on my left arm and I concentrated on drying it with a tissue as I chose my words. "I have my sources." I hurried on, "I won't get in your way. Or Ziegler's."

She raised her eyebrows at the force with which I uttered her partner's name. "Sounds like you got your fur ruffled."

"I may have been a little touchy. So, anything from the coroner yet on how she died?"

She tugged off her earrings and massaged her lobes. "I'm not in a position to tell you anything…Lexy, although by now the police will have issued an official statement that it's being handled as a murder investigation, death officially ruled as suffocation by strangulation."

The use of my first name surprised me although I knew it might be an effort to make me more co-operative. "I'll agree not to disagree for the moment. One thing though—am I a suspect?"

Robbie cocked her head. "Who's questioning who here?"

I winced at her grammar. "We share professions of inquiry. More than

40

that. We're both women in male dominated fields. It's not enough we've gotten them to deal us in—we have to be more card-sharp, know what to play and when."

She said nothing but I sensed an effort to keep her face noncommittal. Then she got out of the car, bending down to look back at me before closing the door. "Go easy on the research, Ms Hyatt. I won't let you ignore a big difference here. I'm a cop looking for a murderer, you are a reporter. Even if you're experienced at crime coverage, stick to police reports. Don't do anything risky." A brief pause. "Of course any information is always appreciated." She placed something on the seat. "My card."

She straightened and I could no longer see her face. Before she could close the car door, I retaliated with a laugh, "We'll see about that."

CHAPTER FIVE

The four-lane highway, crowded with early Saturday evening traffic, angled to the northeast. My wide side view mirror became a miniature painting of a lush Florida sunset. Swatches of clouds were scattered against fading blue and brushed with irregular strokes of magenta. Spotting my destination coming up on the left, I drifted into the turn lane for a cross-over. When I finally caught a break in the traffic, I sped across the two lanes and skidded a bit in the gravel. The rectangular wooden building situated far back from the highway was nondescript, almost ramshackle and in need of painting. The protective bars were rusty on the small windows. Large floodlights protruded from the four corners of the roof and would soon illuminate the lot with stark light, but no ubiquitous neon sign flashed identification. A few scraggly pepper plants across the front struggled in the gravel dust. Only the door had distinction. It was a burnished coppery-brown. I pulled up next to Marilyn's sedan, one of two cars in the lot, along with a gaggle of motorcycles.

I paused on my way to the entrance to examine the bikes, testing my memory of information garnered two years ago for a series on Bike Week in Daytona. A Harley-Davidson Sportster was surprisingly dusty and a Yamaha dirtbike exhibited mud splotches. The Kawasaki Vulcan and the two Honda Magnas leaned in the last flashes of the sun. My fingers itched to trace the swirling deep gold trim on the burgundy Honda Gold Wing, but I had learned that indiscriminate touching was not wise.

Moving on, I discovered that the larger than normal door was real wood and appeared thick and solid. Probably scavenged from some old homestead by an antique dealer and rescued by the Admiral. If an inanimate object could contain a manitou, I wondered how the door felt being the gateway to a bar called Leather Fever.

I stood just inside the door and let my eyes adjust to the dimness. Despite the motorcycles out front and two traffic lights flanking a large jukebox in a back corner, a country western atmosphere dominated. The long bar on the right wall was wood with a brass foot rail. The floor, tables and chairs were wooden and I liked the smell that prevailed. Railroad style lanterns emitted a soft yellow light. A large woman with a Harley-Davidson armband sat at the bar, her tousled, gray-flecked curls bobbing as she talked emphatically with the bartender. Two younger women in fringed leather jackets danced to a slow country tune. Three others shared a small table. All three had multicolored hair rising above Indian head bands reminiscent of the sixties.

"You lost, honey?" The huskiness of the bartender was what my father had described as whiskey-voiced when referring to an elderly aunt, but this foxy woman was no one's elderly aunt.

I shook my head and took a stool. "Looking for Marilyn."

She volunteered no information on the Admiral's whereabouts and turned to answer the phone. Her leather leggings disappeared into black combat boots, but her white blouse was sheer and lacy. Thin leather strands hung from her necklace to nestle against attractive cleavage. She combed her long, dark blonde hair with her fingers as she cradled the phone against her shoulder. I rested my arms on the deep red padding with brass studs that bordered the bar edge, staring at myself in the mirror, and so I saw a door open on the wall behind me. Marilyn and a tall woman made even taller by high-heeled boots entered. The woman's fluid movements bespoke an animal energy and she wore the tight, dark brushed-leather suit like a second skin. Her own brown-buff skin, the distinctive planes of her face and the almond-shaped eyes indicated oriental blood, as did the gloss of thick black hair. Loosely tied at her throat was a delicate lavender scarf.

Marilyn's face registered curiosity when she caught sight of me in the mirror. I twirled around slowly on the stool and she tapped my foot with hers. "Think those so-old-they're-out-of-style cowgirl boots are going to let you fit in here?"

"At least they go with my brown jeans." I tapped my waist. "Got a leather belt too. And look at you—all polyester and knit."

She laughed good-naturedly. "I'm on my way to eat. And if you get more respectful to your elders, you can go with me." To the bartender who had approached us she said, "Have you carded those three, Sheila? Look like reform-school rejects. "

"Checked them the first time they came in a couple weeks ago. They're okay. Work at Disney World and are feeling their way around the gay scene." By our reflections in the mirror, I could tell that the three of us questioned the reference to working at Disney with those hair styles. Sheila added, "They wear wigs on the job."

Marilyn squeezed the back of my neck. "Get this kid a bourbon and water." To me she said, "No Perrier and no limes. Things are more straight-forward...bad choice of word...more simple here." She shifted back a step so that the tall, seductively attractive woman and I could see each other. "This is Lexy. One of The Cat's regulars. C. K. Chen. Manages this place for me."

We gave each other civil smiles and shook hands. I remonstrated, "I'm nearly thirty-five, Marilyn. So when are you going to stop calling me a kid?"

"I call everyone that who is young enough not to be bothered telling their age." She saw my mouth open and squeezed my neck harder. But there was amusement in the exclamation.

The phone rang again as Sheila placed my drink before me. Upon answering it, she gestured to Marilyn that it was for her. The manager leaned on a stool, leaving one empty between us and asked, "Were you at The Cat last night?" Not sure what Marilyn had told her, I merely nodded. She continued, "I liked Darla Pollard. She went her own way without apologies. Good businesswoman too. I could respect that."

"Anything you couldn't respect?"

Her face closed. She looked towards Marilyn. "I'm a good business woman as well. I don't meddle in my customers' private lives. What's your line of work, Lexy?"

I knew a brick wall when I ran into one. I changed to an intimate tone. "C.K.—what does that stand for?"

Her bemused smile was devastating. "I'd have to know you better to reveal that." She stroked my cheek teasingly before she retreated to her tasks. I was glad Marilyn didn't see.

I sipped my drink slowly and watched others enter. The leather varia-tions in clothing and accessories were fascinating: body suits, jackets, vests, boots, belts, suspenders, head bands, armbands, choke collars, hats, bracelets. The articles were oiled, polished, glazed, brushed, embossed, tooled. Though darker colors dominated, here and there were flashes of white, soft ecru, silver blue, dove gray. I did feel out of place in simple denim and a golf shirt.

As patrons and activities increased, Sheila was joined by two others behind the bar. Apparently you ordered your drinks at the corner of the bar and paid as you received. Three pool tables along the opposite side were in constant use as were electric dart boards at either end of the same wall. The dance floor was seldom empty. Marilyn remained on the phone, her back to everyone. C. K. patrolled. Just as I thought I recognized a high-pitched voice nearby, Marilyn bumped a bike dyke from the stool on my left and usurped my attention. "I know a beer distributor I'd like to castrate. Claims he can't make the delivery he promised me. Our dinner will have to wait."

"So what will you do?" While I directed the question to her, I checked out the increasing crowd listening for the high-pitched voice that I was sure was Chrissy...and looking for Jodi. "I'll send Hal over with some cases." After a pause, "Why are you here, Lexy? Branching out or looking for me?"

"First of all, I wanted to see how you were. Got a couple of questions too."

"Wind's in your sails."

I asked, "Have the police gotten back to you yet?" She shook her head no. "Would Pollard's secretary Chrissy Shoemaker know what was upsetting her?"

The vertical line between her eyes deepened in thought. "I don't think so. Darla seldom mentioned her except in connection with the business. How do you even know her?"

"I met her this morning at the insurance office. Just went by. A simple way to start. She didn't know her boss was dead, but I imagine she does now. Jodi was there, too, setting up a date for tonight. Not someone I'd expect her to take out."

Marilyn grunted, then said, "That's not Jodi out there dancing with her."

I followed her gaze and spotted Chrissy dressed in flashy off-white buckskin embossed with flower images. Her partner was almost scrawny slim with an olive complexion. Glossy black hair brushed back from the face into a modified mane tumbled down the back of her neck. She wore fringed leggings and a loosely designed mesh of diamond shapes over a strapless leather bra. Tattoos coiled from her upper breasts over her shoulders and down her arms. Suddenly I remembered seeing her. "She was at The Cat last night."

Marilyn voiced skepticism. "Chrissy?"

"No. The other one. She was coming out of the restroom just as I started in...and right before Melody screamed. I forgot about her when I made my list."

"List?"

"I made a list of everyone I could remember going down the hallway." I punched her shoulder. "Starting with you."

She didn't smile, lost in some thought of her own, then thrust herself from the stool. "Got to get back to The Cat. Sheila, look after this one." Her hand was on my shoulder. "I'll be in touch, Lexy."

Sheila was swiftly and expertly twisting caps off beer bottles and handing them over the counter. I commented, "Not a good idea to run out on a Saturday night, is it?"

She regarded me curiously. "We never run out. C.K.'s too good a manager for that."

"I thought Marilyn was on the phone with some distributor who was letting her down."

The bartender glanced back at the phone on a small desk near the end of the long mirror. "That was some woman who was real pushy about talking to Miss Neff." She pointed to my empty glass, but I declined.

I ran my thumb and middle finger up and down the flat sections of my glass wondering about Marilyn's deception. And wondering if she was really on her way to The Cat. I wouldn't have expected the police to let her open tonight. I was peeved. If she expected my help I expected openness from her. I returned my attention to Chrissy and friend but they had left the dance floor. Sweeping the room, I easily latched onto the bright buckskin at a small table directly across the room from me. I threaded my way toward her.

I touched a chair back. "May I?"

Chrissy didn't appear to recognize me so I added, "I spoke with you in your office this morning." Knowingly committing an indiscretion, I continued, "Jodi was setting up a date with you."

Now she looked totally confused. "Jodi? I don't date—"

She snapped her mouth shut as the slim dark girl materialized at her side spearing me with a hostile look and asking, "Who's this?"

"I don't know. She was in the office for just a minute this morning wanting Darla."

I noted Chrissy's use of Pollard's first name. It also ran through my mind that Detective Exline might not have caught up with her yet. "I'm Lexy Hyatt…a friend of Jodi." Both women stiffened as I looked at the dark one. "You are…?"

Reluctantly she answered, "Janel." She touched the back of Chrissy's hand. "Christine."

Choices ping-ponged in my mind till I decided on one. "Chrissy, do you know about Darla Pollard?"

"I don't understand."

"It would be easier to talk outside. Could we?" She looked up at Janel for guidance so I added fuel. "Darla and Janel here were both at The Cat last night. It needs talking about."

This startled Chrissy. Janel, stone-faced, said, "Outside."

There was a line of rapidly fading light in the west. The parking lot was dominated by trucks and motorcycles. We zigzagged our way to a red and black pickup. Chrissy climbed in on the passenger side and Janel stood against the open door as I said, "I don't know if I should be doing this,

46

Chrissy, but I think it's time you knew that Darla Pollard is dead. Unless you already know."

Her sharp intake of breath and the way her hand flew to grip Janel's shoulder were strong indications that she didn't know...unless she was an actress as well as a secretary. Janel stroked the hand but kept wary eyes on me. I sketched the events of last night much as I had done earlier for Jodi. Chrissy stuttered negative responses to most of my questions but kept darting concerned, if not frightened, glances at Janel. My questions to Janel met with sneering hostility. "Why shouldn't I be at The Cat? Think I'm not good enough for the place? No, I didn't know Darla was there. She's not my mother-figure." Chrissy had winced at that. "And who the hell are you to ask us questions?" Janel ended my detecting by stomping around the front of her truck. Once behind the wheel, she gunned the motor and sped off, leaving me squinting my eyes against the dust and gravel. I stood in the deepening twilight considering the fireworks of emotions I was setting off. I wasn't so much concerned with whether or not it was the right thing to do as whether or not it was the responsible thing to do.

A sweep of headlights and a scattering of gravel brought me back from my thoughts. A large rectangular mirror jutting from a gleaming black truck grazed my shirt sleeve. The truck stopped on a dime, then a figure rose from the driver's side, balancing on the open door and the top. "Sorry, sweetheart. Didn't see you standing there." The voice was coated lightly with the honey of a southern drawl. "Someone foolish go off and leave you?"

I couldn't stop my smile or the appreciative assessment I gave her as she swung out of the truck and approached me with a chattering of chains attached in short loops from all parts of her body suit. She was large and full-bodied and I was startled by a desire to lean into her and feel those powerful arms curve securely about me. Maybe the Admiral was right about the hormonal raging. I was startled, too, and irritated by the catch in my voice as I said, "No, just standing here daydreaming."

"In the dark, sweet thing. I know a lot better things to do in the dark." She nodded toward the bar door now thrust open, emitting two laughing couples and the twang of country western music. "Buy you a drink? Or take you...on the dance floor?"

Instead of embarrassing or offending me, the suggestion drew another smile from me. "Thanks, but no. Perhaps another time." I couldn't believe the sincerity I had put into that. She held my gaze until I lowered them only to become acutely aware of the rise and fall of the chains coiled over ample breasts. I lifted my eyes quickly to encounter a face beaming at my discomfort.

Slowly and deliberately she drawled, "I'll be here for quite a stretch in case you want to come looking. They call me Luke. Best I could get out of Lucille."

When I didn't follow with my name, she measured me smugly, touched the bill of her cap, then crunched off toward the squat building leaving behind a scent of Aramis in the cooling night air.

Back in my car I pounded my steering wheel in frustration for lack of any idea why I had turned Luke down, grabbed up my notebook and checked my last entry. It summarized Jodi's remarks earlier. I added questions concerning the real conversation with Chrissy since Jodi obviously had lied about dating her. I penned some questions about Janel and added her to my list of people in The Cat at the time of Darla's death. Minutes later I was creeping toward the pickup window of a fast-food establishment and the chicken sandwich I had just ordered, chastising myself silently for my eating habits of the day. I ate as I drove and, without really thinking about it, wended my way toward The Cat.

Turning onto the last street I could see that The Cat was dark except for the protective lighting. I pulled into the side lot anyway, noting that the only other car was Hal's. It took two firm series of knocks before Hal's face appeared behind the three triangles of colored glass in the door. It took a couple of minutes more for him to deactivate the alarm system and let me in. "Just ate a sandwich, Hal. Can the house afford to buy me a beer?"

He rumbled laughter in the same manner as his sister and waved me toward the bar. We were shadow figures in the dim light and conversed in low tones as we drank beer from bottles. At my question concerning the whereabouts of Marilyn, he gave me a shrug of his wrestler-size shoulders. "Haven't seen her today, Lexy. I got bored and came in to do an early check on supplies. Called the cops and was told we could reopen Tuesday. She did get phone calls from some woman though. Pushy, I thought, then I decided she was upset, so I finally told her to try Leather Fever."

I asked, "She give a name?"

"Wouldn't. You don't think it had something to do with last night, do you?"

This time I shrugged. "Hal…" As he gave me his full attention, I clinked my bottle to his. "Truth serum, okay?" He grimaced but nodded yes. I continued, "Did you know anything about Marilyn and Darla Pollard?"

His discomfort was palpable. "Marilyn's being gay was never any problem for me. Her getting hurt was. She puts on a show of being tough, but people can really mess her up." He took a swig of the beer, then went on. "She wrote me awhile back before I came to work here, about buying a

48

motorcycle hang-out that was going downhill and her plans for it. Couple of letters later she started talking about this insurance agent babe and how well they hit it off. Even said something about this one looking like it would be more lasting than her usual." He put the beer bottle down with a thud. "Wasn't too long though before she stopped mentioning her. Could guess what that meant."

"So you knew her when she came in here last night?"

"Not right off. At least not really. When I started working here, Sis told me Darla was trying to start up contact again. Told me not to pass on her phone calls."

I twirled my empty bottle between my palms. "Did Marilyn tell you what Darla wanted?"

"No...and I didn't ask." Hal gave a rueful smile. "I never quit being the little brother who toed the lines his big sister drew, even though I'm only two years younger." After a pause he added emphatically, "No way Marilyn had anything to do with that last night."

Softly I said, "I know." But as I watched him rinse out our empties, I wondered if I did know.

We walked out together. Hal held my car door for me, saying before he closed me in, "Everything's going to be all right, Lexy. We'll land on all four feet and The Cat will too."

I nodded agreement but bit my lower lip. Darla Pollard hadn't landed on all four feet. And while her murderer was still out there, how could any of us be sure which way we were going to land?

I preceded Hal out onto the street. At the first intersection we turned opposite ways. A couple of blocks further I caught a red light and sat thinking until impatient honking behind me propelled me through the now green light. A few blocks more I signaled a left turn. Suddenly changing my mind, I angled back into the thru lane and was honked at again. I resisted an urge to give them the finger.

I touched the electric switch and my window lowered. Enjoying the wind ruffling my hair, I sped back east toward Leather Fever, deliberately emptying my mind of everything but the mechanics of driving. When I got there I had to wait for someone to leave before I could park. Still keeping my mind blank, I tugged open the heavy door. Noise and the strong smells of beer and cigarettes assaulted me. I stood bathed in the bright orange-red light of the exit sign above the door and felt the machinations of fate as I locked eyes with Luke straightening from her bend over a pool table. She gave me a tight-lipped, knowing smile and handed off the cue stick. Her approach was neither fast nor slow. She cupped my elbow commandingly and turned my body effortlessly, reaching around me to open the door. She kept her hand on my elbow and guided me toward her truck.

"My carriage, princess," she drawled, "or do you follow me?"

I understood the choice she was giving me and pointed toward my car four rows away.

"Be there before you, hon." She released my elbow and tapped me lightly between my shoulder blades. I heard her truck rumble to life before I sidled through the first row of vehicles. I crossed the last opening before mine in the glare of her headlights, the pulse in my throat matching the throbbing of her engine.

CHAPTER SIX

Luke was a masterful lover, demanding yet considerate. My nipples quickened into hard buds in response to the hunger of her mouth; my legs tensed at the power of her rhythmic thrusting. I had been too long without passion. I yielded my body trustingly as she stroked and feasted everywhere until I cried out my joy and jolted against her soft body. Afterwards we drifted in and out of light sleep.

Towards morning she lay on her stomach, her face turned away from me, but her right arm across my waist. As I shifted onto my side, she withdrew her arm and backed into the curve of my body. I nuzzled her neck below the short brown hair and reached my arm around the larger body to fill my hand to overflowing with a soft breast. She stirred and mumbled. As she reached a hand back to cup my head, I slipped my hand in between her breasts, marveling at the heat. After a moment she pulled it free and guided it lower. I combed her fine silk with my fingernails until her thighs parted enough for me to embed fingers in the moist crevice. With a steady circular motion I drew deep-throated moans that eventually shifted into erratic gasping explosions of air. Her body stiffened and arched away from me before slowly settling back into the crescent of my form.

Then with movements almost swifter than I could follow, Luke stretched, relaxed onto her back and pulled me on top of her. The hard bulges of my small breasts molded into her larger softness. I straddled her and cried as her wide hands clutched my buttocks, grinding me against her with such force that I could feel a blended pounding.

I covered her mouth with mine, extending my tongue as deeply as possible and felt her teeth close lightly on its base, forcing me to withdraw it excitingly slowly. The scrape of her teeth was richly sensual and a jagged moan rose out of me.

I put my hands on either side of her, lifting my upper body away from hers. At the same time she spread her legs and mine dropped between, enhancing our contact. I stared into her eyes, a blue as light as the now early morning sky and increased the movement of my hips to a near frenzy. She gave me the same smug smile of the night before and I wanted to drive through her. Her exultant laugh tore her name from my taut throat as a flood of sensation raced down my legs and up my torso in an endless moment.

I collapsed weakly upon her, succumbing to a gentle stroking of my body and a honeyed whisper of, "Princess, sweet princess. I think you like early morning quickies…and I like that."

She did a quarter turn and I slid to the sheets. Her strong arms tightened me against her and I could feel my own warm breath coming back to my mouth and nostrils from her glowing skin.

I said, "Luke…it was a good night."

She brushed my hair tenderly with her hand. "Did we get all those ol' ghosts put to rest?"

I lifted my head and looked into her eyes now sparkling like star sapphires and waited three breaths before speaking. "Yes…I think so."

Her slightly parted lips drew mine for a lingering kiss. Then I snuggled back into the length of her, entwining her limbs with mine. I knew she was younger than I, but at that moment I felt coddled and protected.

Then I felt regret when she swung out of bed saying, "The shower is tricky. I'll get it going for you."

Forty-five minutes later I stood on the balcony of her second-story apartment, looking down at our vehicles. Her truck wasn't the black I had thought. It was a dark jade green with delicate detailing like silver dust.

I turned as she traced a design across my shoulders. "Those ghosts ever come back…you come looking for Luke, you hear."

I tried to swallow the catch in my throat. "I hear."

At the bottom of the steps I looked back, but she had already retreated into her apartment. Strange how you can feel gain and loss at the same time. Soon after I drove away. Simple hunger pangs drew me back into a familiar world and, shifting into my usual Sunday routine, I drove leisurely through light traffic to a diner near my apartment. A couple of regulars nodded greetings as I sought my customary window booth in the corner. As I slid into the bench seat, my back to the rest of the diner, the matronly waitress put down a medium grapefruit juice and a cup of coffee. I placed my notebook in the window ledge away from possible spills and sipped the strong coffee from the thick, pitted mug. I did some mental stretching, savoring the emancipating night with Luke along with the steaming liquid.

After consuming half the coffee, I downed the grapefruit juice, enjoying the clenching in the back of my jaws at the rush of the tartness. The minute I had finished the glass, the waitress appeared to top off my mug, plop down a *Sunday Ledger* left behind by an earlier customer and take away the empty glass. In the middle of shuffling through the sections, scanning headlines and perusing articles that caught my attention, I realized that for the first time in many months I had not given a thought to how Jodi was spending her Sunday morning. Even now as I thought of her, I knew that Jodi was no longer a ghost hovering over my activities. I lifted my cup and whispered, "To Luke..." and looked directly into the eyes of an elderly couple passing the window. I was accustomed to being caught talking to myself. At the newspaper I was often asked if all those other people in my cubicle got paychecks.

After reading the only comic strip I liked, 'For Better or For Worse,' I 'neated up' the paper—my grandfather's phrase—and stacked it on the table corner to be passed on to someone else. Without a word the waitress placed a bowl of cornflakes with sliced bananas before me along with a glass of milk. As I completed my breakfast, I reread all my notes on Darla Pollard's murder, but felt like I was just spinning my wheels.

I placed a folded dollar bill partially under my cereal bowl and slid out of the booth. Halfway to the cash register I halted at the sound of my name issuing from a table I had just passed. Turning, I met the brilliant black eyes of Rita Burgess. Were her eyes really glistening with unshed tears or was I overly aware of her continuing grief?

"Good morning, Rita. Never seen you here before."

She explained, "Moved into an apartment near here last week." I remembered that she and Dee had shared a small house on a lake near the city.

Seeing my inability to respond, she continued, "It's all right, Lexy. I'm just doing things that need doing...and it is actually good for me. I feel a little like a dog got wet and suddenly discovered how satisfying it feels to shake the water out of my fur." She shook her head and the thick dark hair, held back from her face in a loosely knotted scarf, spread over her shoulders. "Sit for a moment, won't you?"

Glad of this change in her, this apparent movement into the acceptance phase of the grief cycle, I sat across from her. She cradled her coffee mug in the long, beautiful fingers of both hands and lifted it to a mouth more relaxed than I had seen it in months. Different though it was, I knew we were both emerging from the oppression of loss.

Rita said, staring into her cup, "Do you happen to know why The Cat was closed last night?"

"I'm not sure you want me to spoil this great morning."

She raised her eyebrows and with a fluid movement of her hand, indicated to go ahead. As with Jodi yesterday morning, I gave a no-frills summary.

Her voice sounded strained. "Do they know who did it?"

I shook my head. "Did you see Darla Pollard before you left? She was wearing a well-cut purple suit."

Rita hesitated, then she said, her voice quiet, strained, "I wasn't noticing much of anything. Friday night was an anniversary— Dee and I—" She stared somberly out the window, then continued bluntly, "I was at The Cat because I couldn't face being alone, but I couldn't join in either. I'm not Catholic but I do understand the concept of limbo…"

Not comfortable enough to reach across the table and touch her, I spoke instead. "I've learned recently that limbo can be left."

"And that's what I've finally started doing. The apartment was the first step. A cat may be the second…or even a person someday."

An impish gleam flashed in her eyes, "Speaking of which, do I detect a bit of an afterglow?"

She caught me so off-guard that a flush leaped to my cheeks. We both laughed and I felt the ice of her self-imposed isolation cracking. I accepted another cup of coffee from the silent waitress and we chatted as Rita ate breakfast. When she spoke of her life with Dee, her dark eyes misted with tears but I could sense the easing of tension. We talked, too, of my work at *The Ledger*.

Rita asked fiercely, "Do you ever get bothered, Lexy?—By all the badness you have to report on. By the meanness of spirit." She looked out the window again. "Things like…at the end, the doctor wouldn't permit an increase in the morphine dosage for Dee. She was brave about it…but I was angry. I'm still angry… about a lot of things. He had no right to condemn her to that pain. What was addiction at that point?"

Immediately I had a thought but spoke judiciously. "Rita, would it be too stressful to talk about it—if I looked into the pain and drug aspects of terminal illnesses and did an article on it? Might incite some dialogue that could lead to something helpful."

Her response was quick and emphatic. "Dee would appreciate that. Do it." She reached her hand across the table and gripped mine with warmth and firmness.

I felt satisfied by more than breakfast when I left the diner. The sky was as clear this morning as it had been cloudy yesterday. I felt like tilting my head way back, putting out my arms and doing a complete turn under that total blue. What was it Amy Lowell had written?—'Four-souled like the wind am I,/Voyaging an endless sky, /Undergoing destiny.'

Back in my apartment I changed clothes, checked my work schedule for the coming week and planned out an approach for a series on medical treatment and attitudes relating to the last stages of the terminally ill. I was drawn toward the subject by more than Rita's comments about her partner. I would never lose the memory and the unsettled feelings of the first times I had ever seen my mother cry.

At some point during the year before I started school, my mother began leaving me with different people each afternoon. On our return drives home I would stare up at the tears streaking her face and be frightened by her stifled sobs. I never remembered anything she said to me or how long this went on, but I remember how unstable my world suddenly became.

Years later she explained that she had spent those afternoons sitting with her life-long best friend who was dying of uterine cancer. My mother spoke bitterly of the husband who had zealously lobbied his wife and the doctor to avoid pain-killing drugs on the basis of religious convictions. Yet the husband had seldom sat with his wife during her last weeks. That fell to my mother and other friends. My mother concluded the explanation with quiet but unquestionable conviction, "I do not believe in bringing death early, but no one should be condemned to such monstrous pain."

I hugged her then. It was my first physical contact with my mother on equal footing. I felt my childhood slip away and the future approach.

CHAPTER SEVEN

I pretended not to hear Councilman Thawley plaintively calling my name and caught the elevator. Covering decisions about water restrictions was necessary but I wasn't going to hang around and listen to Thawley expound his pet theory about gravel and decorative-stone lawns. The meeting to set guidelines on the use of city water during the coming spring and summer months had been pleasingly short, possibly because recent rains carried a promise of a return to Florida's semi-tropical wet season. But I knew that such promises had faded before and that the state's water table was dangerously low. Old-timers spoke of a need for a slow moving, low-wind, wet hurricane.

Once out of the City Administration Building and back in my car, I considered my choices. It was too early for lunch and I wasn't due back at *The Ledger* until two o'clock, so I voted for The Cat even though it was closed. Should Marilyn be putting in some time there, I wanted to tackle her about the phone call Saturday night at Leather Fever. She owed me the truth if it related to Darla Pollard's death. At The Cat I pulled into a street parking slot behind a patrol car with the blue lights flashing and watched a bulky policeman putting two handcuffed skinheads into the back seat. His beefy face was set in stone ridges and folds to deflect the stream of obscenities issuing from the snarling mouths. Crude designs covered their bald heads and iron crosses dangled from their ear lobes. Supervising from the entrance was the younger, trimmer Officer Romero. Not until the boys were safely maneuvered into the patrol car did he acknowledge me.

He spoke with mock good humor, "We have to quit meeting like this, Miss…"

He knew my name but I supplied it anyway. "Hyatt…but if we are going to keep running into each other, how about making it Lexy." He wasn't sure if I was needling him or waving a truce flag. I said more seriously, "What's going on?" As he hesitated, I pressed, "I'm asking as a friend of people here…not a reporter."

He relaxed a trifle and held the door for me saying as I entered, "A little dust-up in the alley."

"Dust-up?" It seemed an odd phrase for the precise officer.

Pulling himself more erect didn't mask the sheepishness. "I've liked westerns since the first time I saw *The Magnificent Seven*."

My original antipathy toward this man was diminishing. "For Brynner or Bronson?"

I could tell my stock was rising as he responded with a near smile. "Charles Bronson. That set me off on seeing every movie he was in. My daughter got hooked on them, too." With that he ducked into the front passenger seat quickly.

I spoke over my shoulder as I approached Marilyn and Hal at the bar. "Watch out for that little girl. She may be police commissioner one day."

His door slammed shut as the car moved off.

Halfway to the bar I saw that Hal was holding a wet cloth to the side of his face and his thinning hair was mussed. Marilyn, hovering over him, appeared divided between concern and anger. I stood before them and waited.

Marilyn said, "Go on, tough guy, you tell her."

Hal rolled his eyes at me. "Not as fast as I used to be and one of those turds clipped me one before I pinned them both in the dirt. Bet they're still spitting sand."

Marilyn pulled back the cloth. "And you're probably going to have a black eye."

He rolled his eyes at me again. "Won't be my first. It wasn't much, Lexy. Sis thought she heard one of the distributors drive up in the alley. Turned out to be those two guys in a beat-up truck. They were getting ready to redecorate for us with spray cans."

I said angrily, "And I have a good idea of their design plan."

Marilyn took over the narration. "I yelled for Hal to call the police but he decided I needed protection first. Shit, I could have toed their balls and had both of them on their knees." Despite her surly attitude she smoothed her brother's hair. "So I called the cops."

I shifted to the doorway and looked down the hall. Crime-scene tape was still across the door to the supply room. "They won't be able to hold those guys." I turned back and leaned against the wall.

"I know," Marilyn said. "But at least they've found out the cops will come here. And maybe they've got rap sheets to add this to. We take what we can get." The sardonic smile was the Admiral I preferred. "You playing hooky, Lexy?"

"Negative, Admiral. Got a little slack time and thought maybe you and I could talk about phone calls."

She stared steadily at me but spoke authoritatively. "Go home, little brother. I'll lock up after the delivery."

Hal gave her a chagrined glance, tossed the cloth on the bar and then grumbled his way out. Marilyn watched him go affectionately. We both took seats at the bar and talked to each other's reflection in the mirror.

"He's looking tired, Marilyn."

She lowered her head and her voice. "No. He has prostate cancer. It's in remission but that's why I pushed him to come live near me." She raised her eyes to my reflection again. "And you know that what I push for, I get."

The news rocked me. "Should he be working, Marilyn?"

"Of course he should. We wouldn't either of us just lay down to die." She saw the words strike me. "Don't hurt for him yet, Lexy. He'd see it. Part of the reason I got him here was the liveliness…the life force you younger people spread around. I intend to give him as much good time as possible." She looked at herself in the mirror. "He'd do the same for me."

We sat lost in our own thoughts, the quiet of The Cat washing over us. I contemplated the pernicious nature of cancer, not just in relationship to the victim but to relatives, friends, society. I thought of my mother's friend, of Rita's loss of Dee, of the threat to Hal. Where was all the research money going for what seemed so little progress against the disease? Maybe *The Ledger* could catalog and track local cancer monies and see what conclusions could be drawn, as a follow-up to the more patient-oriented approach I was planning.

"Damn!" I startled myself.

Marilyn looked directly at me. "What?"

I replied, "I'm beginning to think like a reporter all the time. Not sure I'm ready to be a Brenda Starr or Lois Lane or whoever…I'm seeing stories in everything."

Marilyn punched me smartly on the shoulder. "'Bout time, kid. Thought I was going to have to take you sailing and see if dodging a swinging boom would scare some sense of who you are into you. Even thought about tossing you overboard and letting you swim for shore so you'd have time to think about it."

"Real poetic, Admiral."

She was facing the mirror again. "And what's with this calling me Admiral to my face? No one's supposed to do that where I can hear. Aren't those the rules?"

I saluted her reflection. "The rules are undergoing changes. At least

58

mine are. And speaking of rules, I thought we had an agreement about you being open with me about Darla Pollard."

She was wary. "So?"

"So…the phone call at Leather Fever wasn't from a beer distributor. It was from a woman who had been trying to reach you here." I repeated more demandingly, "So?"

She turned and stared toward the front door where dust danced in the three shafts of sunlight piercing the glass triangles. I remained facing the mirror. She spoke brusquely, "All right. It was that fake blonde in here with her husband and another couple. And it did have to do with Darla but I don't know if it means anything about her death."

I was peeved to realize that I had left my notebook in the car. Maybe just as well though. Instinct told me Marilyn would get edgy seeing things written down. I urged, "Give me a run through and let's see what I think."

"Okay. We'll sail with your hand on the tiller for awhile. The woman described who she was, said her name was Gloria Driscoll, told me that she knew Darla Pollard and saw that I did as well Friday night. Said it was real important that she talk to me about Darla. Couldn't tell if she knew Darla was dead or not. I agreed to meet her in the side parking for the Centergate Mall."

Marilyn paused but I said nothing. She continued, "When I found her, I got in her car. Didn't want her in mine. She's one of these bird people, always moving. Drove me crazy. Shifted in her seat, played with the steering wheel, adjusted her clothes, checked herself in the mirror…you know. Talked like that, too. I'll see if I can smooth it out for you." She ignored my 'thank you' and plodded on with little emotion in her voice. "She said that her husband believed Darla was connected with their daughter's suicide two months ago. When he saw her come in here and go down the hall, he tried to go after her. Gloria claims she stopped him."

I jumped in. "She may have. I saw them arguing right there in the doorway. I can't really say he got back toward your office but I did see her go back that way. But what did she want with you?"

"Wanted me to warn Darla that her husband was getting rougher in his threats." At my facial response she added hurriedly, "I don't know what kind of threats, but I felt like she wanted something from Darla to head him off. Lexy, I'm condensing everything here but there are threads I don't follow. She said her daughter, Stacy, was assigned to Darla on one of those work-study programs they set up for high-school students. The girl praised Darla, said she was treated like a real person, got to learn things."

Marilyn leaned toward me. "There was nothing said about anyone being gay but I would swear Gloria knew Darla was. And I'm sure her daughter was the kid I saw Darla with those few times before I broke it off." Marilyn touched my arm continuing earnestly, "I want to be honest here, Lexy. I wanted out of that relationship. It was going sour like so many had. I used seeing Darla with the girl as the last straw…but I didn't really see anything to say they were having an affair. The biggest part of me doesn't believe that about Darla. You know we all get tarred with that brush but very few of us are ever guilty."

I nodded in agreement. "If the girl was actually having personal problems and talking them over with Pollard…then maybe committed suicide…?"

Marilyn broke in, "And if that's what Darla wanted to see me about… But why me? Why not the parents?"

"Maybe they were the problem."

"So why was the husband going after Darla?"

"I don't know, Admiral. Something else to look into…or tell the police about."

Marilyn touched my arm again lightly. "Am I asking too much, Lexy?"

I straightened and stretched my back. "No. It's beginning to be like it was when I was teaching. The more I have to do, the more I get done. Besides—" Before I could finish, the phone rang, startling us both. Marilyn quickly rounded the bar to answer it.

"Slow down…and bring your voice down. You're screeching in my ear…Okay, yes, yes, if you must know it was Darla Pollard. That's all I can tell you. The police haven't released details…I can't tell you what I don't know. What? Why? I'll see."

She hung up, her lips compressed. Then she said, "That was Gloria Driscoll. Read that short bit of yours in this morning's paper on a death here. Asked me straight out if it was Darla. Wanted me to forget all about our conversation. She was over the edge. Sounded scared."

"I'd say you should talk to Ziegler." At her frown I added, "He might be able to get to them without including you. The girl did work for Pollard, once."

She tapped me under the chin. "By the way, you had to go and finger The Cat, but at least you didn't identify us as gay."

"Worthington insisted—as a compromise in letting me handle developments on the story." I put my back to the bar. "Why do you think those people happened to be in here Friday night?"

"I asked. Don't think I got the truth. She did a song and dance about the other couple being curious about gay places. Side-stepped my question on how they knew about The Cat since our advertising is by word of mouth and alternative papers. And she flat out ignored me when I said I thought I'd seen her in here before."

A pounding at the alley door announced the soft-drink distributor. His white coveralls smudged with dust and grime, the delivery man expertly and speedily hauled in cases and stored them under the bar. Marilyn checked the invoices against the actual delivery and signed the sheet on his clipboard. Even in the dim light, the stones of her many rings sparkled.

When Marilyn returned the clipboard, he said, "Some bruise you've got there."

She held her hand under a night light directly above the bar and I could see a darkened area below the vee of the thumb and first finger. "Don't know where I got it. Hope that's not a sign I'm getting old."

The sandy-haired man laughed boldly. "Not you. I got thirty-year-old customers you could take down anytime."

She tossed him a cold Gatorade. "I'll take that as a compliment but you better get on your way before I change my mind."

I was about to ask her about the bruise when she returned from locking the door, but a light rapping on the front glass interfered. Peering out first, Marilyn angled me a 'what now?' look as she opened the door to Detective Exline.

By way of greeting, she said flatly, "Pardon me for the intrusion, but I just have a quick question or two, Ms. Neff. I want to ask you whether you noticed a broom missing and to know how many you have."

The two women joined me at the bar but remained standing as Exline explained that a broom with a yellow handle and with 'Neff' and 'Cat' inked along the side had been found in the back of the boys' truck. They claimed they had picked it up in the alley near the trash cans but it was obviously too new to have been thrown away. Marilyn admitted to owning some and placing them at various points.

Exline continued, "Exactly how many?"

"Two anyway. The place is professionally cleaned after closing and the cleaners bring their own equipment, so we just need something for quick clean-ups."

"Would you show me where you keep them?"

To Marilyn's, "Yes, one behind the kitchen door with the mop and pail and the extra in the supply room," Exline responded, "Let's check."

I awaited their return, wondering about the connections of the broom, the skinheads, the supply room and Darla Pollard. Trailing the detective, Marilyn shook her head 'no' to me. Exline passed me without a glance and started up the steps to the front exit. My words stopped her on the first step.

61

"What's going on, Robbie?"

She glared at my use of her nickname and answered curtly, "Police business, Ms. Hyatt."

"Should I return your card?" I got up from the bar stool and stood to my full height, annoyed. "Thought we had a…ladies' agreement to share information?"

- She came down from the step but was prudent enough not to move toward me where she would have to look up. "Why, what do you have?"

"I asked first."

Marilyn barged in. "Stop that silly sparring. Go sit at a table and I'll fix some club soda with lemon for those sour dispositions."

We obeyed, seating ourselves opposite each other. I was wise enough to maintain silence while the detective chewed on her lower lip determining a course of action.

Marilyn placed three glasses on the table, each a turmoil of bubbles pummeling slices of lemon. "Now, I'll referee."

I placed my fingers on the table edge in front of me and slid them toward the corners. "Okay, Admiral. I get the message. I don't know where the touchiness came from, Detective. Sorry."

The hard brown of Exline's eyes softened as the gold flecks returned. "No harm." She leaned forward on folded arms. "Do you have something, Lexy?" The slight emphasis on my name earned my regard.

"What do you say, Marilyn?" Knowing I was referring to her conversation with Gloria Driscoll, she grimaced but agreed. She was uncomfortable with Exline's note taking during her recitation and carefully avoided any reference to her personal relationship with Darla Pollard, glaring me into acquiescence.

Exline asked me, "You saw Gloria Driscoll go toward that supply room?"

I answered, "Not really. She may have been going to the restroom. And someone else said she was crying so the restroom's a logical assumption."

Alertly she queried, "Who saw her crying?"

Automatically I covered for Jodi. That was still my card. "I don't remember. There were lots of people milling around. And I don't have any idea whether or not her husband came from back there or just stood with her in the doorway over there. Do you know anything about their daughter's death?"

She sighed, "Some other team must have caught that one. I'm sorry to say there are more than enough deaths to go around several times, but I'll check it out."

"Is it possible to omit mention of Marilyn when you approach the Driscolls?"

She answered me but treated Marilyn to a long appraisal. "I have an appointment with Christine Shoemaker later this afternoon. If I can lead her into mentioning the work-study program and then the girl, that may leave—what is it they call you?—the Admiral, out of it."

Marilyn reached to touch Robbie Exline's bare forearm. "I don't doubt your ability to lead someone."

I gawked at the blatant flirtation. Gripping the arm tighter, Marilyn continued, "Do you go out on the water? That's a muscle for raising sails."

Exline removed her arms from the table and unnecessarily tugged at her light peach, knit vest. She said, "Haven't sailed in a long time."

A wily campaigner, Marilyn turned her attention back to me. "Now, Lexy, claim your share."

I motioned in agreement and said to Exline, "Your turn."

The detective spoke bluntly. "Darla Pollard died quickly from a blow to her larynx, and pressure on her throat. There was bruising—finger marks as well as a blow with something like a piece of pipe...or a broom handle."

I shifted forward on the edge of my seat. "Take a man to do it?"

"Not an absolute. Today's women play tough sports, work out, pump iron, do martial arts, swim, sail..." She glanced at her arm and then at Marilyn. "We aren't afraid of a little muscle. I could control a man twice my weight with a choke hold, but I hope I never have to prove it."

'Why?" I asked.

"I think it is a dangerous maneuver. Too much pressure or too much struggling...and death is possible." Her face set in a stern frown. "That's off the record, Lexy."

"Understood." As though by general consensus we sipped our drinks and spoke of other things like the weather and city politics, trying to ease away from murder. Shortly, Exline pushed her chair back from the table and rose in an abrupt movement. She said, "I would like this conversation to be between you and I."

I corrected, "Me."

"What?"

Marilyn put a hand on Exline's shoulder. "It's a sign she likes you when she corrects your English. Right, Lexy?"

"Aye, aye, Admiral." I watched her accompany Exline to the door keeping her hand on the detective's shoulder.

63

CHAPTER EIGHT

Back at *The Ledger* I confined myself to my cubicle and filed my write-up on the Water Department meeting. Then I tied up loose ends. Mondays were always my day to complete deadlines and set my schedule for the week.

I even roughed out a memo on each of the research ideas fluttering in the back of my mind, tracing the productivity of cancer monies, determining attitudes, means and responsibility in treating the severe pain experienced by the terminally ill. I printed the two memos and slipped them under the weighted wooden etcetera, a gift from a class teasing me for my constant use of the word. I wasn't yet ready to call attention to myself with Worthington and have to respond to questions about Darla Pollard.

All Monday obligations resolved, I studied my notes on Pollard's murder. I added the information gained from Marilyn on Gloria Driscoll and her daughter Stacy, as well as Robbie Exline's brief explanation on the cause of death. I wondered if the detective was truly sharing information with me or trying to use me, hoping to accrue more than she doled out. Noting all the question marks embellishing the pages, I considered ways of erasing them. I especially wanted time with Chrissy minus the protective Janel. I closed the notebook firmly, but not before my 'Chrissy/Jodi???' notation scratched at my eyes.

Even though Luke had stilled my hunger, and brought me into the present, none of that nullified my past relationship with Jodi or eliminated my very real concern over her presence along the fringes of events. She had been in the back area of The Cat at the same time as Pollard. I was sure of that. She had lied about dating Chrissy. Unless Chrissy was the one lying. I steeled myself to register another thought. She knew karate. Unbidden but taunting, an answering refrain floated up from the recesses of my mind…so did Marilyn…and Hal. I ran my finger hard across the my brow, then rested my head in my hand.

"Miss Hyatt."

I didn't push my chair back far enough before turning to the commanding voice of the Iron Maiden and so cracked my knee painfully on the side of my desk. Her perpetually quiescent face reflected no concern for my pain or opinion of the scatological epithet I uttered loudly.

She said, "Your information relating to Miss Darla Pollard," and extended a small sheaf of papers toward me, then about-faced to return to her corner almost before my fingers closed to secure them. My, 'thank you' was spoken to air empty of her being.

On most of the sheets Darla Pollard's name appeared merely as one of several local independent insurance agents. Apparently she had participated in a series of seminars designed to acquaint single and divorced women with the desirability, nature and language of insurance coverage. There were some references to recognition and award for community service projects and contributions. Very carefully I read the article on placement of high school students with small businesses for both a salary and credit toward graduation. Pollard was quoted as praising the program and the students she had encountered, but there was no specific reference to Stacy Driscoll although there was a Stacia Garrison among the list of students.

A flurry of phone calls demanded my attention. The only one I appreciated was from Tamara Gantt in editing, clearing a headline with me for my article on antiterrorist measures being taken in local government buildings. Hopefully her value would be recognized soon and she would be rewarded with advancement. Her incisive mind made her a fine prospect as a journalist, but there was too much truth in her caustic conclusion that, "As a Black woman speaking and writing perfect English, I scare hell out of the establishment. Makes me an uppity nigger."

When I returned to the information on Pollard, I discovered that the efficient Miss MacFadden had included computer entries that had never made publication, probably because they were deemed unworthy of space or advertising had exercised some control. Most were of publicity relating to Insurance Board meetings, conventions, office expansion and such. However, two were admonitions by a state regulatory board for her failure to acquaint policy holders with the limitations of their coverage and clarify binders. One claimant had been seriously injured in the wreck of his company car due to his own negligence and another involved in a fire that destroyed an in-home, small business. A third entry listed several names of persons filing a complaint against Pollard and the American Health Insurance Company. I circled the three entries in red and placed them behind the article on the work-study program which I also checked before putting them on top of the other sheets. I sat drumming my fingers on the pile wondering if they were only facts of Pollard's life or grist for the mills of revenge. My phone buzzed again. I was surprised by the easy, unconstrained voice of Jodi.

She said, "Hey, friend. How about letting me show off for you?"

"What?"

Her tone was almost glib. "I want to make you eat a little crow. You used to complain that I never finished anything. Well, I've advanced from white through yellow and tonight I go orange."

"Jodi, what on earth are you talking about?"

The laughter in my ear no longer made me ache to curve my hand about her long neck to feel the vibration. I found it a cleansing sound. "Belts, Lex. I get my orange belt tonight. Karate. The studio's on Hibiscus. There'll be a demonstration. I want you to come."

Now I understood. "I'd like to." I adopted a mock serious intonation, "Unless you want to use me in the demonstration. I don't relish the idea of being chop-chopped and tossed around."

A villainous "Ha!" hissed in my ear. "Does the fair maiden fear my advances?"

"I've never been anybody's fair maiden. And I saw where your advances were directed Friday night, my friend. But I'll come watch you play."

"Play! Lexy, you are impossible." Her tone became serious, "I do want to see you though. Need to talk about a couple of things."

I regretted the shift but capitalized on it. "Your dating Chrissy Shoemaker for one?"

Jodi met that with silence, then concluded the call. "Be there by seven. Got to run. Bye."

I continued to hold the receiver to my ear until the dial tone disrupted my thoughts. I put it down, saying softly, "Don't do a take-down on me, Jodi. Don't be in trouble."

I looked around, hoping that no one had heard me. Realizing that Marilyn's soda water and lemon had served as my lunch, I decided to supper at Feathers. 'To supper' was another phrase picked up from my grandfather, reflecting his midwestern roots. Friends learned early on to pin me down on whether I meant a noon or evening meal whenever I suggested dinner.

Since Monday evenings meant fewer customers for most restaurants, I didn't hesitate to claim a large, comfortable window booth. The waitress delivered a glass of ice water in the light green solid goblet that I loved to hold, but, knowing my preferences, kept the menu tucked under her arm.

66

"Really good vegetable and beef soup tonight. And some of that sweet corn bread you like." A slight flatness of tone indicated the true southerner's disapproval of sweet cornbread.

"Suits me fine. I'll probably want two bowls. Skipped lunch."

She admonished me with a lifting of severely plucked eyebrows. "I'll hold the second till you're ready."

I smiled my thanks. Watching her move off brought the booths along the back wall into my line of vision. Only one was occupied. In it, his back halfway to me, was Detective Ziegler. Facing him was a young woman, possibly college age. Quickly I averted my eyes as the girl, her face set in defiance, turned her eyes from Ziegler and brushed with mine.

I reached for the goblet of water, my fingers curved under the bowl and touching the stem. Jodi claimed that my delight in goblets was a tantalizing trace memory of my having lived in medieval times. Coming from past lives and going to future ones is a nice thought for someone not sure of the truths of life…or of death.

To escape both Ziegler and Jodi, I opened the mystery novel I had with me. I was scarcely two pages into it when my first bowl of soup arrived. I crumbled corn bread into the bowl and ate as I read. My second serving arrived as I finished the first, along with an additional square of cornbread. The nourishing food elevated my curiosity as well as my body reserves, and I considered attempting conversation with Ziegler when he finished his meal.

I waved away the waitress on her offer of dessert or coffee and scrutinized the girl with Ziegler. She had close-cropped, sun-bleached brown hair jutting out in all directions from her crown. Wide-set eyes, a long nose, and a full mouth gave balance to a rectangular face. Three gemstones studded her left ear and some kind of amulet nestled in the hollow of her throat. When she got up to go to the restroom, I glanced over my book at the sight of her as she strode off, her soft, rust-colored harem pants billowing above dark brown granny boots.

Returning my attention to Ziegler, I could see the sag in his broad shoulders and wondered at his relationship with the girl. Then I realized that while I couldn't see a resemblance in their faces, it was his walk she had. I put down a tip, picked up the check and my book and made my way to his booth. The look in his eyes when he recognized me was a cross between relief and aggravation. Actually I didn't know if the emotional conflict was aimed at me or the momentarily absent girl, or an undetermined half and half.

I said, "May I join you for a moment, Detective?"

He gestured to the empty side and I slid in. We both remained silent as the waitress efficiently cleared away the dishes. Ziegler made a nervous movement toward his jacket pocket and then shook his head ruefully, saying, "Gave up smoking years ago but I still reach for one after a meal."

"Tried gum?" I asked.

He produced a likable grin. "Makes my jaws tired." Then his face became a placid mask. "You in a better mood than the last time we talked, Ms. Hyatt?"

I had forgotten my antagonism outside my apartment the night of the murder when he had asked about my being gay. I narrowed my eyes and he continued hastily, "I want to apologize for my bad manners. I..." He ceased abruptly as the girl reappeared.

I started to shift out of the seat but she stopped me, holding a hand up. Her voice was deeper than I expected and full-toned. "Don't bother. If you'll just hand me the bag in the corner." She turned toward Ziegler and I saw the matching, tense jawlines. "Thanks for dinner, Dad. I'll be in touch." The boots thudded on the tile floor at her hurried and determined exit.

Ziegler looked rueful again. "Now I need to apologize for her bad manners."

I put my elbows on the table and rested my chin in the cradle of my fingers. "It goes with being young. Most of them work it out."

"You really think so?" He saw me glance at his left hand. "Divorced. She lives with her mother. I thought this dinner was a get-together. Found out Casi wanted backup on moving out into her own place."

I asked, "How old?"

"Nineteen. As in I can take care of myself and I don't need anyone looking over my shoulder."

"I've been there. Haven't you? What does she do?"

He sighed. "Goes to the community college and works at the Copy Shop on Sunshine Avenue. Thinks she can support herself now that she was made manager of her shift." He sounded proud.

I removed my chin from my fingers. "I'm stepping in where angels would fear to tread but I'd say it's time to give her control of her life." He rubbed a knuckle against his chin and I added, "With maybe a little discreet looking over her shoulder."

He pierced me with a level stare. His dark eyes reminded me of a cocker spaniel I once had. I saw him start to say something and then decide against it. Had I not been aware of needing to leave soon for Jodi's demonstration, I might have pushed. He caught my glance at the wall clock and checked his bill, saying, "I guess I've kept you from getting to your subject of choice. It wasn't intentional."

68

"I know that. I was wondering about that broom business and the Driscolls, especially the daughter's death…"

Ziegler's face was still again and the eyes unreadable. "The broom was out of place. So were the Driscolls." He looked at me abashedly but I let it pass. "But when I can really check them out, they may fall into place. I've learned to look for the out-of-place things in sudden and unplanned murders."

"You think Pollard's death was unplanned?" I hadn't considered things from that angle.

He answered, "At the moment it's a possibility." He watched me digest that then reached over and tapped the mystery novel at my elbow. "Don't take those too seriously, Ms. Hyatt. Solving murders is police business…and for good reason." At my general stiffening he said, "And don't go acting like my daughter. Looking for a murderer is a bigger deal than looking for your own apartment."

Reluctantly I acknowledged his point. "Granted. But I can't turn off my interest or concern. Not when it involves a lot of people I happen to know and identify with. I was there. It's not just that I'm a reporter snooping after a story—I guess I also feel, well, protective." I relaxed with a shrug. "And I'm not going to act like your daughter. I'm not going to stomp off to avoid things."

Ziegler lifted himself from the booth on strong legs without bending. Ridiculously, I was glad that my hiker legs made the same movement possible. He waited for me to precede him to the cash register. I dropped my few coins of change into the S.P.C.A. canister as he placed his bill and the correct amount on the counter.

Walking behind me to the exit, he said, "Appreciate your passing on the bit about Gloria Driscoll to Detective Exline. We owe you one."

Apparently Robbie had not indicated her part in the exchange. Without turning I said, "And I'll be putting in a claim."

At the door I ignored his movement to reach around me and push it open. Instead I shoved my way to the sidewalk and held the door for him. He crooked his mouth. "You are a strong-minded woman."

"As is your daughter." I was puzzled by a sudden withdrawal in his manner as he tossed me a cold good night and strode to his car. This time I had no idea what I had done to engender his reaction.

On the way to the karate studio I listened to a light-rock station seeking to ease a growing tension concerning why Jodi would wish to see me. Once I located the correct strip mall, only the cars in the parking lot told me there was an activity taking place in one of the connecting properties. When someone opened a door second from the left end, I could see bright light and people milling about.

Meant to be a store, the room inside was square and painted an uncompromising oyster white. Much of the floor was covered in gray-blue mats, and folding chairs lined the back wall toward the parking lot and the two side walls. At the back were many students in the traditional loose uniforms with colored belts. I assumed the people seated around the three walls were family and friends and I chose a seat.

When a young boy took a seat on the other side of me, I asked him if he knew what would be going on. Still at an age to like explaining things to adults, he gave me far more than I needed, peppered with martial-arts terminology. Condensed, it amounted to the information that the students who had advanced to a third level were in a back room receiving their orange belts from the master in private. Soon they would demonstrate their skills. I didn't know if this was an Americanized approach or reflective of Asian roots, and I wasn't inclined to ask.

Within a few moments the students wearing white and yellow belts scurried to seat themselves crosslegged around the perimeter of the mats. In the silence that followed, a line of students wearing burnt orange belts came through an archway in the back wall and took up positions on the mats in three lines of five each. Stepping in front of them, the master greeted the spectators and gave a short speech about the value of the training.

I had expected someone inscrutably Asian but this man was white, large and loud-voiced. So much for my preconceived notions. His speech was followed by demonstrations of kicks and punches, clearly aggressive. Then two or three pairs at a time would take to the mats and appear to attack and defend with much bowing and gutturally explosive sounds. Eventually the lower-rank students produced rectangles of boards and wooden posts which the others then cracked or shattered with rapid kicks and powerful hand chops. I was so wrapped up in watching Jodi, the set of her face failing to completely dispel the hint of cynicism in her nature, that Janel escaped my attention until she took the center area with a tall, muscular man. Her face was a hard visage of obdurate antagonism. I shuddered at an image of that narrow foot or that hard, rigid hand being driven into Darla Pollard's fragile throat. A clipped, low moan escaped me as my mind cast Jodi in a similar scene. I pretended I was responding to the fierceness of the demonstration to avoid solicitous inquiries by my neighbors.

The performance concluded and Jodi approached me with a mockingly brazen swagger. The peripheral vision that had served me so well in the classroom enabled me to see the alert stance of Janel and the cold disdain glazing those dark eyes.

Jodi bowed to me. "Need sand kicked in anyone's face, Lexy?"

We had once laughed together over the Charles Atlas body-building ads in old comic books at a fair I was covering for the paper. "I think your cohort Janel would like to kick some in yours, if not something more violent."

The playfulness went out of Jodi's manner. "She's part of what I want to talk to you about. I'll be back as soon as I change." Some of the play came back. "Watch yourself. There are some delicious morsels around but every one of them could swift-kick you into next week."

I shook my head at her retreating back, marveling at the ease I felt with her since my night with Luke. Now I could appreciate her animal elegance without a clenching of thighs. I could let her alluring voice wash over me teasingly without a quickening of breath.

The blade of Janel's voice cut into my thoughts. "Are you two a thing?"

A quick glance assured me no one was in earshot. "Are you and Chrissy partners?" I tried to toughen my stance and my tone. Jodi's grace was the insouciance of late afternoon sun and heat. Janel had the stillness of a night animal watchful and ready to react. I was wary of her.

"Her name is Christine. Use it."

"Mine is fancier, too. But I don't mind Lexy." I decided to ease the situation. "Jodi and I are now just friends." I regretted the now as I saw awareness register in her eyes.

"Then give her some advice. Tell her to stay away from Christine. She had Darla Pollard. What's she need with the secretary after she's had the boss?" Janel started for the door, then whipped her body back towards me. "Remind her that I can take her down as easily off the mats as on."

CHAPTER NINE

I got caught in a small traffic jam leaving the karate demonstration and heading for Swan Lake, Jodi's choice of a meeting place for our 'talk.' When I finally reached Swan Lake, a small park near the downtown area and beautifully tended, Jodi was already seated on a bench under a towering magnolia tree. It would be a good six weeks before the air would be laden with the sensuous redolence of the large, pearl-white blossoms, but the lighter aroma of the bark drifted on the still night air.

My mind vibrated to a fluttering of pain as I remembered our last conversation under that tree. Jodi and I had huddled in windbreakers too flimsy for an early winter cold snap and the chill off the water had only increased our bleakness at separating. I wondered if she had chosen this spot perversely or if the choice was another serving of the indifference that had now provoked, now wounded me. I stood behind the bench and placed my hand lightly on her right shoulder. "Good night to watch for shooting stars," I said.

Jodi gave my fingers a single stroke. "Look at Orion. Takes up nearly half the sky." She watched me come around and seat myself leaving half the bench between us. She continued, "March first…a new moon night. Never did understand that term when it's really no moon. At least it's no visible moon."

"That's why it's also called dark of the moon." Though I was at peace now with our separation, I found the setting disquieting. Or was it the discovery that a modicum of hunger remained? I thought it time to focus and said, "What are we here to talk about, Jodi?" I hoped she didn't hear the constraint in my voice.

She shifted, stretching out her long legs and putting her hands in her pockets. "Things, people…me. The lies I told Detective Ziegler when he interviewed me today."

"Jodi!"

She straightened, turning toward me and pulling one leg up on the bench. The pinkish glow of a halogen lamp overhead highlighted the frown disturbing her strong features. "Don't moralize, Lexy. I seem to remember you subscribing to Emily Dickinson's 'Tell all the truth but tell it slant.'"

"Slanted truth and lies aren't the same...and you know it. And maybe that's why you want to talk to me. Right?"

The bold lines and calm planes of her face reasserted themselves. "Maybe. I just know I don't feel comfortable about things. I need your ear." She extended an arm and tugged at my ear lobe with thumb and forefinger. "Is that a part of you I can still have?"

"Always, Jodi. Always. But can I ask some questions first?" At her affirmative nod I asked in rapid succession, "What's the problem with Janel? Did you have an affair with Darla Pollard? What's with Chrissy?"

Silence settled in the space between us. I waited for Jodi to break it. Finally she responded, "Yes. I had an affair with Darla. I was restless after you and I broke up. I wandered in and out of casual relationships. None of them meant anything special. I liked it that way. Light and easy seems to be what I'm best at."

I asked, "Was it different with Darla?"

"No. We didn't even spend a lot of time together. The sex was okay but we didn't have much to talk about before and after." She tapped my knee and her expression was roguish. "That's what I miss the most, Lex. The way we talked."

I gave a disgruntled laugh. "You sure know how to make a woman feel good." Then I confessed, "I miss it, too." Then quickly I steered the conversation back on course. "When was the fling with Darla?"

"About six months ago. I wound things down fast after she had me run her by Leather Fever one evening to drop off some papers for the owner. I knew that the place was managed up front by C. K. Chen, but I had heard that Marilyn was the real owner. On the way there, Darla bragged about having had an affair with the owner. Before I could detour her onto another subject, she told me she would have liked for the affair to continue, but the woman was too restrictive about some things."

"Like other women on the side. The Admiral plays a fair game."

Jodi agreed. "I know. I like her as much as you do. That's partly why I let things die off between Darla and me. And there were no problems about it. We weren't important to each other." She exhaled a deep sigh and stretched out again. "So I don't know why I didn't tell Ziegler I knew her...except that I didn't want it getting back to Marilyn."

I was confused. "Why? Marilyn doesn't meddle in our lives. A little advice here and there, but no interference. What's the rest of it, Jodi?"

She laughed self-deprecatingly. "You know me, Lexy. You know I like my image. I kind of let Darla pick me up one Sunday afternoon at the Out of Bounds bookstore and I floated along behind her for awhile." Her eyes were clearly somber even in the darkness of the moonless night. "I've always known Marilyn thought more of you than of me and I didn't want to lose any more ground with her." Her voice dropped lower. "And it still matters to me what you think…even if I don't always show it."

I drew her into my arms and rubbed my nose in her pliant hair, inhaling the clean scent. We weren't meant to be each other's life but I would always want to protect her from the fear of her own frailties. After a moment I felt her gather herself to withdraw from my embrace and so, released her myself, but the warmth of closeness remained.

"Chrissy and Janel?" I reminded her.

"No big deal." She shrugged. "Silliness. Darla liked me to meet her at her office when we were going out so we could leave from there. I liked talking with Chrissy. Found out she was into cross-stitch and took her all those I never finished or even started. Remember?"

"How could I forget! I impaled myself on enough of the needles. Did she finish any?"

Jodi's tone swelled with pleasure. "Absolutely. She did the one I cared about…the tilting mailbox in front of the old log fence with all the wild-flowers. Had it framed and gave it to me." Her voice grew sober. "Darla was good to her as a secretary but not as a person. She kept bullying her and Chrissy would take it like you would from a big sister you admired."

I said, "Are you sure it was bullying? Maybe it was the big sister/little sister kind of sparring."

"No. It was more like mean teasing. One day when I was waiting for Darla, Chrissy was feeding the fish in the tank by her desk and baby-talking to them as they came to the top to feed. Darla came out of her office and made fun of her. Then she started on her about picking up strays, especially Mexican strays." Jodi got up from the bench putting her hands in her back pockets. She turned back to look down on me, her face shadowed. "That was the only time I ever saw Chrissy stand up to Darla. Said that Janel was not a stray and that her family was from Lebanon. Told Darla to leave her alone about Janel."

Jodi continued, "Darla put on a cruel smile and told me that Janel was Chrissy's tough dyke lover. Lexy, Chrissy was horrified and hurt! We had never spoken about our lesbianism though I had guessed and she couldn't believe that Darla had just tossed it out in the office like that."

"What did you do?"

"Not enough. I pushed Darla toward the door and winked at Chrissy, trying to tell her it was all right and didn't matter."

I got up and walked a few steps nearer the lake's edge. Star reflections winked as a light breeze rippled the dark water. "So what are your problems with Janel?"

"She has the problem, some big chip on her shoulder. Being mistaken for Latina when she's Lebanese, that kind of thing. I'm sure she confronts racism all the time. What can I say—she's just butch to the core!"

I sighed. "And I can imagine she's had to walk away from family, tradition and religion. Not all of us are as lucky with our families as you and I. But, Jodi, she seems to go out of her way to confront you."

Jodi bent down and picked up a stone which she then sent skipping toward the center of the lake. "The first time I met her she was more than just confrontational. Chrissy had heard me tell Darla that I was thinking of taking up karate and had told me about the studio where Janel went. I signed up there. On my third time I spotted Janel by the description Chrissy gave. I introduced myself and tried to shake hands. I didn't even have time to breathe before she'd tossed me over her shoulder. I landed hard on my ass."

I couldn't keep the amusement out of my voice. "And you've stuck with the karate! I'm proud of you."

Jodi adopted an aggrieved tone. "You think I'd let someone younger and smaller run me off? Come on, Lex. But she didn't stop there. Before I could put down my hands to lift myself, she turned me on my stomach with one of those arm and shoulder twists and told me to stay away from Chrissy!"

"What was round two like?"

"There wasn't one. Janel stomped off out the door and I stuck with the class, trying not to look anyone in the eye. Which was easy since they were all shorter than me." She touched the back of her hand to my lips to stop me from my habitual correcting—something about me that had irritated her.

I smiled, enjoying the easy camaraderie between us. "I suppose Chrissy had talked to Janel about you and she had jumped to wrong conclusions. Do you think she treats Chrissy rough?"

Jodi said resolutely, "I don't. The few times Chrissy spoke of her there was a softness in her voice...a protectiveness. Which was sweet considering it was coming from someone who seemed to need protecting herself. I made a point of going by the office when I knew Darla would be out and talked to Chrissy about it."

"And?" We walked back to sit on the bench. Above us the limbs and foliage of the magnolia tree stirred in the eddies of increasingly strong wind.

"Chrissy was upset about what happened but she still defended Janel. Said that she had made the mistake of telling Janel that Darla tried to convince her Janel wasn't good enough. Then Chrissy felt like she had added to the mistake by talking about me too much and how nice I was to her. Janel decided that Darla must have put me up to it to lure Chrissy away." Jodi voiced chagrin. "I wanted to say that I wasn't into cradle robbing but I didn't think that would help anybody's ego. It wasn't long after that when I backed out of things with Darla."

I scooted forward on the bench, gripping the front board with both my hands. "What do you know about Darla and Janel both being at The Cat Friday night?"

I couldn't tell if Jodi was hesitating or thinking. Finally she said, "When I saw Darla come in, I figured it didn't have anything to do with me."

"But you left the bar area right away."

Jodi leaned forward looking at me severely. I felt the camaraderie slipping away. "I didn't want any contact with her," she said. "I didn't want her talking to me in front of any of you."

I couldn't stop. "Did you see her before she was found dead?"

Again the hesitation. "No…but I heard her. When I went back to the restroom later, I had forgotten about her until I heard her in Marilyn's office. I couldn't hear the other person but I figured it was the Admiral. I told Ziegler about hearing voices but said I couldn't recognize them. Actually I stood there trying to hear. I was holding on to the restroom door so hard while I concentrated on listening that poor Rita had to really tug so that she could get it open to come out. We laughed about it. Then when I came out I had to push my way through that arguing husband and wife…" Her voice trailed off and I knew we were both remembering our conversation outside Pollard's office Saturday morning when she had denied knowing Darla and pretended she was dating Chrissy. She had even denied going back to the restroom.

"Jodi…," I whispered intently.

"Don't go judging, Lexy. You know how I like to keep things smooth with people. I didn't feel good about my affair with Darla. I wanted to hide it, camouflage it. How was I to know she was going to get herself killed? After I fudged the truth with Ziegler this morning, I kept thinking about that quote from Mark Twain about not having to remember anything if you told the truth in the first place." She was warm toward me again but it didn't reassure me.

"And you didn't see Janel at all?"

Jodi shook her head no. "Maybe she followed Darla there. For all I

76

know she killed her. I don't know all the ins and outs of their connections. Maybe Janel had more than she could take of Darla's interference."

I dug in. "So why were you at Pollard's office Saturday. Why were you talking with Chrissy…and what about?"

"Is this the reporter, Lex? Or my friend?"

"Always your friend, Jodi. But all this has to get cleared up." I took her hand. "Level with me."

She exhaled loudly. "The truth sounds dumb. When I got home late Friday night, more like Saturday morning, I had two messages from Chrissy on my machine. One was left Friday afternoon saying she wanted to talk to me about a problem Darla was having—"

I interjected, "A problem Darla was having? Not one she was having with Darla?"

"Right," Jodi answered. "Then a later call said to forget the first one. So I went by out of curiosity. Chrissy insisted that she had just overreacted to something. Was sorry she bothered me. You know…" She squeezed my hand. "I'm giving you the truth, Lex."

I hoped so. We sat for a long time while looking out over the lake, holding hands with the tentativeness of adolescents. Long enough for Orion to drop partially below the western horizon. My mind was filled with Darla, Marilyn, Chrissy, Janel…Jodi. I didn't know what filled hers.

Eventually Jodi released my hand, cupped the back of my head and pulled me near. Her kiss was gentle—the flick of her tongue the beat of a butterfly wing. Her voice was husky in my ear. "Don't give up on me, Lexy. You know I'm not a bad person."

I wanted to know it.

CHAPTER TEN

The police permitted The Cat to reopen on Wednesday, not my usual day to go, but I went out of support. Since my talk with Jodi, I hadn't made any further headway, and thought it might be good to start all over at The Cat again. The well-muscled woman bouncer in leather pants wasn't hard to miss, someone Marilyn had hired from the Leather Fever, no doubt. I nodded to her and then took my usual seat at the bar while Hal prepared drinks for a few early customers. I noticed that the hallway was well within the bouncer's scope from her position at the front door, but I resisted the urge to glance down its dull length, now cleared up of all the crime tape. Darla Pollard haunted my mind—her hair displaced, purple jacket askew, her sightless eyes staring.

Hal made more of a flourish than usual, presenting my bourbon and lemon-flavored Perrier. He let a wedge of lime plop into the glass saying, "This one's on Rita."

At my questioning expression he added, "She was in here this afternoon hoping you might be here. Said she's going to be running a booth over at the fairgrounds from tomorrow on through the weekend. Wanted to buy you a drink. Said it was for last Sunday."

I laughingly shook my head at his presumptuously raised eyebrows. "We shared some breakfast-time Sunday morning and we talked. It was good for both of us. I'm the one who owes her a drink—she gave me a good idea for an article, maybe even a series."

"What on?"

As I was opening my mouth to answer, I checked the response, painfully mindful of Marilyn's private disclosure of his cancer.

Instead I made a joke of reporters needing to protect their ideas from the journalism thieves who, like industrial spies, no doubt hid electronic devices in limes as well as olives. Hal took no offense and moved down bar to draw draft beers for a newly arrived foursome. He delivered the beers himself as Alice was still readying tables. The four women were having an animated

78

discussion and I noted Hal's embarrassment at comments or questions directed to him.

When he returned behind the bar, I asked, "They giving you a rough time, Hal?"

His frown bore no enmity. "Wanted me to cast a deciding vote on whether or not centerfolds in lesbian magazines were okay." He paused. "How about it, Lexy, are they okay? Or like one of the ladies said, just more of the same old pornography?"

"Haven't really thought about it. The few nudes I've seen in magazines like *Girlfriends* haven't offended me. In fact I thought there was some clever nose-thumbing going on."

Hal leaned on the bar in front of me. "I don't follow."

I said, "Well, the women in those centerfolds have seemed natural and at ease with who they are. They don't reflect the manipulation or exploitation of most of the men's magazines. There's no sense of someone else posing them as though they are just so much T and A. But I'm not comfortable with all this business of what's PC, which is one of the reasons I got out of teaching."

He looked perplexed.

I laughed. "Talk to Marilyn about it, Hal."

His face stiffened, emphasizing deep wrinkles. His words were heavy with anxiety. "I've got to talk to her, all right. Had to go to the police station to be interviewed by Ziegler again this morning. He's good at his job. Talked real nice. Hid the hard questions inside a lot of easy ones. Let me hang myself good."

I was immediately interested and concerned. "Care to explain that?"

"Yeah. Maybe it would be a smart idea to practice on you before I face Sis." He lowered his voice. "I kept telling Ziegler that I didn't know Darla Pollard, that I never noticed her come in here, that I didn't know if Marilyn knew her. After awhile he switched to questions about Marilyn being a lesbian. What I thought about it. Who'd she go with. Stuff like that."

"How'd you answer?"

"Told him I didn't consider it any of my business. Or his. I'll give him credit; he said it wouldn't be any of his business if no one had been murdered."

I followed a sip of my drink with, "How did he trip you up?"

He gave the bar a vigorous swipe with his clean towel. "Pulled out an application for an insurance policy and tossed it in front of me." At my quizzical frown he explained, "I had forgotten all about it. When Darla kept calling Marilyn, I thought I'd check her out and see if I could tend to things. Get her off Marilyn's back."

"Did the Admiral know?"

A flash of his sister's sardonic humor brightened his eyes. "Oh, no. Big sisters can do things for little brothers. Not the other way around. I went into Darla's office saying I was interested in some medical insurance. Wanted to look her over and see what I thought before I really started meddling. Shit...always thought that was something only women did."

I saluted him with my glass. "Working in a women's bar is raising your consciousness, Hal. Didn't you think she'd connect your last names?"

"I had a reason enough to be there and keep Marilyn out of it."

I kept my face bland knowing that the cancer was his reason.

He continued. "I hate to admit it, but she did a good job talking to me about extra insurance. Was blunt on how anything I could get would be impossibly high. Made a couple of suggestions about things I might check on someplace else. And she talked nice about Marilyn. Nothing to indicate any intimacy between them. Made it sound like they just had a good business relationship." He folded the towel. "I left the place figuring I'd stay out of things."

"But now Ziegler's brought you into them."

"Yow." Hal grimaced. "He found the application she had me fill out in case she ran across something. I tried to make out like I had gone to lots of places looking for insurance and hadn't remembered one from another." He rubbed the back of his neck. "But he did that same waiting bit Marilyn does. Just stared at me easy like until I finally told him how it really was. But I tried to put a no-big-deal slant on everything."

"That may be for the best, Hal." I wasn't sure I believed that.

"Maybe. Sure hate to tell Marilyn though. Got to do it tonight. She's supposed to see Ziegler tomorrow."

Hal returned to preparing drinks and I to my thoughts. I was having increasing difficulty distancing myself from Darla Pollard's murder. When I reviewed my notes and perceived clues relating to my friends, my mind shied away from pursuing them. I was even uncomfortable with calculations of Janel or Chrissy being involved. I sympathized with Chrissy's apparent need to strengthen as a person. And Janel's feisty belligerence earned my admiration, muted as it was by her concern for Chrissy. I actually liked her insistence that her partner be called by the more adult Christine.

I couldn't even begin to fantasize lethal connections with the unknown Driscolls, the bigoted skinheads, or the accidental plumber without feeling guilty. Some crime reporter I was turning out to be.

I spun my glass down the polished dark wood toward Hal, shaking my head 'no' to another. More women than usual for a Wednesday night were scattered about the lounge. Several were unfamiliar. I supposed that word of suspicious death had brought some of them. A buoyant clamor of voices from the alcove beyond the dance floor was infused with the discordant rhythms of clicking billiard balls and the electronic beeping of dart boards.

I recognized Marilyn's back hunched over the lighted slots and numbers of the large jukebox where she was rapidly punching in a starter set of songs. The band provided live music only on Thursday, Friday and Saturday nights. I knew her selections would run heavy toward rhythm and blues. Hal, too, was watching Marilyn. I saw him look away from her toward the opening front doors and the gloom darkening his face was dispersed by the warmth of a smile.

I lifted a hand in greeting to Melody who was descending the steps with ponderous grace, her airy personality and tranquil temperament in counter-poise to her hefty dimensions. Skittering along beside her was her petite partner, Victoria Nugent.

Magnanimously, Melody always ignores rude stares and snide remarks prompted by their disparity in size; Victoria was oblivious to them. Victoria's rapid-fire manner overshadowed any meagerness of frame and flesh. Even the strands of her ginger-brown hair whipped and fluttered in concert with her darting hands. The only stillness about her lay in the remarkably large amber eyes, dominating an elfin face. More than once I contemplated the pleasure Melody must feel when drawn by those eyes.

I still feel embarrassed when I think about my introduction to Victoria. At work behind the bar, Melody had pointed to a table of three and told me to go meet the allegro to her andante, phrasing which I understood later. I assumed, prejudicially I now realize, that Victoria was the largest of the three and ignored the petite young woman who got up from the table and passed me as I approached. I had engaged the other two in conversation making especially complimentary remarks about Melody to the tall, broad-hipped woman in a floor-length silk dress.

After a few moments of meager responses, I had turned back toward the bar and the sight of Melody's glowing cheeks and wide grin as she jerked her thumb toward the diminutive figure returning from the restroom. Back at the bar and trying to avoid Melody's gleeful eyes, I constantly twisted my head to keep a rapidly stepping Victoria in my line of vision. I very nearly sat on my hands to keep from stopping her twirling the stool next to me and I never saw the drink Melody handed her reach her lips long enough for a real swallow.

That same night, at Melody's urging, I had gone with Victoria and the other two women to a supper club where, with two others, they formed a jazz dance combo. They had played to more than appreciative applause. And when Victoria soloed on her clarinet, her tones ricocheting from dark to light, she had captivated her audience.

Now Melody signaled me to join them. As I sat, she said, "Seems like weeks since I've seen you, Lexy."

She motioned to Hal for two wine coolers but I declined anything. The drinks, a refreshing primrose pink, were delivered by Alice, a straight woman about thirty and a single mother. She had walked in a couple of years ago, told Marilyn she was a good waitress or barmaid, that she was tired of being hit on and that she had heard that lezzies didn't grope the help.

Alice created her own acceptance when it was discovered that she could do fancy needlework designs on T-shirts and sweatshirts and would do so at fair prices. Now when her daughter played kiddie soccer on Saturday mornings, there was always a contingent of Cat regulars cheering from the sidelines.

Before Alice could leave our table, I said, "You served this area last Friday night. Do you remember the straight couples?" She indicated that she did and I continued, "Remember anything they said that might have had something to do with the dead woman?"

"Maybe. I was seeing if they wanted another round when Marilyn walked by taking that woman to the back. One of the guys got all bent out of shape and kept trying to get up. His wife kept trying to keep him at the table. The only thing I heard was him saying something like, 'Damn dyke changed my...' oh, I've lost the name."

"Could it have been Stacy?"

"Yeah. I think so. That mean anything?"

"I'm not sure. Did you tell either of the detectives?"

Alice half-closed her eyes and hesitated before saying, "I didn't talk to anyone. When I asked Marilyn if I could leave before the cops got here, she just said something about how could I be here on my night off. She's a good woman."

I agreed with her about the Admiral but I was becoming less and less happy with Marilyn's apparent circumvention of the truth. I hoped she would lay things out clearly for Ziegler tomorrow. Her evasions were being discovered and I didn't want the detective giving them more weight than they merited. The same went for Jodi's meanderings on and off the path of truth. And Hal. How far would he go to protect a beloved sister?

Melody's "Come back, Lexy," drew me from the clutch of concern as she said, "I saw Detective Exline this morning. She kind of walked me through that night. Had me tell a lot of little things...like what drinks I

82

served to people, topics of conversations with regulars, new people I noticed. Made me remember things."

"How so?" I asked.

"Now don't get upset but I found myself telling her about keeping an eye on your reactions to Jodi and sending you off to dinner. That made me remember Jodi being back in the restroom after Marilyn took Darla back there. What I really remembered was her having to get past the arguing hus-band and wife over there in the doorway."

I was glad that Marilyn had already told Robbie Exline about Gloria Driscoll's phone calls and meeting with her. I wasn't as happy with the emphasis on Jodi. I asked Melody if she had recalled any more.

"Yes. When I was describing new people, I remembered that little, dark one with the leather mesh and tattoos. Noticed her right away because she stayed up on the steps looking over the room. Looking for someone I'm sure. Watched her check out the game room and the dining room. Then she headed back towards the bar, for a drink I thought, but went on down toward the restroom."

"Wonder why I didn't notice her?" I said.

Melody twirled strands of her champagne-blonde hair. "Because you had eyes only for Jodi and tuning out like you were doing a minute ago."

"Watch out, Melody, she's going to hiss at you," Victoria inserted.

I frowned at Victoria but remained silent.

Melody added, "I meant to watch for her to come back. She seemed real uncomfortable and only here looking for someone. But I guess I forgot about her until that Exline took me back over everything."

I thought about Ziegler's comment on out-of-place things and sudden murder. Janel had definitely been out of place at The Cat. And now I was wondering if Janel's antagonism toward me was less a matter of my con-nection with Jodi and more a matter of my having seen her leaving the restroom just as Darla Pollard's body was discovered. That was a disquiet-ing thought.

Just then I heard Marilyn's gruff, good-natured voice carrying over the jukebox as she greeted her patrons at tables and at the bar. Hal squared his shoulders as she neared him and spoke a short sentence to her. She gave him a curt nod and watched him move off, twisting caps from bottles of beer to hand Alice. I assumed he had made arrangements to talk privately with her later.

Melody said in a solemn tone, "I envy Marilyn."

Victoria and I turned toward her questioningly.

She explained, "Harold's attitude toward her. He doesn't care that she's a lesbian. They're really close. I lost my brother when I came out."

An unusual stillness settled over Victoria as she laid a hand gently on her partner's forearm. She even spoke more slowly. "I read somewhere that we grow on our losses…that we improve. You've never needed improving. The loss is your brother's. He'll know it someday."

I blinked back unaccustomed tears as Melody placed a hand on Victoria's and they descended into each other's eyes. Quietly I removed myself from the table, waved to Hal, and gave him a clenched fist as I glanced at Marilyn. He grinned and nodded understanding.

Moments later I sat in my car in the parking lot scribbling additions into my notebook on Hal's and Melody's detective interviews. I couldn't see anything particularly meaningful in any of it. I wasn't sure there was anything meaningful in the whole notebook.

Suddenly I heard the dull poof of an air rifle and the ping of a BB striking metal. As a kid I had put in more than enough hours pinging BBs into soft-drink cans not to recognize the distinctive sound now. I lowered my window a couple of inches and listened carefully. This time the poof of the air rifle was followed by the shattering of glass as one of the floodlights in the parking lot exploded.

Foolishly I leaped from the car, looking for the culprit. A door was open in a dirty truck two rows back, and the dim interior light was enough to show me the bald heads and bare arms of skinheads. Wisely I dove back in the car as I realized the one using the door for an arm rest was aiming the rifle at me. This time I heard no pinging sound but I felt the impact of the BB on my shoe. I kept my head down and started to press the horn but then froze at a cacophony of sounds behind me. I risked a peek. A slight figure was attacking the rifleman with deft punches and kicks. The driver gunned the truck motor and screamed obscenities. His tires squealed as he pulled into the street, his pal scrambling into the back. I opened my car door again and watched Janel retrieve the rifle and strut toward me.

CHAPTER ELEVEN

"Dumb asses!" Janel hefted the air rifle like a trophy. "Not even tough enough to have a real gun."

"For which I am more than a little thankful." I had removed my loafer and was plucking the BB from the scuffed suede. After replacing the shoe and rising from the car, I extended my hand toward this scrappy bantam of a woman. "And I'm more than a little thankful that you happened along."

Neither of us blinked until Janel warily, and briefly, gripped my hand. She spoke with little inflection. "What were they after you about?"

I closed the car door, backed against it, and pointed to the broken light. "It's The Cat they're after. I didn't see them long enough to tell if it was the same two arrested here Monday when they wanted to decorate the walls with their own special slogans." Her somber eyes under tapered brows narrowed in angry understanding. I added, "They could have been buddies putting in their half-cent's worth."

This time her intonation was brittle with antagonism. "So you high class queers catch it too."

I muffled my irritation. "We're not high class, Janel. We all make choices, have preferences, develop our own styles. If lesbians can't be tolerant of our own differences, how can we expect it from the straight world?"

"They never give it to us." There was such cold conviction in her steely voice.

"Some do. Come in The Cat with me while I tell Marilyn about this out here and let me buy you a drink."

"No!"

Thwarted and impatient, I hissed. It so startled or confused her that there was a softening of her hardness.

She said less harshly but in clipped phrasing, "I can't take the time. I'm looking for Christine. I was checking this parking lot for her car. I need to get on with it." She walked back toward her truck, swinging the air rifle effortlessly but with less cocksureness.

I followed her a few steps. "Janel." She stopped and looked over her shoulder at me challengingly. Bluntly I asked, "Are you worried about her?"

She turned fully toward me and I could see the struggle for words in the soundless movement of her lips. There was more than the checking up on a girlfriend going on. I risked another request. "Let me run back inside just a minute. Then I'll tag along with you. Extra pair of eyes and all that." She remained motionless, the dark eyes revealing nothing. I rolled the BB between my thumb and forefinger where she could see. "A little pay back."

Not knowing if she would wait, I hurried back into The Cat and reported the incident to Hal, leaving again as he called the police. I told him what little I could about the two skinheads and their dingy truck while asking him to leave Janel out of it. Might give me a little leverage with her.

She had pulled her red and black truck to the slight incline into the street, the dark portions gleaming with the reflected colors of pulsating neon signs. The idling motor ran smoothly but, as I crossed in front of the vehicle, the soft purring became a sonorous rumble. I neither flinched nor jerked my head to glare.

Once I was settled on the passenger side, Janel said in a neutral tone, "Sorry about the leg room. Christine and I are runts."

I ignored the flagellation. "I know a skinhead out there who doesn't see you that way. And I hear you tossed Jodi over your shoulder." That surprised her into almost smiling. "And you accomplished something I never did."

Her swift look before concentrating on the traffic was an obvious question.

I answered, "You made her mad enough to stick with something."

She half-commented, half-questioned, "She couldn't stick with you?"

"Not so much that as we just couldn't blend enough to ever really live together."

"How much...blending...does it take?" I knew she was thinking of Chrissy and herself, and waited to see if she would add anything. She did. "Christine and I were okay until a few months ago. Then Darla and Jodi had to mess with us."

"Maybe Darla...not Jodi." Despite the contemptuous disbelief in her look, I argued on, "Jodi told me how much she admired Chrissy for standing up to Darla about you...and how she disliked Darla's behavior. And she doesn't interfere with other people." We paused at a red light and I said very softly, "Don't let senseless jealousy..."

Janel seized my upper arm with a force I knew would leave bruises, and spat through clenched teeth, "I'm not jealous. I care. I'm wor—"

The light flashed green, and she gunned the truck through the intersec-

86

tion. I made no reply and resisted the urge to massage my arm. If Janel truly wasn't jealous, what was she worried about? And how could I get her relaxed enough with me to explain?

Eventually we angled into an apartment complex of several two-story buildings in a shabbier part of town. No landscaping and a littered cement parking lot intensified the drabness even under cover of darkness.

Janel read my sweeping glance and said defensively, "I wanted us to move in together and get a better place as soon as my raise came through at UPS. But when it did, Christine said it had to wait for awhile. I know Darla was pushing at her about something...not just me."

We drove further back into the complex until Janel stopped in front of a building dark except for one apartment. She said exasperatedly, "She hasn't even been home. There's no light on."

"How about the office? Maybe there was stuff that had to be done. Business goes on no matter who dies." I experienced a twinge of guilt at my cavalier dismissal of Darla's importance. Back in traffic and heading for Pollard's office, I chose another approach to reduce her hostility. "Janel, I understand what it is to be worried. I'm worried about who killed Darla Pollard. I don't want it to be any of my friends..." I bounced bruisingly against the truck door as Janel swerved into the curb and hit the brakes. Stopping my forward plunge with hands against the dashboard, I yelled, "Hey!"

It didn't cut off her, "I ought to put you out here! You want my Christine to be the one who did it? Just so long as it's not your precious Jodi!"

We both breathed heavily in the ensuing silence. Presently I was able to say calmly but with firmness, "Look. I want a truce. I don't want Jodi guilty. I don't want Chrissy...Christine guilty. I'd like for no one to be guilty. But it doesn't work that way."

The rapid rise and fall of her small breasts beneath the light-weight sweatshirt slowed gradually. A rising March wind detoured through the truck cab and lifted our hair. A palpable silence hovered between us. I resisted the desire to brush it aside with another statement, waiting cautiously for her to resolve her own turmoil.

Janel touched a small, delicate dream-catcher—a silver and blue web with three trailing feathers—dangling from the rearview mirror, and stilled its motion. She said tentatively, "It doesn't come easy to me, but I'll try a truce."

Wisely I maintained my silence until we pulled into the stripmall containing Pollard's office. Chrissy, her back to the wide window, was clearly visible at the aquarium along a side wall near her desk. With fluid movements, Janel slid from the truck, ran up the sidewalk, and tapped lightly on the window. A startled Chrissy dropped something in the aquarium as she swung about abruptly. Immediately, relief flooded her face as she recognized Janel, and she hurried to unlock the door.

I had opened my door but hadn't yet exited the truck. As Chrissy held open the office door, Janel indicated with a jerk of her head for me to join them. Considering that her first active acknowledgment of our truce, I hastened to enter the office before she changed her mind. Chrissy held the heavy glass door for us with one hand. In the other was a plastic freezer bag bulging with water. I walked to the aquarium and, seeing that she had dropped a small net scoop into it, carefully immersed my hand and half my forearm to retrieve it.

I watched the zigzagging, exotically-colored tropical fish while listening to Chrissy's girlish voice eagerly explaining to Janel. She had spent the morning going over files with two insurance agents who were going to absorb Pollard's business. That afternoon she had prepared material for transfer to the other offices. She was pleased to have been offered a job with one of the agents, and chattered excitedly about more money and a chance for the two of them to move together into a safer place. I turned from the aquarium, rewarded with a glint of comradeship sparking Janel's ebony eyes and the flicker of a smile.

Janel perched on the corner of the desk after brushing an area clear of clustered supplies, and we both listened to Chrissy's continued account of her day. Toward the end of the afternoon Darla Pollard's half-sister from Greenville, South Carolina, had come by. The police had released the body for burial in Greenville, and she was trying to close out Darla's private affairs as quickly as possible. She had selected a few personal items from the office and told Chrissy to take or dispense with the rest as she chose.

"So I've been boxing up things I want. And I got to thinking they might cut off the power anytime. I couldn't stand it if anything happened to the fish." There was no missing the appeal in Chrissy's wide-set eyes or the coquettishly pleading tone.

Janel shoved herself from the desk, taking the plastic bag half full of water and holding it open in front of her. "Okay, okay. But you have to catch them. I don't know what you want with fish. They don't do anything."

I shifted out of the way and held the scoop toward Chrissy, causing her to fully register my presence for the first time since Janel and I had entered the office. I told her Janel had helped me earlier with a little problem and that I was returning the favor.

Janel explained uncomfortably, "We were looking for you. I didn't think about checking here."

Hastily Chrissy said, "When I thought to call you, you'd already left work. And later I didn't get you at your place."

"It's all right. We'll get the fish and stuff in my truck. I can shift my hours tomorrow and help you in the morning. I need to get Lexy back to her car."

"I've got time. Let me help," I responded. I was hoping to gain more insight or information about Darla Pollard from the slackening of tensions.

With surprising efficiency Chrissy netted swiftly dodging fish and deposited them in the water bags held by Janel, and which I then sealed. I marveled at the iridescent colors and the variety of gauzy fins as I propped the bags against one another in a small box. Then Janel and I carried the aquarium gingerly out of the office, and placed it in the bed of her truck. It still contained some water because of the plants and was made even heavier by a thick bottom layer of white, blue, and green sand supporting mottled rocks and ledges. The few other boxes Chrissy had ready were light by comparison.

I held the box of fish while Chrissy closed up the office, then handed them to her in the cab once she settled herself close to Janel, making room for me. We talked little but I could sense Chrissy's uncertainty about me. Janel offered to take me immediately to The Cat, but I countered with an offer to help her get the aquarium unloaded first. She neither accepted nor declined but drove in the direction of Chrissy's apartment.

Carrying the heavy and unwieldy aquarium up a flight of outside stairs winded us both. Once we put it down on a wrought-iron stand, I flexed my cramped fingers to ease the ache. "Don't think I'm as strong as you, Janel."

"Take up karate," she teased unexpectedly.

Though ill at ease, Chrissy said, "Sit down, Lexy. Janel and I will get the rest. Then I'll make coffee."

I queried Janel with a lift of my brow and a widening of eyes. A shrug was all the support I was going to get from her on the invitation. I sat and surveyed the small living room. I would have expected pastels, softness, and cutesy. I saw earth tones, comfortable furniture, and cross-stitch patterns in dark frames on the walls.

Once the last box was stacked inside the door, Chrissy made coffee. I was handed a mug marbled in blue and yellow, the dark liquid within emitting a whiff of chocolate. After I took a sip and proclaimed my pleasure, Chrissy said, "This was Darla's favorite. Chocolate macadamia nut. I started to throw it out, but then I thought maybe it would be right to drink it and think about her." She looked uneasily at Janel who kept her face noncommittal.

I said, "Are you going to South Carolina for the funeral?"

"No." Her voice dropped lower by half an octave. "I was told it would be family only."

"Of course!" Janel exploded scathingly. "When someone queer dies, the family pretends they never had any friends." Directed to me. "And don't tell me it's not like that."

"It too often is," I said succinctly.

Chrissy mused, "It's sad about Darla. She wasn't close to her family. It'll be like strangers burying her." More strongly she said, "She was a pretty good person even if she didn't listen to other people much and pushed things through her way all the time. And she did some good, too. I think she really wanted to help Stacy."

Her blue eyes clouded, indicating regret for that last statement, but I pounced. "Who's Stacy?"

Janel answered, "Someone else dead. Right after Christmas."

I kept my gaze on Chrissy, willing her to continue, and realizing I was reaching out again for unknowns to be involved in Darla Pollard's mysterious death. Chrissy responded to my level gaze with some information. First she explained what I already knew about the work-study program and that Stacy had been part of it her junior year. Then that past summer and fall Pollard had given the teenager some part-time work.

"But there was something wrong," Chrissy said. "Sometimes I could tell she had been crying. Darla would close her office door. Or she'd drive off with the kid."

I lowered my head to hide a smile at Chrissy calling someone a kid.

Janel spoke up. "I told her maybe Stacy was being beat up at home. I had a friend who went through that." Her throat seemed to close on those words.

Chrissy shook her head slowly. "But I didn't see anything Janel said to watch for. She never wore dark glasses. Her throat and arms and back were bare lots of times, and I never saw any bruises."

"Did she talk to you about school?" I asked.

"No. When she first started there, I asked her about things she did…clubs, sports…you know. But she said she didn't have time for any of that."

"Girlfriends…boyfriends?"

Again Chrissy shook her head. "Last spring I asked her if she was going to the prom. She said her folks wouldn't let her date. I didn't think there was anyone like that any more."

I continued probing. "Was she gay? Do you think she and Darla..."

Janel said impatiently. "No way. I can smell my own kind even when they don't know it themselves."

"You agree, Chrissy?"

"I think so. I don't think it had anything to do with whatever the problem was. Oh, I know there are people who commit suicide over being gay or being found out..." She halted abruptly as Janel jerked herself upright and left the room, but not before I glimpsed the whiteness about her drawn mouth.

Chrissy and I made small talk about her cross-stitch work until Janel returned with the coffee pot and topped off my mug. I barely heard her whispered, "It's all right, Chris."

For some reason it pleased me to hear her use that abbreviation.

As Chrissy lifted her mug for a refill, Janel questioned, "Where are your bracelets?"

Putting down her coffee, Chrissy retrieved two thin golden bracelets from her pocket. "Didn't want to get them wet chasing fish." She patted the oversize pockets in the tartan vest. "Must've left one on my desk."

As Janel passed by me on her way back to the kitchen with the coffee pot, I wondered at a fleeting expression of anxiety.

Without any manipulation on my part, the conversation returned to Stacy. I listened without interruption as Chrissy related a scant narrative of the young girl's death. She had come by the office one Saturday morning to pick up her check. She had thanked Chrissy for the Christmas gift of a key chain with a clear plastic circle protecting a cross-stitch of pink flowers around a fancy initial 'S.' Shyly she had dangled it in front of Chrissy, complete with keys, as proof she was actually using it.

Chrissy claimed that Stacy had appeared in a decent frame of mind, that she had spoken briefly with Darla, without closing the office door. Chrissy's voice was strained as she then told of reading the newspaper account of Stacy being found dead of carbon-monoxide poisoning. She was found across the street from Pollard's office in a parking lot which served a restaurant and multi-cinema complex.

"People coming out of one of the shows saw her fallen over in the seat. It was that week it got so cold and surprised everybody. They were worried about the oranges and everything." Chrissy shuddered. "It bothers me to think of her dying alone like that."

I said almost to myself, "And the police called it suicide?"

Quickly Chrissy retorted, "The paper didn't say that. There was something about it being an old car and needing a new muffler. Darla said she might have been running the motor for the heater and waiting for some friend to come out of the movie."

I considered the chances of parents who wouldn't let a high school senior date allowing her to stay out alone that late but, not wanting to reveal what I had gathered from Gloria Driscoll's call to Marilyn, I said only, "Could it have been suicide?"

"I think so." This from Janel. "I went to the funeral with Christine. There was a thickness in the air...like people feeling guilty." That taut mouth and stiff jaw again. "I've been around that before when I knew it was suicide and the people were right to feel guilty." The bleakness of the words chilled the room and I was glad Chrissy leaned comfortably against her where she perched on the arm of the couch.

I asked Chrissy, "How did Darla take things?"

"She didn't talk about Stacy and wouldn't let me bring her up...but I could tell it was rough for her. And I know she had some run-ins with the Driscolls but—" At a frown from Janel, she ceased in mid-sentence.

I put down my empty cup. "Pick up on anything unusual?"

Chrissy was perplexed. "Like what? People die. Other people get upset. That's all normal stuff. "

"There was the phone call." Janel turned her face, sculpted in distinct lines, to me. "Darla called here late that Saturday evening. Made me mad. There wasn't any good reason for it. She was using her car phone. Said she had been out to dinner and had just passed Leather Fever, and remembered that she had to go over the new insurance with the owner."

Chrissy took up the narration. "Asked me where the file was in case she went back to the office on Sunday. Like she couldn't find it herself?" Her blue eyes narrowed. "I never misplaced files. She never went in on Sundays. And I swear I thought she was in the office right then, too."

Simultaneously Janel and I said, "Why?"

Chrissy motioned to the aquarium. "For over two years I've heard the hum of that air filter and the light. Thought I heard them in the background and that Darla was using the phone on my desk." She hurried on before Janel could speak, "I didn't mention it because you started fussing about her calling the minute I hung up."

Surprisingly, Janel had the grace to look sheepish.

Thoughtfully Chrissy resumed, "There was something else about Stacy. Or about Darla. I don't know which way to call it. Darla wanted me to think about letting Stacy move in with me for a little while when she turned eighteen in February." She stroked Janel's thigh but avoided looking at her. "I didn't want to. I wanted Janel and me to get our own place. I told Darla that.

But she kept at me. Said it would just be until Stacy graduated in June and could get a full-time job and afford her own place."

I asked, "Did Darla tell you why Stacy wanted to move away from home? Say anything about the parents?"

"No. And I've never been any good at pushing people to tell me things."

I grunted, accepting her insinuation. "You've been very helpful. Thank you."

Janel toyed gently with Chrissy's sand-brown curls. "We going to make a pact, aren't we Chrissy?"She locked eyes with me over Chrissy's head. "You're going to get a little tougher. And I'm going to get a little…"

"Milder," I suggested.

She twisted her mouth wryly but accepted the word. "…milder."

I got up and thanked Chrissy for the coffee, receiving a similar response for my assistance. She acquiesced to Janel's suggestion that she stay put while Janel ran me back to The Cat.

Once again in Janel's truck, we rode in a comfortable silence. I considered the additions I would be making in my notebook concerning Darla Pollard and Stacy. I also lodged a mental reminder to check on the teen's death with Ziegler or in back issues of *The Ledger*.

As we were slowed by an increase in traffic, Janel sighed loudly. "Lexy?"

I waited.

She said, "Do you really think things will get better for us?"

"As lesbians?" I was sure that was her focus.

"Yes."

"I have to think so. It's the way I am." A short pause and I added, "But we have to take part in it."

"By coming out?"

"Not necessarily. That's one way but there are other ways, too. Like not tolerating offensive jokes. Bringing up things in conversation like praising the tennis contributions of Martina or the detective fiction of Forrest and Redmann." I grinned. "Taking somebody straight to *The Incredibly True Adventures of Two Girls in Love*."

She grinned, too. "How about to dance at The Cat or shoot pool at Leather Fever?"

I laughed. "Depends. Might be a bit too much for them."

A sternness iced her features. Her hands became fists clenching the steering wheel. Her words barely rose above the sounds of traffic. "I was born in this country. My first…lover was born in Lebanon. Came here when she was six. I always thought it was really something that she spoke better

93

English than me…'cause she worked at it so hard, I guess. I was her first, too. We were just high school kids."

I kept my eyes forward, concentrating on the changing light patterns as she continued almost emotionlessly, "Her family made her quit school. They arranged a marriage with a cousin so he could stay in this country. She tried to escape by telling them about us." She bit her lip, possibly to stop tears. "They kept her away from me. They broke her. She committed suicide a month after the marriage."

My sight dimmed with tears.

Janel spoke with fervor, "I don't mean to be hard on Christine. I just don't want to lose her too. There have been others but we were just…moments for each other. I want Chris and me to be forever."

Assuming that they were in their mid-twenties, I knew there were years of potential pitfalls ahead. Still, I was coming to respect Janel's intensity, and I had seen the caring in Chrissy's eyes. I said, "In the office and at the apartment, I saw the blending…"

She glanced at me for a second only, but I caught the glow of gratitude and the smoldering of resolve.

CHAPTER TWELVE

The next two days seemed to be full of deadlines and meetings about stories that meant little to me. Meanwhile at the back of my mind Darla Pollard's death nagged me so that I couldn't sleep well. Friday night I even avoided The Cat, now feeling I needed some distance. I wanted something to gel, to fall into place. I wasn't making any headway, but then neither were the police. I needed someone to talk to. I needed a break. And that's when I remembered the drink Hal gave me on behalf of Rita Burgess. I decided to go to the fair and see what she was vending. Maybe talk about the article I had started on about terminal cancer and pain treatment.

The narrow two-lane road snaked around low rolling hills where there had been rows upon rows of orange trees only a few years ago. Those groves had been decimated by a pre-Christmas freeze, unusual in its severity. A couple of years later while enjoying a Sunday drive with Jodi I had been stunned by the unbearable cheerlessness of the gray-white trunks rising life-less above the earth, surrounded by wind-broken twigs and branches.

Now the land was an uneven checkerboard of new growth. Stands of young pines backed large plots of corn developing toward a spring harvest. Nearly depleted winter gardens abutted rectangles of recently turned, dark soil being prepared for April plantings. I was glad I had chosen this back way to the Old Florida Arts and Crafts Fair. It was a tonic for my eyes and my mind.

Turning onto a four-lane artery, I began to watch for signs. Suddenly a large, sweeping shadow encompassed me, then slowly skimmed ahead. I was delighted by the brilliant red, yellow, and orange of a hot-air balloon, the elongated oval vivid against the gentian blue of the early March sky. I barely lowered my gaze in time to catch the sign announcing a right-hand turn for the fair at the next intersection.

I skirted a field containing two more balloons and a scattering of people awaiting rides. One balloon was a random display of lightning bolts against a deep purple background, the second was striped, top to bottom, in rainbow hues.

Teenagers in fluorescent orange vests, obviously enjoying their power, directed the parking with broad, emphatic gestures. A gray-haired, full-cheeked woman, whose abundant body strained at her plaid shirt and faded jeans, cheerfully stamped the back of my hand in exchange for five dollars. Watchful from beneath a pink and white golf umbrella, propped on the ground, was a small brown and white dog, the stubble of its muzzle gray with age.

A light rain last night had settled the dust and augmented the onion pungency of recently cut field grasses. A dozen steps into the crudely fenced fairgrounds, however, and I was assaulted by milling humanity and the odor of food. I sauntered toward a tented stage as a crowd gathered to listen to a country western band.

Along the way I observed the offerings of various booths. Quilts with African-American images in glorious colors were crammed next to simple clay pottery and intricately woven baskets on one side, the pastels of hand-dipped candles on the other. A booth selling dark, rough-hewn cypress knee sculptures was flanked by the Salvation Army first-aid tent and a 'Save the Manatee and the Florida Panther' exhibit. Shelves of home-canned fruits and vegetables were interspersed with delicate dried-flower arrangements. I enjoyed the blur of color and sound.

Passing the stage area, I continued leisurely toward the north end of the grounds, visually sampling the wares and displays. No booths covered the fencing at the end. To the left on the outside I could see junior riders putting their mounts through the rigors of barrel racing to much shouting and applause. In a field well off to the right two women's fast-pitch softball teams were warming up for a game—lime green and black against turquoise and navy blue.

Laughter and the thud of a ball hitting a glove rode the strong breeze stimulating my memories as I began my trek along the next aisle. I paused to admire the purple balloon with its lightning bolts pass overhead. I laughed at my momentary desire to sail the air in such a vehicle when I still refused to submit to the speed and convenience of commercial air flights.

"What's so funny, Lexy?"

I scanned the booths to my left and discovered Rita Burgess in front of an attractive one, its shelves covered in khaki and dark brown burlap, and tented over with loosely stretched yellow cloth. I joined her, noting the many small glass cases containing odd objects against red satin backgrounds.

Pointing to the swiftly rising balloon, I said, "The thought of me in one of those! I can't face air travel, let alone the space age. I keep my feet on the ground."

"How about boating?"

I grimaced, exaggerating my trepidation. "Only when the Admiral grabs me by the scruff of the neck and throws me on deck. She makes me feel like the dog I used to have to force into the car for a trip to the vet." I moved closer to her displays. "What are these things?"

"The tools my great-grandfather made himself for repairing watches, radios, and cameras in the early part of the century. Actually he worked up through World War II. My dad was just a kid then, but later he told how he would help Grandpap in the garage shop. Told me that the town boys overseas would even send Grandpap their watches to be fixed. He never charged, and those who came back brought him clocks." She gestured to a high shelf behind her holding mantle clocks of diverse construction and design.

I ran my fingers over the smooth wood of a small case on the first shelf containing old watches beneath the glass. The satin in this case was stripes of red, white, and blue.

Rita said gently, "Those belonged to boys who never came back. Their families wanted Grandpap to keep them." Her voice strengthened. "I pick a few fairs every year and trot these out. Kind of a celebration of a man who died the year I was born." A shy smile softened her face. "I have a thing about dates, celebrations, anniversaries…that kind of thing. Guess I'm out of step with modern times, too."

Her dark eyes glimmered above the smile and I was struck with how they differed from Janel's. Where Janel's ebony glowed and deepened, Rita's black irises seemed to shimmer below water. Her bracelets clinked together as she waved toward a cooler. "Offer you a cold drink, Lexy?"

"No, thank you. By the way, thanks for the one you provided for me at The Cat. It wasn't necessary, but it was appreciated."

Her jaw stiffened. "Have you started the article?"

"Yes, I have actually. I came to talk to you about it. Hal told me you'd be here. I've roughed it out. Started gathering info yesterday. Interviewed a nurse I know who works in ICU. She's inviting me to a nurses' party. Says I'll get more honest comments in a casual setting."

Rita nodded in understanding. "I'll hunt up the names of Dee's last nurses. Most of them seemed so sympathetic. A couple actually coached me on how to approach the doctor to get more help."

I replied, "That's why I'm starting with nurses. They're more frontline."

"Got the time, Rita?!" The contralto voice was teasing. The tall, well-proportioned woman standing a few feet in front of the booth welcomed Rita's light hug while candidly appraising me over her shoulder.

As they moved out of the bright sunlight, I admired the shape of her arms extending from the rolled-up sleeves of her burnt-orange denim shirt, and couldn't help noticing how her mocha pants tapered from firm thighs down slender calves into brown boots. Undaunted, she watched the journey of my eyes. Her face was nearly square, a straight mouth below a narrow nose. Her eyes, green as velvet moss, challenged me to remain as still for her survey. The breeze ruffled the short wheat-blonde hair. Appreciatively she noted the sharp rise and fall of my bosom; a slight smile parted the finely shaped lips.

The roaring in my ears nearly blocked Rita's introduction as she said, "Wren, this is Lexy Hyatt, a *Ledger* reporter. Wren Carlyle, design artist."

We shook hands. Hers was firm and cool. I withdrew mine reluctantly. Politely I stood aside as they exchanged information about shared acquaintances. No attempt to drag my eyes from this attractive woman succeeded. My senses had been invaded as never before, becoming jumbled and disoriented. At one point I swallowed self-consciously feeling her lambent gaze slide over my exposed throat. Her voice was now burnished, now musky. I thought of the flavor of vanilla as I watched the slim fingers trace the shape of a tool.

"Lexy?" Rita's insistence made me realize that she had spoken my name more than once in a bid for my attention. At last having it, she said, "Don't you play fast-pitch?"

I felt the need for moisture in my mouth, and was afraid my voice would crack. "Used to. Not much any more. It's a peak performance kind of game. Now I mostly watch."

Rita continued, "Wren here is going to watch her niece play. Maybe you'd like to join her and explain the finer points of the game."

I probed her face for signs of matchmaking, thrusting me on her friend like that, but her lips were relaxed and her eyes ingenuous.

Wren gazed out over the crowds, seemingly unconcerned, but I saw a brief flutter of coppery lashes at my weak, "Be glad to."

A small group arrived to investigate the contents of Rita's booth. She prodded Wren and me on our way with gentle shoves. Admonishing us to avoid foul balls and spilled drinks, she tossed us a slim roll of paper towels. I snatched it from the air a foot above my head.

"I guess you did play ball," Wren observed.

We turned sideways in unison as we worked our way through a swarm of children brandishing food and drinks. I asked, "Did you?"

Rustling laughter. "Not me. I saved my hands for sketching and cutting and pasting."

We progressed toward the exit gate pausing now and then to examine or comment on some offering. I bought a key chain because I admired the simple sketch of a weeping willow cut and inked into a pliant square of yellow leather. Wren paid for a delicate four-inch carving of a heron, asking to set it aside till she returned.

Eventually we scuffed our way along a well-worn path of loose sand. Reddish dust dulled the sheen of Wren's high boots and coated my worn, low pair. I said, "Wren? As in those little darting birds?"

"No. As in William, Rachel, Eliot, Norma." She went on to explain that her parents had hoped to have two children, a boy and a girl, planning to give each the paired names of their own parents. "But my mother was a diabetic and my birth was hard on her…it was dangerous. The doctor stressed there should be no others. So…" Her smile was devastating. "I was given William's W, Rachel's R, Eliot's E, and Norma's N."

We reached the ball field and climbed up five rows of dilapidated bleachers along the third base side. We dusted sections with Rita's towels, shoving the soiled paper into the cardboard cylinder. I enjoyed the pre-game. The catcher struggled into her gear, the pitcher curried the mound, the umpire checked numbers. Taunts and encouragement issued from the stands.

Wren pointed to the third baseman wearing shirt and shorts of lime green with black pinstripes. She looked barely out of her teens, medium height with an athletically sturdy build and dark hair in a single thick braid. "My niece."

I challenged without thinking. "How does an only child have a niece?"

She kept her patrician profile toward me and answered without rancor. "She's the daughter of an ex-lover who remained a true sister." Slowly her head turned full-face to me. "Don't you have any nieces or nephews like that?" The eyes sparkled teasingly.

I wanted to dive naked into those eyes and feel the copper lashes close over me. I wondered if she was seeing the gray that I've been told dominates mine whenever I struggle for balance or am uncertain. The green in mine only deepens when I'm making love, or so the likes of Jodi have told me. Not ready to know what she saw in my eyes, I quickly shifted down two rows, stretching to lend a hand up to an elderly woman. I settled back a row below Wren next to her booted feet.

In silence we watched the first inning of the game. Wren's niece batted first when her team came up in the second half. She hit the third pitch over the shortstop's head just out of glove reach. She made first base easily and then stole second on the catcher, but she died there as the next three batters struck out. She came up second in the third inning, and positioned herself to hit from the other side of the plate. I turned to look up at Wren framed against the whitened blue of the afternoon sky. "Switch-hitter."

I returned my attention to the field just in time to see Wren's niece choke up on the bat, step toward the pitcher at the point of release, and slap the ball into the infield dirt as she left the box area. Before the pitcher could regain her balance and scramble for the ball, the fleetfooted girl was standing on first base. Then she stole second on the disgruntled pitcher, made third on a teammate's bunt down the first base line, and was driven home by a solid single. Wren clapped a hand on my shoulder as she stood to cheer, and I felt my blood quicken. As she sat down, she slipped a finger under my collar and tugged. "Come back up here."

I would have resisted a command, but there was a quietly assertive force to her words that drew me unresistingly.

"That's better. I didn't want to talk to the back of a head."

I hoped my smile was casual. "So talk."

Before Wren could speak, we were interrupted by a call. "Hey, Ms. Hyatt."

I greeted a former student who climbed toward us and seated herself at my feet. I was pleased to learn that she was a first-year social studies teacher at a nearby junior high; we exchanged opinions on the educational system— the challenges and problems. Wren shifted to the right and leaned forward concentrating on the game, granting me a sense of privacy for our conversation.

My former student pointed out a younger sister in the bleachers on the first-base line, and said, "I'm really sorry you're not teaching any more. My sister gobbles down books like a garbage disposal gone wild, but she needs you to teach her how to recognize and appreciate quality. Every time I notice something special about what I am reading, I know it's because of the skills you gave us."

"Do you pass on any of them to her?" I prodded.

She grinned understandingly. "Of course!"

We shook hands on that, then she hugged me and swung off the side of the bleachers. I followed her with my eyes, feeling as I always did after an encounter with a former student—a rush of emptiness.

"Why did you leave teaching?" There was no curiosity in Wren's tone, but there was a directness.

"I'm not sure I've ever made that completely clear to myself. It's lots of factors. No single one." I glanced at her, enticed into continuing by the alert expectancy. "I was lucky to start out with a principal who understood that it was his job to help the school work rather than to make it work. He protected his teachers from much of the bureaucratic mumbo jumbo and let us have our own styles. Mine was a by-the-seat-of-your-pants style. I just discovered what to do and could never explain it!" I sighed. "Then came the principal who either hid behind the bureaucracy or believed in it. He was stifling and destructive of everything that had made the school superior. And it was happening in other schools, too. It was like a conspiracy from the legislature down through the administrators to create a climate of fear and constraint. The fancy word was 'accountability.' It got so it took half my energy to keep all the negatives out of my classroom." I shrugged in a helpless gesture.

Wren said nothing and I was acutely aware of the continued waiting. I looked her way again noting the sweep of her arched eyebrows.

"All right," I said testily. "There's more to it, but it is very hard to put into words...even for an English teacher." I matched her level gaze. "In fact, I never have."

Excited cries from the field caught our attention. A clean out at home plate earned our applause. The scoreboard indicated that her niece's team still led by the single run. Not sure if I wanted to continue, I stayed quiet.

Wren said, "I'm not being nosy, Lexy. There was obvious respect in that girl's voice. I want to know why you walked away from that. I would think it would be hard to do."

"It was. But it was also part of why I got along with all my students and managed to teach with success because I did have their respect. And I had it because I earned it with honesty and fairness. The administrators try to make teaching complicated when it is very simple. Just know your material and be up front and fair. And you don't have to be perfect. Kids will forgive you your mistakes if you admit them."

Wren commented, "I have a feeling that caring enters into it."

I straightened and pulled back my shoulders, trying to work out some of the tension the subject had engendered. "Of course. And the caring is also part of why I walked away. I had their respect and I cared...and I lived a lie in front of them everyday. Had I taught elementary school or even junior high, I don't think I'd have had a problem with it. But I was teaching sixteen to eighteen year-olds. Near adults." I glanced around. "And look at me now. Checking to make certain there's no one near enough to hear."

"You couldn't come out at school." Wren's empathy reached me.

"But I couldn't keep watching the terrible struggle of those facing their homosexuality in the horrendously cruel environment of adolescence...and live with my own inability to offer assistance. So I ran." I bit my lower lip hard, wanting the pain.

When I didn't release my lip, Wren touched my cheek lightly with the back of her fingers. "Ease up, Lexy."

With my tongue I felt my teeth marks. Then staring intently ahead, I spoke with little inflection, "It was the third suicide that did it. I had heard of two others, a boy and a girl, who had committed suicide because they were gay and couldn't live with it. I believed it was probably because they couldn't get others to live with it. But I knew the third one. A boy I had taught. I had liked him for his dry humor and the clever way he had of adapting the latest fads to his own style. I admired him for his talents. He was so at home with the arts—writing, drawing, music—but he was also an energetic soccer goalie. Dumb me. I thought he would go out into the world and pluck pearls from oysters. I never thought about his being gay, so of course I never thought about what it must be like to be gay in a family whose military traditions went back to the Revolutionary War. Two older brothers had already gone to West Point."

There was a shared pain in Wren's eyes and the lift of her square chin. I wanted her touch again. "He committed suicide the summer after he graduated from high school. I felt that I had failed him somehow. That my hiding the truth about myself added to the conspiracy." I attempted a lightness of tone. "So I quit teaching."

"And now you hide in newsprint." Wren's tone was not accusatory but I jerked my head back in anger. Wren responded, "Don't you dare dump that anger on me. We both know where it goes."

I closed my eyes and hissed slowly through my teeth.

"Interesting defense mechanism," she said tartly.

My eyes flew open. "You don't give much ground, do you?"

"I don't give any."

"Is that a warning?"

Her momentary silence was not a hesitation. More a testing. "Would you heed it?"

My own silence was a hesitation. I had avoided commitment since I left teaching. I chose, "No."

We had crossed a line. The next steps could wait. We gave our attention to the ballgame.

CHAPTER THIRTEEN

All Sunday I willed myself not to stare at the phone. A ridiculous phrase kept zipping through my mind—a watched phone never rings—a watched phone never rings...

At the end of the ballgame the day before, I had joined Wren in congratulating her niece and teammates for their play and the win. On the way back to the booth area, we had spoken of Rita Burgess and the death of her life partner Dee. I had admitted to having only casual knowledge of them through sporadic contact at The Cat.

Wren had said, "I met them about eight years ago when I was peddling some of my detailing designs to Sea Lane Boats. Dee worked in accounting and Rita out on the line. It amused me that going by their builds and their general appearances, you'd expect a reversal of their jobs. Dee was nearly six feet and muscular from working out regularly." Wren's face had clouded. "Watching that firm flesh melt away and the skin hang from that large frame..."

She had not finished the statement, and we had walked back in silence, wrapped in the late afternoon light. When Wren had stopped to collect her carved heron, I had strolled on to Rita's booth where a group of volunteer teenagers were assisting in the take-down process. I had admired the way Rita supervised with a light manner but a vigilant eye while I perched on a crate and answered questions about the ballgame. At one point between issuing orders and listening to my responses, she had inserted, "And my capable friend—what do you think of her?"

As Wren was approaching within earshot, I had limited my answer to, "I expect to be thinking a lot."

And now I sat doing just that. Thinking about the sweep of hair like fall grasses bending and following the curve of the warm earth. Thinking about the prickling of my skin at the touch of those velvet green eyes. Thinking about the deep voice and its casual offering as we separated to seek our own cars. "I'll call you!"

I got up suddenly from the couch, scattering the still unread Sunday paper on the floor. I stretched my arms toward the ceiling then brought them down, clasping my hands at the back of my neck, trying to press away the images. I seated myself at the counter dividing the living room from the small kitchen, continuing to avert my eyes from the phone at my left elbow.

Dispiritedly, I flipped open the orange notebook containing my notes relating to Darla Pollard. I considered my latest entry, added last night upon returning home from the craft fair. Rita had spoken of Hal when I helped carry some of the small cases to her van. "I'm worried about Hal, Lexy. Sometimes his eyes harden like Dee's used to when the pain was just starting. And his hands shake sometimes. He spilled a glass of wine in my lap that Friday night." She furrowed her brow. "But to be honest, I'm not really sure if that was caused by his hands shaking or because he was watching Marilyn coming back right after she took that woman in the purple suit down the hallway."

I had sidestepped her concern for Hal, and asked if she had seen more of Darla Pollard.

"No," she had said. "I tried to make Hal feel all right about the spill, then went to the restroom to sponge off my slacks. I was sorry it happened...for Hal. I didn't want to cause him any embarrassment. And I remembered how important it was to Dee to keep seeming in control of her body. Like I said, Lexy, I'm worried about what I saw in Hal."

A thought flickered, and I thumbed back several pages. I found what I was looking for. Jodi had heard voices from Marilyn's office after that. Now it appeared that Marilyn couldn't have been one of them. If so, who was talking with Pollard? I tried to visualize the area behind the bar. Had it contained both Melody and Hal at that point? I wasn't sure. I made a note to ask Rita if she had recognized voices when she left the restroom.

I started at the front of the notebook and skimmed each page. Hal, Marilyn, and Jodi dotted the pages like primary colors. Chrissy was a tint but Janel, a darkening shade. The Driscolls and their daughter Stacy were indistinct streaks of gray. I closed the pad and ran a fingernail down the tightly coiled binding. It was over a week now and the sightless, colorless eyes of the murdered woman continued to float in the darkness behind my own. Was the price for closing them more than I wanted to pay? Could I live with discovering that a friend of mine had immobilized them into a perpetual stare?

Propping my elbows on the counter, I lowered my head and pressed my closed eyes against the hard heels of my hands. Dull colored patterns of lines and dots played against my eyelids. When I lifted my head, the dark screens of my eyelids brightened and paled with fluctuating surges of orange-red. It was a game I had played as a child when forced to lie down in the afternoon for a nap. 'Soaking time' my mother had called it, a lovely hovering between sleep and wakefulness. I wanted to be soaking with Wren Carlyle.

Opening my eyes, I turned my head very slowly to glare at the phone, so mockingly still. I reached over, tracing the outline of the receiver as though to make it ring.

My whole body jerked in surprise at the sudden jangle that disrupted the heavy Sunday quiet of my apartment. I forced my hand to grip the receiver without lifting it while my heart thudded in my chest. I ended the torture in the middle of the third ring. "Yes?"

"Exactly the answer I want." While not as stirringly throaty over the telephone, Wren's voice lapped at my ear.

"Do I get to hear the question?" I hoped my own voice was as nonchalant as I intended.

"Join me for a light dinner Tuesday evening? Someplace simple but pleasant."

I wanted to kick something. "I'm sorry, but that's the one evening I am committed."

"I understand." Was that easy acceptance in her tone or unconcern?

I rushed to explain. "I'm attending a going-away party for a nurse. She's not anyone I know. I'm going as a reporter." Realizing how implausible that sounded, I stumbled on. "It's a special situation. I—"

"No diagram needed, Lexy." Was she being polite or irritated

"I need to be clear, Wren. Indulge me."

"Just what I had in mind."

My thighs quivered and I let out a long breath. Then, feeling that Rita would not mind my sharing the circumstances with a friend, I told her about my article on the issue of dehumanizing pain endured by the dying. I explained that I wanted to find out what assistance was available, and whether or not it was provided.

Her few comments were sympathetic and understanding. Then she lifted me with, "Would it be rude or awkward for me to attend with you? I spent a lot of time in the hospital with Dee. I got to know some of the nurses." She spoke sincerely, "I wouldn't want to get in the way or complicate any-thing—" A little teasing, "—or interfere with the independence of the reporter."

Quickly I said, "You wouldn't. And there is a bit of exaggeration to that image of being an independent reporter."

"What about Lexy the person? How independent is she?"

I pitched my voice nearly as low as hers. "That's still being determined." Somehow I knew we were both smiling.

Wren said, "Will this be one of those potlucks?"

"Yes," I replied. "My nurse friend said for me not to worry but I'm going to pick up some chips or such."

"Why don't you let me tend to that? A little compensation for my including myself. Deal?"

I could think of several deals I would like to make with Wren Carlyle. "Deal."

Now that the gnawing desire for the semi-promised phone call from Wren had been alleviated, I expected to be at ease with the day. But I wasn't. I brewed some tangy orange-spice tea, but drank only a few sips. I rustled through the many-sectioned paper, concentrating on nothing.

Eventually I found myself fingering Roberta Exline's card and wondering if her Sundays were sacrosanct. I decided to risk a call only to receive a recorded response. I gave my name, requested a call back, and concluded with my number.

I placed my mug of tepid tea in the microwave, and the phone rang midway through the reheating countdown. It was Detective Exline for Ms. Hyatt. We had returned to the formality square. I explained my wish to know more about the Driscolls, then thought to apologize for interrupting off-duty activities.

She said, "Actually I've just come off a tour of duty that began at four this morning and I'm on my way to the Body Shop. I can talk some while I work out if you want to meet me there."

I agreed and verified the location. Soon I was pulling into a lot that had once served a large grocery chain. The distinctive design of the building remained, but the brick-red and soft yellow colors had yielded to stark black and grays. The wide plate-glass windows were safe behind spiraling wrought-iron bars.

Plenty of people were using the gym on a late Sunday afternoon. All were in spandex or sweats. Some were resplendent as peacocks, strutting through their workouts. Others pushed and pulled their bodies with the concentration of robots. I inhaled deeply, identifying sweat, powder, oils…

Even in my softball days I had resisted the body-building routines. My mind recognized the value, but some atavistic gene recoiled from the constructions of metal slats and pipes, chains and wires.

"You look like you think they're going to attack you." Robbie Exline had appeared at my side. I admired the muscled thighs clad in black spandex, the firm breasts scarcely concealed by the hot pink halter-bra.

I said pointedly, "You should invite the Admiral here."

Her mouth dropped open slightly, then closed, but there had been a brief acknowledging glimmer in her eyes. "She's invited me sailing some early morning."

"Going?"

Her manner sobered. "Not as long as the Pollard case is an active file."

She pulled on workout gloves and moved toward a rowing machine. I waited while she settled herself, adjusted the resistance, and began a series of disciplined strokes. My shoulders ached just watching her.

As her breathing integrated with the strokes, she said, "What are you expecting from me, Lexy?"

Had Wren Carlyle not been encompassing me like a shielding aura, I might have responded suggestively. Instead I remained serious as I sat on the floor nearby. "I've picked up tidbits on Darla Pollard and the Driscolls. Can you add to them?"

She spoke unevenly between rowing strokes. "I talked with Christine Shoemaker, the secretary. Got a little more on the Driscoll's daughter being upset and Pollard seeming to help her out."

I asked, "Did Chrissy tell you about Pollard wanting her to take in the girl for a few months?"

Her eyes narrowed and the gold flecks faded. "No. But that backs up something the school counselor told me."

"How so?" I listened to the detective's narration, in between her rhythmic breaths. She and Ziegler had examined the file on Stacy's death in January. The case had been closed as death by accidental carbon-monoxide poisoning. But the investigating detective had included notes on his dissatisfaction with some evasiveness on why the girl had been out so late. Also, spoken to separately, Mr. Driscoll had claimed to be in bed sleeping whereas Mrs. Driscoll said they were watching a late movie and waiting up for Stacy. The husband explained away the discrepancy by saying he had forgotten that he had fallen asleep on the couch.

Ziegler had sent Exline to check out the girl with the school. Her counselor had spoken of her as a good student but uninvolved in any school activities and apparently part of no special groups. Based on Stacy's test and aptitude scores, the counselor had urged her to consider applying to business school. The girl had said things like that would have to wait until she was on her own.

"Telling me about that made the counselor remember Stacy asking about the school rules concerning a student living away from home. She asked sometime before Christmas. She was told she would have to be eighteen and her parents would have to sign some papers."

I mused, "So Stacy Driscoll really did want to leave home."

"Stacy Garrison."

"What?"

Exline answered, "Her name was Garrison. Her real father is dead. Driscoll was her stepfather."

"But she went by Driscoll." As I said it, I remembered the article back in my *Ledger* desk listing a Stacia Garrison in the work-study program Pollard participated in.

Exline continued, "The counselor explained that they try to accommodate the students as much as possible in what they want to be called. She described it as bolstering their self-esteem. Said they have to keep records under the official names, but she had an empty folder filed under Driscoll saying see Garrison. Called it another sign of the decaying times." She stopped rowing. "Your name the same as your parents?"

"Yes."

"Mine's not." She stared unseeingly into space. "My father left us. When my mother remarried she thought I would want to change my name, too. But it was all I had of my father. For reasons I've never tried to understand, that made me want to keep it."

Exline shrugged off the private revelation and got up from the rowing machine. I regained my feet as well, and followed her to a mat where she did a series of stretching exercises.

After awhile she said, "Quid pro quo time."

I gave a quick nod of agreement and told her relevant parts of my Wednesday night contact with Janel and Chrissy. I emphasized Janel's firm assessment of the closeness between Darla and Stacy not being a gay thing, and Chrissy's remarks about the Driscolls hounding Darla after the girl's death. I chose, however, to omit Chrissy's reference to the phone call Darla pretended to make from her car on the night Stacy died.

Exline queried, "Who's Janel?"

Not sure how much I wanted to give away, I answered carefully and identified her only as Chrissy's companion. I shifted uncomfortably under the detective's calculating gaze. She said, "You're not leveling with me, Lexy." Then added, "And don't pull that protecting-sources maneuver on me."

I turned my head and hissed at the wall. I wasn't ready to place Janel at The Cat the night of the murder for the police just yet.

Exline backed off a little. "Did you arrange the evening just to pump Chrissy for information on Pollard?"

More at ease, I told her about the skinheads, the BB in my shoe, and

Janel's victory. I let her think that the evening simply evolved from there without revealing that Janel had been searching for Chrissy and seemed overly anxious. I indicated that I was certain Hal had reported the incident to the police when she stressed the importance of documenting everything possible against the skinheads. I could tell we both thought it would be nice if the murder lay at their door.

In a change of direction, Exline said, "You seem to be surrounded by people who take karate, hoist sails, work out…maybe somebody's trying to tell you something."

I laughed. "No, no. That's all too demanding and aggressive for me."

"Just how aggressive is your friend Jodi?"

I stood very still, feeling like a mouse frozen under the chilling eyes of a cat. Exline stepped from the mats and positioned herself against the wall where a contraption of rings and pulleys permitted her to work her arms and shoulders. I moved in front of her, feeling as though she were aiming for my chin with each thrust.

With a flat tone, her eyes unwaveringly on mine, she said, "According to my interview with one of the bartenders, Jodi was the one who parted the arguing Driscolls. That puts her in the back with Darla Pollard alive or recently dead. And she's in my notes from the interview with Christine Shoemaker as well. Obviously she was a good friend of Pollard."

I tried not to react to the slight emphasis on friend.

The detective continued. "I checked your friend's interview…" Again the emphasis. "…with Ziegler. Not exactly lies, but definitely sins of omission."

"Something you'll have to discuss with her." I kept my voice level and, I hoped, impassive.

"I will. Or Ziegler will. And we'll be talking to Marilyn again. Seems she was less than honest, too." Her voice softened. "It's my job, Lexy."

"They're both good women, Robbie," I spoke as softly.

"I don't doubt that." She released the rings, removed her gloves, and began massaging her hands. "But I haven't found any proof that Darla Pollard was a bad one. A little high-handed maybe…but not bad."

"What about the Driscolls? What have you found out there?" I couldn't keep a swipe of sarcasm out of my voice. "If a lowly reporter may ask."

I saw her lips twitch toward a smile before she controlled them. Her response was probably a gift to counteract the news about Jodi and Marilyn. "Ziegler is going to tackle him at his job tomorrow and I'm going to see her at home. There is something interesting, though."

As I lifted my head expectantly, she cautioned, "But don't ask where I got it. Gloria Driscoll dated a cop in between the death of her first husband and her marriage to Edward Driscoll." She broke eye contact as she pulled on her gloves. "A female cop."

My mind rushed through possibilities. Gloria Driscoll and Pollard...an angry husband...the Admiral mentioning thinking she had seen Gloria Driscoll in The Cat with another woman...a confused daughter...

Exline interrupted my flurry of thoughts. "May not mean anything. Happens sometimes to women suddenly alone, and lonely. It seems she took a course after her husband's death, offered through our Community Services department—Self Defense for Women. Met a female uniform there. They spent some time together." She returned to her arm and shoulder workout, continuing to aim at my chin.

I watched the roll and bulge and stretch of her muscles as I considered the attractive possibility of one of the Driscolls as the murderer of Darla Pollard. That would mean The Cat wasn't involved at all—or any of her people.

I saw Exline's dark eyes focus somewhere beyond me, and shifted my weight to turn. Not breaking her rhythm, she said, "No! Christine Shoemaker just walked in. There's a wiry, dark woman with her...has tattoos. That bartender, Melody, described someone like that checking out The Cat the night of the murder...maybe looking for somebody. Your Janel?"

"Chrissy's Janel. I thought she was a pain in the ass at first, but she's all right. Her rough edges are mostly for show. They're defensive. When you question her..." I glanced at her hands. "...wear gloves."

Her jaw slid back and forth in a quick movement. "Your loyalties come in quite a variety."

"Only when earned." I knew there was more certainty in my tone than in my mind.

CHAPTER FOURTEEN

At the *Ledger* I sat watching my digital clock-radio click toward midafternoon, its woodgrain motif out of place on the gray metal desk dominated by the white plastic of my computer, calculator, stapler, and other desk accessories. I had bought it for my bedside table to wake me to light-rock rhythms and the dulcimer tones of disc-jockey Krystal Kay. But when I switched off the light, I was so shocked by a turquoise glow that defied even the tissues I draped over the changing numbers, that I exiled it to my *Ledger* cubicle the next day.

I was to meet Wren in the parking lot outside at two o'clock. She would be 'collecting' me and driving to the party for the nurse moving to Atlanta. The timing of the party was to accommodate those nurses both beginning and ending shifts at three-thirty. I had worked steadily all morning and through lunch via my computer and telephone. I was ready to escape—ready for Wren Carlyle.

I was unaware that I was resting my right foot only on the toes and rapidly jiggling my leg until papers in the hand of the Iron Maiden touched my knee. I straightened, feeling like a child caught considering libidinous deeds.

Unsmiling, Barbara MacFadden handed me two sheets of paper. "These came through relating to your request for information on Darla Pollard."

As usual my 'thank you' was said to her back. The first was a grainy news picture of a self-satisfied, smiling Pollard handing a solemn teenager a certificate. Standing slightly behind her daughter, Gloria Driscoll's smile was weak. To her left was a scowling Edward Driscoll. I noted that Stacy was listed as a Driscoll in the brief copy under the picture.

The second was a short statement issued by the State Commissioner of Insurance announcing that his office found insufficient evidence of intentional wrong-doing on the part of American Health Insurance and the local agents offering their coverage. I found my folder on Pollard and re-read the clipping relating to a complaint against Pollard and American Health. I shuffled both sheets to the back of the folder, fearing that my hope of finding a trail leading away from The Cat was becoming a serious handicap.

I fingered the picture of Pollard and the Driscolls. Time I found a way to approach the wife. Irritably, I slammed the folder away in a desk drawer. The irritation fled, however, at the sight of the disjointed blue lines registering one-fifty-five. I fled to the parking lot.

Descending the few wide steps, I saw Wren wave from a white Buick with a dark, padded top. I slid into the passenger seat and tugged the seat belt into place before turning to greet her. We laughed together and Wren whipped a hand through the sweep of hair across her forehead when we saw that we were dressed as twins in reverse. The gray of my corduroy slacks was echoed in her charcoal mock-turtleneck. The cranberry of her stirrup pants was two shades darker than my Oxford shirt. Simultaneously we checked each other's feet. At least my black walking shoes were not like her dark gray boots.

Wren's chuckle glided into a teasing comment. "If one of us is going to change, I vote for you. You clash with your notebook."

I had brought one of my orange spiral-bounds with me. I placed it on the floor saying, "I don't plan to take it in with me. Just want it handy when we leave. We're interlopers at this party as it is."

Wren started the car and cocked her head toward me. The green eyes widened questioningly. "Directions?"

While keeping an alert eye on the traffic, she told me of a recent conversation with Rita Burgess. "Went by her new place last night. It was easier to be with her in a place she hadn't shared with Dee. I think the inner crumbling has stopped. It's like she's pausing before she changes directions."

"That's a nice way to describe it."

She didn't turn her head but I saw the twist of a smile. "It was her description of you." She overrode my startled 'oh.' "Said she had watched you for about a year now, just hovering." I knew she was aware that I stiffened. "She didn't elaborate. I just assumed the…hovering…was between a relationship ended and one not yet begun." She eased to a stop at a red light and turned my way. I met the challenge of her eyes silently. Her smile deepened.

Once we arrived at Brenda's modest house, Wren inserted the car, with an admirable economy of maneuvering, into a tiny space. She retrieved two foil-wrapped trays from the back seat, handing me one. We entered behind two women in white pants, teal smocks, and athletic shoes.

Inside, I was hailed by Brenda Jarrell who motioned us to the Florida

112

room where card tables were awaiting food. With a "Let's see what this is," she took my tray and pried away the foil covering. Wren placed her tray on the table and followed suit, identifying the triangle sandwiches as cream cheese and pecans. The other tray contained cucumber and dill on rye.

Brenda raised her eyebrows, first at the sandwiches and then at me. "You didn't make these, Lexy. Nobody changes that much."

I laughed away the hit and made introductions. Brenda and I had been lovers one distant summer. Our affair had soon drifted into friendship. Now I was uncomfortable with her obvious effort to read my relationship with Wren. She compounded it by hugging me and whispering in my ear, "I trust you licked the cream cheese from her fingers."

I was certain that Wren had heard.

The next three hours passed swiftly. Brenda commandeered Wren while I drifted from room to room and group to group. Sometimes I skirted the edges, merely listening and at other times, I settled and asked questions. While there was a heavy lacing of shop talk among the nurses, a variety of topics ebbed and flowed in the conversational eddies.

"The knee replacement in A bed is a sweetie…" "My son doesn't understand that his head is going to roll when those two girls find out he's asked both of them to the Prom…" "The ulcer bleed is convinced he'll get AIDS from the blood transfusions…" "You didn't hear it from me, but Dr. Viella is nailing the admissions clerk in Emergency…" "We've got to fight this business of not wearing specialty identifications or the patients won't be able to tell us from Housekeeping…" "That dirty old man may have burned hands but he bit my tit…"

Most of the nurses were obviously enjoying the opportunity for uninhibited chatter and good food. I found it remarkably easy to insert myself and, with minor fictions, direct short discussions toward pain and its treatment. Many did not hesitate to express strong views and present personal observations. I was the only one disconcerted by the incongruity of the subject matter as party talk.

When I caught Brenda alone in the kitchen and commented on this, she gave a knowing grunt. "I told you, Lexy. Nurses are frontline. If you ever turn your head or step back, you're done for. You won't be any good any more. Nurses could make a lot of difference in healthcare in this country, if we were consulted."

"Well, I'm asking and I'm listening. But I'm not taking any notes. Think any of these women would talk to me privately some other time?"

Brenda removed a container from the freezer and cascaded cubes into an ice bucket. "If you'll let me smooth the way first. I'm sure it was the same way with teachers. You have to be careful just how close up and personal you get with a reporter. But I know the strings to pull."

I snorted. "You always did, Puppet master."

Her close-set eyes twinkled. "But not yours, my friend. You kept them waxed, or oiled." She pressed the lid of the ice bucket into place. "What about the cool beauty?"

I ignored her question with one of my own. "Where is Wren?"

"I settled her with Karen when I found out she had lived in Atlanta for awhile. She'll help Karen think about the pleasures of going more than the sadness of leaving."

I said meaningfully, "Puppet master."

She grinned and kissed me lightly on the lips. I stepped back to discover Wren in the doorway, her slitted eyes masking their color.

Brenda hugged the ice bucket to her body with one hand as she scooped up a bowl of potato salad with the other. She gleamed mischievously at Wren who had moved out of the doorway to let her pass and said, "Just a peck between ex-lovers. I'm sure you have your share of those."

Wren's eyes widened; I could see a splash of deep ocean green. She leaned against the door frame. "She doesn't mince words, does she?"

"Never did. And I think that's why she's not superintendent of nurses at the hospital. The nurses respect her, and she knows how to make doctors listen, but administration is another matter. Scared to death of a blunt, powerful woman."

"I'm not sure she doesn't scare me a little." Keeping the butcher's block island between us, Wren began smoothing and folding foil into neat squares. "When were you lovers?"

I removed a patch of foil from her hands, waiting until she looked directly into my eyes before speaking. "Years ago. After my first experience, at college." I adopted an exaggerated melodramatic tone. "I had been devastated by desertion. Thought I would never love again." I became serious. "Didn't have the sense yet to know that what I thought was first love was really first lust. Brenda helped me see that. Got me to relax a little about it all. Taught me about the naturalness of being a lesbian. Taught me more about friendship."

"And now you know it all."

I held her eyes for a moment. "Even as a high school teacher, I remained a student. There is always more to learn."

Before Wren could respond, two nurses entered the kitchen carrying dirty glasses which they began rinsing in the sink. By silent agreement we returned to the Florida room, where I ignored the candid appraisal of

114

Brenda, and resumed my quest for information. Wren joined a group on the small patio.

I realized there had been a shift in the composition of the guests. Most of the wives and mothers had said their goodbyes, and left for home and family responsibilities. The remaining nurses were younger, probably single, and a few of them gay. Several I talked with were harsh in their criticism of older doctors for dismissing the pain of the dying as a natural by-product of terminal conditions not meriting treatment. I learned, too, that many doctors refused to permit their patients access to devices where they themselves could control the dosage of pain-killing drugs. When I voiced concern over purposeful or accidental death-inducing dosages, I was informed there were reliable safeguards preventing such. One nurse told me of a doctor who regularly arranged for the hospital's pain management specialist to see all of his patients who were expected to recover, but never for his terminal cases.

I was struck also by how many of the younger nurses emphasized the patients' rights to know the details of their conditions and participate in the decision-making. I was saddened but not surprised to hear bitter acknowledgment that, in dying as well as living, women continued to face discrimination and mistreatment. I pondered what Rita's partner Dee must have faced, and how heavily it must have weighed on both of them. My mind skipped to Hal and his cancer threat. What lay ahead for him and Marilyn? Would his being male assuage that threat?

Brenda thrust a plate of food in my hands. "I don't think I've seen you eat anything, and the pickings are getting slim. You do need looking after, Lexy. Your creamy blonde may just be the one to do it." She faked an aggrieved expression. "Don't frown at me and pull yourself up tall." She shook her head in amusement at my prudently short hiss, and nodded toward the sliding glass doors. "Go join her. Now."

I obeyed. I joined Wren at a patio table she was sharing with two others. I nibbled on my food as they discussed how rapidly the automotive industry had recognized and capitalized on the female market for trucks. How they had redesigned their products to blend comfort and exciting colors with utility.

As the two nurses rose to go indoors, one commented, "Too bad other fields aren't as smart, especially ours. You wouldn't believe how long it took us to get out of those starched dresses and into pants."

The other one added, "And those caps. My mother struggled with hers for years. When it fell off in a full bedpan, that was it."

We all chuckled at the image.

The glass doors closed and the large, powder-puff bush rustled at the corner of the patio as the early evening breeze quickened. The sun had dropped below the treeline, and a hush was settling over the backyard. I was acutely aware of how close Wren was, and wondered at her thoughts.

She startled me by answering my unspoken question. "I like this time of day...night...in-between. I like watching the darkness roll in."

"Melville Cane taught me to see it a different way."

"Melville Cane?" Wren shifted in her chair, turning toward me.

I explained. "A poet. There is a short poem of his describing the approach of night as color going out of things rather than darkness coming to them. Look at the powder puffs. Watch the rose color fade out of them."

She turned her head, and I wanted to trace the tautness of her neck. Her face infused with pleasure as she perceived what I had suggested. Then, gazing my way again, she lifted a hand to touch the flow of hair above my ear. She said, "The red highlights are almost gone." She glanced down. "And the color of your shirt won't last much longer."

I prayed to whatever goddesses there be that Wren couldn't see the hardening of my nipples. I could not draw my eyes from hers. I could no more pull back than dive into the ocean and breathe water. I was lost as I had never been before, and happily so. And Wren Carlyle knew.

Brenda tapped on the glass doors and motioned us inside. The party honoree was leaving, along with the few remaining guests who helped her carry gifts to her car. She thanked Wren warmly for information and advice concerning Atlanta. As I had not even met her, I received only a passing, quizzical glance. I felt a tad guilty, even though my purpose had been to avoid darkening her party for her. Then only Brenda, Wren, myself, and a student nurse remained. I had noticed her earlier, listening as intently as I was to the responses of the older nurses.

Brenda tossed me a garbage sack. "I'll trust you to gather trash, Lexy. Be warned, Wren. She's not very handy around the house."

I frowned and flashed a warning toward the back of the young nurse collecting cups and saucers. Brenda wrinkled her nose, and shook off the warning. She and Wren moved off into the kitchen, where dishes rattling and doors opening and closing rose above their low voices.

"Why were you asking those questions?"

I scooped two limp paper plates into my sack, then gazed at the mildly troubled face of the young woman. "I'm a reporter. I plan to do some articles on pain in dying patients, and how it's dealt with by the medical profession. Wanted to start with how nurses see it...bothered by that?"

She spoke slowly. "No, not bothered. Things to think about." She gave

116

me a tentative smile. "This was my first week on the floor. Not a bit like the books and classes."

"The real thing never is. Feeling all right about your choice—being a nurse?"

A rush of enthusiasm. "Oh, yes. I knew that the first day. But I began to see right away how much it can take out of you if you're not doing it just for the money. If that makes sense?"

"Oh, it does. I've never worked just for a paycheck, so I've had a lot taken out of me."

She knelt to retrieve some paper plates from the floor for me. I leaned over, holding the sack wide, noting her heart-shaped face with a strong mouth above the pointed chin. She asked, "Does it get easier?"

I straightened, hesitated, then gave her truth. "No."

She shrugged. "I didn't think so from what I heard."

Two short beeps of a horn took her attention. She hurried to the kitchen with a precarious stack of cups and saucers, calling, "My ride is here, Brenda. Thank you for including me."

Brenda walked her to the door, an arm around her shoulders. "Anyone on the floor is part of us. Don't forget that." I stepped behind Brenda at the door and waved a hand to the young woman's over-the-shoulder 'thank-you.' Then I reached around Brenda to prevent her closing the door all the way. I had recognized the driver of the car. It was Casi Ziegler.

The student nurse slid into the passenger seat further than necessary, and kissed Casi on the cheek. As Casi held up a warning hand and jerked her head toward the house, I pulled the door into place.

"Not like you to spy, Lexy."

"Not spying, Brenda. Understanding." I went back to gathering trash, considering that I did understand Detective Ziegler's gruff behavior now. He had been trying to find a way to talk to me about his lesbian daughter.

CHAPTER FIFTEEN

As Wren pulled away from the curb, she said casually, "Do I get to hear Brenda's last comment?"

I knew she was referring to the whisper accompanying the goodbye hug she gave each of us. "Do I?"

Her jaw stiffened. Displeasure or an attempt not to smile? "No."

"Likewise." But Brenda's words ricocheted off the walls of my mind: 'Don't be stubborn, Lexy. Don't play that hesitation game of yours. This may be the one you've been waiting for.'

I was having trouble inserting the metal end of the seatbelt into the narrow slot. Wren's touch startled me as she lay her right hand on my left to assist. She asked, carefully unemotional, "Do I need to deposit you at your car right away?"

"No." I made certain my response was as unemotional. We rode in silence for awhile. Then she asked about the information I had gathered from the nurses. It was relaxing to talk about it with her as I scribbled notes in the orange spiral-bound I reclaimed from the floor. Her few additional comments were incisive and helpful.

At one point Wren said, "The no-pain-no-gain philosophy is part of the problem. I'm not talking sports or body-building. I mean the religious concept that pain and suffering win you admittance to Heaven or the Elysian Fields or whatever. And the glorification of gritting one's teeth and bearing it. Never thought much of that either. I watched both Dee and Rita do that. I know they saw it as being brave for each other, but I saw it as trying to deny the need for each other as though that would lessen the final terrible separation."

"It couldn't possibly work."

"Of course not." Wren's shoulders sagged with the memory. "On one of my last days with Dee, she wiped the tears from my cheeks, then whispered with what was left of her voice for me to make Rita cry when it was over."

"Did you?"

She shook her head sadly. "She wouldn't let it happen. Said that if Dee could take all that pain without tears, she could take the pain of losing her as bravely."

I closed my notebook. "One of the nurses told me that sometimes the ICU was so charged with unspoken grief and unshed tears, she wanted to slap people into letting go. But she said it was worse when the place was empty of visitors because they couldn't face seeing the pain. Said she hated it when all she could do was offer a hand to be gripped." Wren touched my thigh briefly. "Keep at it, Lexy. And let me set up interviews with Dee's last nurses and sitters."

"I will. And Brenda told me a doctor who would give me sympathetic copy and another it might be worth confronting. I appreciate this, Wren."

"No. I owe Dee. I let her down with Rita. Maybe this is a way to help balance things."

It was fully dark now; the glitter and pulse of neon signs vibrated against the night. Eventually they diminished as we entered a section of the city dominated by apartment complexes and small parks. These soon yielded to an unfamiliar country area. Not until we topped a small rise and Wren backed the car onto a grassy area did I realize our general location. Clearly visible through the wide wire mesh of the high fence across the road were the brilliant approach lights to one of the long runways. In the same instant that Wren switched off her headlights and engine, my heart thundered in response to a massive passenger jet seeming to drop from the sky, a barely visible outline splashed with tiny lights. I gasped, and held my breath until the noise and moving blur rapidly receded beyond us.

"You liked that." A statement, not a question.

Still I responded with a quick nod. "Do you come here often?"

"Not often. Now and then when a design won't gel, all that commotion with the little bit of threat coerces things into place." After a pause, she added, "First time I've been here at night."

There was an expectancy to the quiet as we looked through the windshield at the array of lights punctuating the darkness. We turned toward each other and, I could see the intensity of her gaze. In simultaneous movement, her hand reached out as I leaned forward. It was as though a part of me stood aside recording sensations. The fingers of her right hand entered my hair. Her left hand splayed over my hip. I arched my breasts into hers. At the pressure of her moist demanding lips, I uttered a short, guttural moan, parting my lips for her tongue.

My moan lengthened and deepened as she swirled her tongue about mine, sucking it sensually into her mouth. Then there was only our deep

119

breathing. I nestled my face into the side of Wren's throat. She stroked my temple and my cheek while touching her lips lightly to my eyelids. The muffled roar of another approaching jet attended the trailing of her fingers from my cheek to my breast. Then the jets deafening rumble obliterated my cry as her thumb circled my nipple, swollen rigid with desire. I sought her mouth hungrily. As I strained toward her, wanting total body contact despite the complications of steering wheel and armrest, Wren gripped both my shoulders and forced me back into my seat.

"Wren?"

"Not now, Lexy. Not here. Not like this."

I turned my head and bit my tongue, trying to show a calm I did not feel, trying to still the rise and fall of my breasts with slower breathing.

"Angry?"

I whipped my face toward her so hard I felt a snap in my neck, but the sharp retort lodged in my throat. I was angry. Angry at being betrayed so easily by my body. Angry that control lay so obviously in her hands. Angry because I knew she was right. Angry because I wanted her—and would wait for her to beckon.

Wren touched the back of her fingers to my cheek. I lifted my chin and half closed my eyes. The craving of my body waned slowly.

Since there were few cars left in *The Ledger* parking lot, Wren ignored the aisles and drove diagonally to mine. We had been conversing as polite strangers, and I was tense with the strain of keeping my eyes from her hands and mouth. She didn't cut off the engine as I bent to search the floor for my notebook. I froze at the light touch on my shoulder. "Lexy?"

I stayed bent. "Yes?"

"I'll call."

I inhaled deeply, whispering huskily on the exhale. "I'll answer." I straightened, then exited the car without looking at her. When I closed my own car door and turned the ignition, she pulled away.

At the street we turned opposite ways. I watched her taillights in my rearview mirror until blocked by other cars. Knowing I was running for refuge, I headed for The Cat. I was glad to find Hal manning the bar alone. I was in no mood for the scrutiny of the Admiral or the perceptiveness of Melody. It was a quiet night for The Cat, and Hal was spending more time watching the basketball game on television than serving drinks. He raised a hand indicating he would be with me as soon as the play in progress ended.

Feeling the need to be defiant, I stood on the footrail, and leaned over the bar stretching for a glass. Then I placed it under the draft spigot and pushed the handle, getting nearly as much foam as beer. As I sucked up some of the foam, Hal approached, shaking his head and making the flesh of his cheeks and jowls wobble. "Do you know what Marilyn would do if she caught you at that?"

"She'd box my ears and fuss about her license. But she's not here, and I don't think any of them are ATF agents." I waved my arm toward the few customers, speaking more harshly than I had intended.

Hal took my glass and tilted it under the spigot, filling it properly. "You mad at somebody, Lexy?"

Chastened, I ran my fingers through my hair, which was a mistake in that I relived the twining of Wren's fingers. "A complicated day, Hal. But I wasn't ready to go home yet."

"I know. Sometimes you're glad to live alone. Sometimes not."

I knew he was thinking about himself. I took a long slow drink of my beer as he continued, "Marilyn has started in on me about moving in with her. It's not time for that yet. May never be." Concerned that he had said too much, unaware that I knew of his cancer, he started to return to the basketball game.

I stopped him with a question. "The police get anywhere with those skinheads in the parking lot last week?"

He brightened. "Yeah. Seems they were trying to make a night of it. They'd shot out windows at the abortion clinic before they hit here. But they got more than they expected later at The Corral. Marilyn heard about it from one of their bartenders. Said the bald shits were chunking rotten oranges all over the front of the place. Figured no one there would take them on."

I laughed. "Big mistake. The Corral is not known for a limp-wristed clientele. Those city cowboys take that western stuff seriously."

Hal grinned. "For real. A bunch of guys came out and lassoed those scummy bastards right out of the back of the truck where they were standing to throw the oranges. Tied them to the hitching post out front and threw a few oranges themselves. Then they called the cops. Bet that was the first time those skinheads were glad to see a police car come up."

Though this was one gay-bashing incident with a halfway happy ending, I knew the gain was infinitesimal. The fear and hatred that put us in jeopardy was a constant threat, and the retaliation of the gay men at The Corral would have its price. I doubted that Hal understood that.

Without asking me, Hal replaced my empty glass with a full one. I ran my finger up the cool side, catching a trickle of beer, then drew my finger across my lips. I reached into my hip pocket for money, but Hal shook his head. "Your money's no good tonight, Lexy. The Admiral said your next few drinks were on the house. Set up that tattooed toughy too, when she was in here Saturday night."

Surprised I exclaimed, "Janel! She really came in here?"

"You bet. Edgy as hell, too, until Melody got hold of her and the date she brought in. Made them sit at the bar for awhile. Talked to them that special way she's got."

I understood. Melody would spot people who were uncomfortable and talk to them as if it were the most natural thing in the world until they began to relax. She was especially good with those venturing into a lesbian bar for the first time. And she had noticed Janel before. But winning over Janel would take some doing. I resolved to talk to her about it. Hal broke into my thoughts. "You know, Lexy, I recognized the femme."

"What do you mean?"

My next swallow of beer did not go down well as he said, "She was outside here the night that Darla Pollard was killed."

I sat my glass down with a thunk. "You're sure?"

"Sure I'm sure. She was in a pickup truck on the street end of the alley. Couldn't see her face 'cause of the way she was leaning forward on the dashboard. But my impression was that she was crying. I'd gone out to check on the noise we heard. Remember? We thought it might be somebody using the side door."

I did remember. Despite the beer, my mouth felt dry. "How come you're sure if you couldn't see her face?"

"The hair, for one thing. But mainly it was that light-colored leather jacket with doodads all over it. She was wearing it Saturday night."

Alice whistled for Hal's attention and he moved down bar to prepare drinks for a table of recent arrivals. I sat sipping beer while considering Hal's news about Chrissy. Janel had been in the restroom with Chrissy not far away on the outside that Friday night. When Melody noticed Janel, had she been looking for Pollard or her partner? Had Chrissy been crying and, if so, why? And I still had a hard time swallowing Janel's story that she was looking for Chrissy at The Cat the night the skinheads plunked a BB in my shoe. I wondered if Robbie Exline had interviewed them together yet. Someone else to talk to again.

My glass contained about an inch of beer. I tilted it and rotated my hand, watching the stream of amber roll with the motion.

"You going to drink that…or just play with it?"

Lifting my head to look in the mirror, I saw Glen Ziegler standing behind me. I turned to face him, noting that the laminated ID was not dangling conspicuously from a pocket or clipped to a lapel. In fact, he was

122

attired in jeans, a crew-neck T-shirt, and a light windbreaker. Seated on the high stool, I was able to look at him without tilting my chin up. "You're not dressed for work, but I wouldn't think this bar would be your choice for a nightcap."

"You don't give any quarter, do you?" The tone was challenging, but the cocker spaniel eyes were mild.

I answered with, "Buy you a drink, Mr. Ziegler? I am assuming you are off duty."

He slid onto the stool to my left and called to Hal, "A light beer." To me, he said, "Make it Glen if you're going to pay."

"Actually we're drinking on the house tonight. The Admiral's trying to make me feel better about my run-in with the skinheads the other night."

Ziegler stuck his tongue in his cheek and his eyes sparked with humor. "Exline passed on the story. Uniforms caught up with them later that night."

"I heard." Then I gave him a hard look. "They going to check on The Corral for awhile?"

He shifted uncomfortably. "They'll do what they can."

I grunted sarcastically.

He took a swig of beer and rubbed a knuckle over his chin line. "It's not an easy situation, Lexy. There's more crime than we can cover. There's more anger and frustration and violence. And there's more not caring...and that's the worst of all. It leads to the worst. Here we are on the rim of a new century and it's like we're dropping back into the pit." The bleakness of his voice was disturbing.

I said, "Maybe those of us who do care should be trying to claw our way out...and take as many with us as possible."

"Hell, I couldn't even keep my family together." The bluntness of his statement was like a jab at his own body.

While I was mentally scrambling for a remark, three women took bar stools near us, their laughing camaraderie a marked contrast to Ziegler's sudden moroseness. On an impulse I motioned to Hal. Leaning forward and speaking low, I asked him, "What's the chance of the detective and me using Marilyn's office for a little privacy?"

Hal's tone was neutral but he pinned Ziegler with a meaningful look. "Don't push at our Lexy too hard, Detective." He handed me a key.

Before Ziegler could respond, I said to Hal, "I think you better worry about Glen here. He's about to meet teacher-tough Ms. Hyatt."

Ziegler shrugged at Hal and, curiosity lightening his features, followed me down the hall to Marilyn's office. I had never been in her office before. It was a hodgepodge of cast-off furniture, definitely more utilitarian than esthetic. One side wall was an exception. It contained small, ledgelike shelves mounted randomly. Each held a ship model. The range was from a narrow Viking longship to the bulk of a German fivemaster.

Ziegler shifted along the wall, perusing the models. I cleared a corner of Marilyn's desk with a couple swipes of my hand and perched on it, tapping my heels lightly against the thin wood veneer.

I spoke to his back. "What brought you here tonight?"

He answered without turning. "I called *The Ledger* late this afternoon, but you had already gone for the day. Called your apartment later. No answer. Went out to eat. Drove by here on the chance…saw your car." He turned from the ship models, noticing that the only chairs in the office were the Admiral's padded, high-backed, wheeled desk chair and a worn captain's chair, the varnish flaking from the thin arms and the sagging cloth an ugly green. He opted for the captain's chair.

"Were your plans to grill me or arrest me?" I relented when I saw the struggle going on behind his eyes. "Or did you want to talk to me about Casi?"

His mouth dropped open. Then he closed it firmly and looked away. He mumbled, "Is she that obvious?"

"Am I?" I stopped tapping my heels.

He stared at me a long moment, then gave me a tight-lipped smile. "No. Nor are most of the women I've met on this case."

I wondered if he knew about his own partner. "Nor is your daughter. I just happened to be in one of those right places at the right time. But this conversation might go easier if you said it out loud for starters."

He tried to joke. "I do believe you were a tough teacher."

When I neither spoke nor blinked, he sucked in his cheek and bit down on it. Then he said, rapidly running all the words together, "Casi thinks she's gay."

I gripped the edge of the desk and pulled back my shoulders. Ziegler got up and paced in front of the closed door. I kept my eyes trained on him, even though he refused to look at me, and continued my silence.

Finally he planted himself before me on wide-spread legs, trying not to clench his fists. He said in a strained voice, "All right. My daughter is gay. That what you wanted to hear?"

I relaxed my own tension and pointed to the chair. As he sat down again, I said, "That's what I wanted you to say…for starters. Maybe we'll get lesbian or homosexual out of your mouth next." I saw the words hit him like blows and felt sympathy but not regret.

He stretched out his legs and stared at his feet as he spoke, "Being a cop handicaps a marriage. I thought things would improve when I moved out of uniform into detective. But Eileen didn't see it that way. She said it was good not to have to worry so much about me getting hurt or killed…but I was home even less. And she claimed that when I was home, my mind was on my cases." He looked at me. "And I guess she was right. We divorced two years ago, right after Casi graduated from high school."

"And what about Casi?"

He sighed. "We always did alright. Except for a couple of her teenage years when she thought all adults were…'plastic,' she called us. And these last few weeks…" He left the chair and faced the ship models again. "Eileen called me over one Sunday to discuss a problem with Casi. When I got there she hit me with her description of a 'perversion phase' Casi was going through." He turned toward me. "Said it was my fault. Said I hadn't been around enough to give her the right picture of men."

"She's just trying to fix blame somewhere for what she doesn't understand and can't accept. Did you talk with Casi?"

Ziegler's laugh was harsh. "I tried. Talk about two left feet and all thumbs. My mouth felt like it had forgotten how to form words. But it was really a matter of not having any idea what to say."

"Casi have any problem knowing what to say?"

A mildly bewildered shake of his head. "Oh, no. Never did. Even as a little girl. And as a big girl, she just got blunter. If you don't mind, I'll…what's the word?"

"Paraphrase?" I suggested.

"Right. She said that she didn't have any problems with men no matter what her mother said. But her interest extended to friendship relationships only. When it came to…to intimacy, she preferred her own…gender."

"You having trouble with the word 'sex,' Glen?"

"Damn it, Lexy! This is my daughter we're talking about." He sprawled into the captain's chair again.

"Listen, Glen. Try to set that aside. Try to see her more as a young woman separate from you structuring her life." I had his full attention and continued, "If you don't want to lose her, you've got to show a willingness to enter her world. You have to recognize it as her world. And one as valid and potentially satisfying as any you and her mother ever imagined for her."

"How do I do that?"

"Watch for some simple way. Ask if she is seeing anyone on a regular basis. Ask if you could have dinner with them. Give her a chance to let you have a little fringe contact with her gay life." He grimaced at that. "Even if she doesn't jump at the chance right away, don't push. Just show her you are

125

interested in an open-door policy."

"But how do I deal with it in here?" He tapped his temple. "How do I handle what I know about how…" He struggled with the words. "…how homosexuals are treated? I want to spare my child the ridicule, the venom, the harm. Is that wrong?"

"Not wrong. Just not possible." I slid from the desk and leaned against the front. "I'm a lesbian, Glen. It's not a choice I made the way I chose a car. It's not something I can change the way I changed professions. It's as indeterminate in its origins as my being a morning person. It's part of who I am…part. I ask the people who matter to accept that part of me as they accept the others."

Neither of us spoke right away. Then he said, "I hear what you're saying. It's going to need some soaking in time though." His smile was shy. "Thank you."

There was a sharp rap at the door which immediately swung inward. The Admiral stood in the opening, one hand on the door knob, the other on her hip.

"A woman's office is obviously not her castle," she said.

Ziegler scrambled to his feet while I stayed relaxed and still. I concentrated on keeping my gaze steady as I fibbed. "Needed privacy, Marilyn. The detective had a few questions for me."

Ziegler added quickly, "And I have a couple more for you as well, Miss Neff." He ignored my frown.

The large chair squeaked as Marilyn settled into it and pulled herself flush to the edge. "The hour I gave you yesterday wasn't enough? Oh well, ask away, Detective. But you and Lexy both look naked without those orange notebooks. Were you planning on me taking the notes?"

I took over the captain's chair and said soothingly, "Okay, Admiral, Okay. This was an off-duty, off-the-cuff conversation. Nothing to do with Darla Pollard. I suppose it was bad manners on my part to push Hal into giving us your office, but we really did need the privacy. And if I could explain more, you would understand."

She pushed back slightly from the desk. "No problem, kid, now that you are leveling with me." She looked at Ziegler, her manner less formidable. "I never let my regulars get away with lying to me. Bad for my ego."

Ziegler had regained his composure. "Am I forgiven enough to ask those questions anyway?"

Marilyn gave a single nod. "But I've given you all there was. No more contraband below decks. I've given you everything straight out."

He seemed to be musing to himself. "I know the restrooms are back here and that people dining, dancing, drinking would naturally use them. And I suppose I can accept the coincidence of some of them being people who knew Pollard." His voice toughened. "You really didn't come back to this area after you put her in here?"

Marilyn held a many-ringed hand toward him. "That's not what I said. I said I never saw Darla again after I put her in here…not until I saw her dead in the supply room. I did come back here to show the plumber the problem and later to get the checkbook to pay him. That's when I discovered that Darla wasn't here any more. I assumed she got tired of waiting for me and left."

"Were you curious about that?"

"More like pissed. If what she wanted to talk about was so big a deal, she could have waited longer. I was thinking about that when I got out the checkbook. This damn drawer sticks and I ended up slamming my hand in it." She flexed her hand, and I could see the fading discoloration. A week ago she hadn't remembered what caused it.

"Problem, Lexy?"

I knew Ziegler was responding to my narrowed eyes. Carefully I widened them. "No. I was just remembering something. When Jodi made things clear…" I hesitated and raised my eyebrows.

Ziegler answered my unspoken question. "She did do that." He turned back to Marilyn. "And she said in both interviews that she believed she heard you talking angrily with Pollard in here a good bit after Pollard arrived."

I spoke hurriedly before the Admiral could make an angry retort. "That's what I was remembering. Jodi told me that, too. But a few days ago Rita Burgess told me—"

"Who's she?"

Marilyn answered, "A regular. Nice woman."

I continued, "Rita told me that Marilyn was at the bar when Hal spilled wine on her. Rita then went to the restroom to wash it out. That's when Jodi was back here, too, and heard the arguing. So it couldn't have been Marilyn."

Ziegler said, "I'll check that out with Burgess." He gave me a long look. "And there is something I wanted to check with you. Exline thinks you're holding back on this Janel Kabani—"

"The butch who saved your butt from the skinheads?" Marilyn interrupted.

Smiling, Ziegler lowered his head while I sent a cold glare both their ways.

"She dates Chrissy Shoemaker." I hoped I could leave it at that.

127

But Ziegler went on, "And, therefore, knew Darla Pollard. And your woman bartender placed her here the night of the murder. Either of you see her?"

We both said 'no' but I saw a memory stir behind Marilyn's eyes. I knew she was remembering when I identified Janel by sight at Leather Fever as someone I had seen in The Cat's restroom right before Melody screamed. She read my silent plea and pursed her lips.

Ziegler appeared not to notice. He said, "She pops up several places. Run-ins with your friend Jodi, I hear."

I shoved the chair back against the wall, getting up. "I'm tired of this 'your friend Jodi' business." I stopped at the clear surprise on both their faces.

Ziegler shrugged and shuffled his feet. Marilyn stared in open curiosity and concern.

I let out a long sigh and said, "Sorry. It's been a long day." I ruffled my fingers through my hair. Again unbidden, there was the sensation of Wren's fingers lightly pressing me toward her for that first kiss. Without a further word and without looking at either the detective or the Admiral, I left the office and The Cat.

I had tossed and turned so violently seeking sleep that both sheets had escaped their moorings. Damn! I was starting to think in the Admiral's analogies. Fifteen minutes ago I had silenced the pudding-soft FM music. What I wanted was the raging of Janis Joplin testing the survival capacity of my sneakers. What I wanted was to find the off switch for my mind.

There would be no explaining my brief emotional tantrum and stomping off to either Ziegler or Marilyn. I couldn't explain it to myself. He probably thought it was a gay thing and Marilyn no doubt classed it a hormonal thing. Neither would believe that the reference to Jodi had been a grain of sand tilting the delicate balance of my day. The first disturbance had come at *The Ledger* when I had quarreled with Worthington over the increasing control of advertising in sensitive news areas. I had stomped off there, too, when I had realized I was having the same argument as I had years ago with my principal. Only then the issue had been the encroachment of religion and politics into the realm of teaching.

Then came the party at Brenda's home and the disquieting images drawn by the nurses. Like so many, I had become hardened by television and movies to the true nature of death. Seldom did the nurses deal with blood gushing and bodies rendered into parts. They participated in the invasion of machinery, the loss of control and dignity, the nightmare of dehumanizing pain. I thought of Hal and feared for him.

And then—Janel. I balked at believing she could have killed Darla. Her feisty and cross-grained exterior was armor worn to protect tender sensibilities, and to empower championship of Christine. Somewhere in my amateur sleuthing I had added them to my heart's list of those I did not want to be guilty.

My bed creaked as I heaved myself onto my other side. I tried to stifle the flood of questions beating against the shores of my mind concerning Janel and Chrissy, Marilyn, Hal, Jodi. But there were still the Driscolls and their agitation with Pollard. Tomorrow I would try to connect with Exline again.

Tomorrow…would there be a call from Wren? This time the flood was not of questions but of sensations coursing through my body like whitewater rapids. Suddenly I knew why I had snapped at Ziegler. While talking with Hal and then the detective, I had been concentrating on not concentrating on Wren. I had been forcing my eyes to stay open, wide and staring straight ahead so that I couldn't look inward and see what she had stirred and changed.

Ziegler's reference to Jodi had broken my control. With the awareness that I was now truly at peace with my past with Jodi came the rush of knowing the future I wanted with Wren. Frightened and unnerved, I had ducked and run.

I changed position again and my feet lost their covering. I pleaded into the darkness for the sandman of my childhood…or the cupped hand of a goddess offering me water from the river Lethe.

CHAPTER SIXTEEN

I leaned against the gray railing at the entrance to the precinct, warming my hands on the large styrofoam cup of coffee. I regretted not having gone back for a windbreaker this morning. The wind teasing my hair and collar had too sharp a bite for the thin broadcloth of my long-sleeved shirt.

I had put an end to an abbreviated night of catnaps at five-thirty. Not long after struggling from the chaos of bedclothes, I called the station and learned that Detective Exline was due in early. Now, watching for her, I wondered if seeking information on her turf was a good idea. But it would have to be. I wanted my life back. I wanted to be courted by Wren Carlyle, emotionally free of all entanglements. I wanted Darla Pollard's eyes closed.

At that thought, I closed my own eyes, then opened them with a start as a hand joined mine about my cup.

"You're about to spill that." Robbie Exline was attractively attired in an orange and brown plaid jumper, and a tan blouse. Long spirals of gold dangled from her ears, matching the flecks in her eyes. Uncomfortably aware of my admiring appraisal, she added in a neutral voice, "I have to testify in court later this morning." Then with a telling emphasis, "I've come in early to get some paperwork done."

"Connected with the Pollard case? Maybe your interview with Gloria Driscoll Monday?" I sipped coffee carefully from the nearly full cup.

"You should have a lid on that." The gold flecks had dulled.

"My coffee or my interest in Darla Pollard's death?" I spoke low and even.

Grudgingly, she smiled.

I said, lifting my cup, "Don't like to drink from a jagged-edge hole. Don't like my friends being suspected of murder."

Exline sighed, "Follow me." Over her shoulder she said, "And try to act like I'm the one in charge."

"Yes ma'am," I said with exaggerated meekness.

Inside the station I was surprised by the number of police until bits and

130

pieces of conversations reminded me that seven o'clock was change of shift. Officer Romero, checking a clipboard of information with another officer, nodded curtly as I passed. Turning to follow Exline down a corridor, I muttered, "Probably hopes you are arresting me."

"Romero? He's all right. Some cultural bias about the place of women. But he's coming along. He actually shook hands with Janel Kabani over that skinhead ruckus." She ushered me into a small room crammed with four desks and chairs.

"You questioned her Monday?"

"Yes. And Jodi Fleming. Ziegler interviewed Christine Shoemaker and Mar...Ms. Neff. There were, as I'm sure you know, discrepancies that needed attention." She sat at a desk near a window, bright with morning light. Then she motioned me into a chair opposite her. The brightness behind her made it difficult for me to read her eyes or facial expression. I wondered if that was on purpose.

She said, "Your Janel carries around a lot of hostility."

I hardened my lips, then parted them with an explosive breath. "What's with this 'your' business!? Your Jodi...your Janel..."

"You take a protective stance with people, Lexy. It's not an arm-around-the-shoulder thing, but it's there. I admire it. And this is unprofessional for me to say, but I hope our perp doesn't turn out to be one of your women." She retrieved a folder from the desk drawer. "I know that Glen is having a hard time believing that another woman could do in Darla Pollard with some kind of chokehold or blow. But you and I both know that all the women involved, except maybe Christine, have the strength or skills to manage it."

I made no comment, and concentrated on downing my coffee as Exline continued, "And they were all connected with Darla Pollard. Two ex-lovers, a brow-beaten employee and her angry partner, an agitated mother—"

I interrupted, "Gloria Driscoll. What about her?" At the detective's silence, I entreated, "Give, Robbie. You know I'll warn you when I'm in the reporter mode."

I waited. Exline spoke to me while continuing to sort the contents of the folder. Her attention was divided, and I assumed the material related to her later court appearance, "Gloria Driscoll is a sad case. She wants to be her own person but doesn't have the strength of character to achieve it." She looked at me and seemed to be measuring how far she could go. "Sister talk, okay?"

"Absolutely."

She continued, "I tracked down Officer...the officer who dated Gloria. She's now an investigator in the State Attorney's Office. She talked off the record, of course." She waited for my nod. "Their affair was short and limited. Gloria could never loosen up enough. My contact couldn't decide if the woman truly wasn't gay or didn't know how to let herself be. Said they did more talking than anything. I'll give you the short version."

I pushed back my chair, stretched out my legs, and crossed them at the ankles. The short version was informative, though not necessarily pertinent. Gloria Driscoll appeared to have had a decent childhood and adolescence. Her father worked in a dairy plant and her mother stayed home, but there was the repressive atmosphere that existed in many Jehovah's Witnesses' homes. She married Ben Garrison, a church member approved by her parents. Probably selected, I thought. Garrison died when Stacy was only ten. Somehow I wasn't surprised when Exline said it was of a rare bone-marrow cancer. I was beginning to feel hounded by the disease.

I asked, "How long before she remarried?"

Exline answered, "About two years. She and the officer she met at those self-defense classes had contact for around six months. Gloria's father had recently died and her mother had settled in with church activities. My source thinks that their relationship happened mostly because Gloria was feeling abandoned and lost, so she didn't push things."

"Sounds like a good woman."

"She is." Something careful in the inflection told me that Robbie Exline at one time had had reason to know just how good. I lowered my eyes and rubbed my fingers along the desk edge indented with pencil and pen grooves.

Exline went on with her narration. Gloria had started working at Florida Home Furniture store and met Edward Driscoll there. He was divorced—dated her—they married. She had stopped her involvement with Jehovah's Witnesses. "That's where my information ends, Lexy."

"Can't be. You had to get something from Gloria herself. Because of the daughter, there was something going on with Darla Pollard."

"And that is police business."

There was a firmness in her voice I knew I wouldn't get around. I straightened in my chair, finished the coffee, and tossed the cup in a waste can. "I'll buy you a cup of coffee sometime for all that information. No cream. No sugar." I couldn't sound as peeved as I wanted.

She laughed. "That's the way I like it. Go play reporter, Lexy. On somebody else's case."

I saluted and left. I had no need to report to my own job yet, so I drove by Christine Shoemaker's apartment. I turned into the complex and cruised slowly. Not seeing Janel's truck, I pulled into a slot. My stomach rumbled,

132

complaining of not having been fed since Brenda's party.

I sat, adding the data on Gloria Driscoll into my notebook until I heard a door slam. Chrissy was descending the steps. I got out of my car and spoke to her over the roof as she manipulated her keys. She jumped at the sound of my voice, dropped her keys and a folder of papers. I scooted around my car to help her catch them before the wind lifted them away.

"Sorry. Didn't mean to startle you." I could see that her face was less pinched by tension than usual.

"I didn't expect anyone. What...?" She didn't finish as she accepted some of her papers from me and placed them in the folder.

I explained. "I just thought I'd see if I could catch you before you left for work. I know the detectives talked to you and Janel Monday." Her face went slack, and her eyes darted away. "Wanted to see if that created any problems for you two."

"Why should it?" She sounded more like Janel than herself.

I walked around to the passenger side of her car and gripped the door handle. "Let me sit here and talk with you a minute." She hesitated, staring at me over the roof of her car, and I urged, "Let me be a friend, Chrissy. No one ever has enough of those."

She unlocked her door and then flipped the electronic door release. Quickly I opened the door and slid in before she could change her mind. "What did the detectives seem most interested in?"

Chrissy frowned. "About Janel being at The Cat the night Darla died. Janel thinks you told."

I noticed she did not include herself in being there and that she said 'died' instead of killed or murdered. I said, "Other people saw her there. It came out in routine questioning. She should have expected that. Why was she looking for your boss, Chrissy?"

She flinched. "I didn't want her to. She was mad because Darla had threatened to fire me. She wanted to tell her I was going to work a one-week notice, and that I wanted the back overtime pay owed me."

"Is that what you wanted?"

"I wasn't sure. It's scary to quit a job when you don't already have a new one. But Darla had been getting harder and harder to work for."

I asked another question. "Why did she threaten to fire you?"

Chrissy smacked the steering wheel with both hands. "For something I didn't even do. She accused me of eavesdropping on her and Mr. Driscoll. Said she couldn't keep a secretary she couldn't trust. When I tried to explain, she said we'd talk about it later."

"Explain it to me."

133

She took a deep breath and blew it out with puffed cheeks. "She was going over some policy changes with me when Mr. Driscoll came in. All of a sudden she's telling me I can leave early since it's Friday and I might like to beat the traffic. She rushed me out without letting me clear my desk. But before I got in my car, I thought about the fish…" Her expression was almost childlike. "I needed to turn up the heater in the tank for the weekend. I went back to do it. Darla's door was open, and I could hear her arguing with Mr. Driscoll. I rushed so I could get back out of there but I knocked the dipper on the floor. She heard me and came out. She really looked mad but I didn't think it had anything to do with me…until she started saying those mean things."

I resisted touching her arm. Somehow I knew that would scare her rather than comfort her. "Could you tell what they were arguing about?"

She shook her head. "Sometimes you don't hear words. You just hear feelings."

I was impressed by her perceptiveness. "Was anger the only feeling you heard?"

Another shake of her head, light curls bobbing. "More than that. They didn't like each other. Really didn't like each other."

"Did you explain all this to the detective?"

I felt her withdrawal. She said, "No. On our way to the police station, Janel told me to be quiet about problems with Darla. Said it would just give them silly ideas. I told them about Stacy working there and that there was some kind of problem with her parents but I didn't know what. And I told them that Janel's only problem with Darla was wanting her not to put me down so much. But that it wasn't any big thing."

She didn't see me roll my eyes at that. Everything to Janel was a big thing. "Do they know you were waiting for Janel outside The Cat?"

I was sure she was considering lying. Finally she spoke, her eyes averted toward a fluttering piece of paper trash near the steps to her apartment. "I didn't think to mention it. Janel made me stay in the truck…and I was crying."

"Did you know Darla was in The Cat?"

She turned toward me, her blue eyes disturbed. "When Janel came here and found me crying, she was going to go see Darla by herself, but I made her take me with her. We checked her home first. Then went back by the office, saw her pulling out and heading south. Janel followed her to The Cat. We stayed in the truck awhile and I tried to talk her out of going in after Darla. But she was too upset. She went in anyway."

"And you stayed in the truck the whole time?"

She began to get huffy with me. "What difference does it make? I thought about going in after her when she was in there so long, but I was afraid I'd make things worse."

I changed direction. "Did you see anyone in the alley near the side door?"

Her impatience increased and her tone sharpened. "I wasn't paying any attention to anything but how I was feeling, and worrying about Janel. I have to get to work. It's a new job and I don't want to be late."

"Just one more question, Chrissy. What did Janel say about Darla when she came out?"

She started the car. "She never saw Darla. She checked around, then waited to see if Darla would come out from somewhere." The soft lines of her face hardened. "Leave us alone."

I got out of the car. Back in my own, I again brought my notebook up-to-date with the little I had gleaned from Exline and Chrissy. A thought sent me shuffling back several pages. I found what I wanted, and considered the import. Although somewhat indirectly, Chrissy had denied hearing what Driscoll and Pollard had been arguing about the afternoon before her murder. But Jodi had spoken of a recorded phone message from Chrissy asking to see her about a problem her boss was having. Was that an indication that, accidentally or not, Chrissy had overheard specifics? I felt like I was stabbing in a boiling pot of tumbling spaghetti, trying to secure a single strand. I was beginning to doubt that I would ever be able to determine the consistency of anyone's statements.

CHAPTER SEVENTEEN

I reported to work early after my brief contact with Chrissy, and was rewarded with good news. I had been taken off the tiresome City Water Department beat, and my first installment on the problems of pain management was scheduled for a Monday feature.

Also, being early enabled me to claim a coveted chair. Sports Editor Bill Rylander was taking delivery of the new chair he had requested, and had shoved his old one unceremoniously into the outer hallway just as I arrived. It was smooth, dark wood with soft, worn leather, and tilted way back for thinking. I seized it even before it stopped moving, and whirled it into my own cubicle. My old chair of unyielding plastic and coarse cloth I thrust out to be claimed by a later arrival.

Good luck continued to flit in front of me like a dragonfly skimming air. I breakfasted on a hearty slice of sausage and cheese quiche, placed before me by Barbara MacFadden, accompanied by an admonition to wash the microwave-safe plate thoroughly before returning it. When I did so, she ignored my effusive praise. With the barest of eye contact, she said in the softest voice I had ever heard from her, "My sister died of cancer when she was ten. She faced the pain bravely. More so than I."

A throat tight with emotion made it impossible for me to respond. I nodded, returning to my desk but unable to focus on my work for some time. Then I yanked my folder on Darla Pollard from the bottom righthand drawer.

The picture of the Driscolls kept trying to speak to me, so I taped it to my computer screen, and stared at it. Though standing somewhat behind his wife and Stacy, Edward Driscoll was clutching the shoulder of his stepdaughter. Even in the grainy picture, I could see the strain in his hand and her arm, as though she were trying to pull out of his grip.

Then I returned to the folder and re-examined each piece of copy. I was repeating the process I had used in teaching. Whenever I had difficulty determining the worth of a student's paper, I would put it aside, then return to it again and again. I never had a feeling of progress but eventually I would consider the paper and know what grade to give it. Though reading through the Pollard data and my notes again gave me no sense of accomplishment, I hoped that an unconscious pattern was developing.

I was about to slam the folder away in the desk drawer when I realized something was missing. Shuffling though the papers once more, I was angry at myself for not having catalogued them on the inside of the folder.

At the sound of Worthington's voice as he left his office, I recalled our argument about advertising influence, and I remembered an article in my file referring to Pollard and American Health Insurance. I moved quickly to confront him in the hall space outside my cubicle. He tried to sidestep my confrontation by pleading urgent business, then finally yielded to providing a skeleton explanation. The word had come down from the Managing Editor that American Health had bought a full-page ad for every Wednesday and Sunday, and that all copy relating to the insurance company was to be routed his way for determination of 'newsworthiness.'

I stared at Worthington in disbelief, if not contempt, when he claimed that Barbara MacFadden had erred in sending me copy that was flagged in the computer as not to be dispersed. Snow in Key West was more likely.

The open nature of the room had taught everyone to appear to concentrate on work even when listening to semi-private conversations floating above the confines of individual cubicles. I seethed with the knowledge that Worthington's remark about the Iron Maiden finally making a mistake would spread like a crown fire in a stand of pines.

First, I didn't believe it. Second, I hated being responsible for it.

I completed my work cloaked in an anger that kept everyone at a cool distance. Then, stomping toward the exit to the parking lot, I was intercepted by Barbara MacFadden. At her direct gaze, I noticed for the first time that her eyes were so darkly blue that in anyone else I would have suspected colored contact lenses.

Without a word she handed me a folded piece of gray paper and then pushed ahead of me out the door. Outside on the steps, I unfolded the paper and read in her small, meticulous script: *Billet—one mile west of Kumquat Mall—any time after 6:30.* I looked up in time to see her swing herself effortlessly into a gleamingly polished white Jeep Cherokee. She did not glance my way.

Checking my watch I realized I had time for the errand still on my mind before looking her up. Flipping down the visor to protect my eyes from the stabbing glare of the late afternoon sun, I headed for Florida Home Furniture. I wasn't waiting any longer to determine where Gloria and her husband stood in the waiting list of suspects. I trusted Exline and Ziegler, but they were hampered by police protocol. I didn't plan to skirt the rough terrain.

The intense sunlight and the lowered visor nearly caused me to miss the store. I swerved into parking area too fast to warn the driver behind me.

The entire front of the building was glass combined with interior sky-lights to create a sense of space and brightness, and to blunt the massive aggregation of furniture pieces. As I entered, I tried to walk purposefully while scanning for Gloria Driscoll, attempting to outmaneuver three sales-men zeroing in on me.

One of them outflanked me but I waved away his card and erased his fake smile as I said I was being helped by Mrs. Driscoll. He lifted a hand vaguely toward a far wall of bedroom suites; I saw her seated on a cedar chest, writing on a pad. Before I could reach her, she was joined by a cou-ple whom she accompanied to a high counter in the back where she handed over the paperwork. I tagged along behind, standing back a few feet as she shook hands and spoke platitudes about how happy they would be with their choices.

Marilyn was right about her hair and clothes. The blonde was too glossy and the clothes were too young. As she walked past me, a hand flew to pat her hair and then to check her belt.

"Mrs. Driscoll?"

Her eyes shifted to the large clock on the wall behind the counter, its hands at four-forty.

She said, "Yes. Can I help you?" Her voice was thin, empty of force and resonance.

"Not with furniture," I replied. "I'd like to talk with you about Darla Pollard."

One hand went to her slightly open mouth. The other became a clenched fist at her side. "Are you another detective?"

It was too soon to risk a lie. "No. It's just that I was at The Cat the night she was killed."

"If you're not with the police. Why are you asking me questions?"

I introduced myself and briefly, but obliquely, explained my connec-tions with people who knew Darla Pollard and were at The Cat that Friday night. I concluded with, "I'm trying to track down information that will help all of you who just happened to be there. I don't think the police are con-centrating enough on some skinheads who were in the area." I did cross my fingers on that. "I've talked with the people I know who also knew Darla. Now I'd like to talk with you...if you don't mind."

I was afraid she might dash off like a mindless squirrel. Her feet were moving as though she wanted to go in any of four directions. I believed if I were to touch her she would leap up and crash through a skylight. Instead I offered just an empathetic smile and said, "Are you due to get off soon? Or take a break?"

"I was due off at four-thirty." She regretted saying that immediately. "But I have things to do. I—"

I interrupted. "I don't need much of your time. Just a few minutes. I'm not trying to get anyone in trouble, Mrs. Driscoll." I felt I should have my fingers crossed on that one. I could tell she didn't know how to get rid of me, or escape me. I wondered how she managed to sell furniture. But then I thought that her nervousness channeled into a chirpy manner probably worked with retirees and new arrivals looking for their idea of a Florida image in home decoration.

I straightened into an unyielding stance and waited—another trace of my Uncle Kurt that had made my mother smile even when disciplining me.

Finally she said, "All right, come back to the woman's lounge. We should be the only ones."

I followed her down a hallway lined with wall units and through a mud-brown door brightened with a wreath of dried vines and flowers. The lounge furniture was damaged cast-offs from the floor. I chose a pool chair with flowered cushions.

Gloria Driscoll curled in the corner of a plastic-covered sofa dominated by brilliantly colored parrots. She removed her high-heeled shoes with a sigh and massaged a foot, then began tracing a parrot on the arm of the couch with jerky movements of her finger. "I don't really know much about Miss Pollard. Just what I heard from…from my daughter."

"I know about your daughter's death and I'm very sorry. I've worked with kids her age. I know how wrong their loss is." I held her eyes for a moment. "According to Christine Shoemaker, she was a fine girl and liked working for Darla Pollard."

"She did. Working in that office was the only thing she ever got involved in outside of her classes. I had never been permitted to join in with different activities when I was in high school. I had wanted her to," her face clouded, "but my husband thought…he wanted—"

"You were at The Cat with your husband. Right?"

She responded quickly. "We were there with friends who wanted to see a…" Her hesitation was because she had just realized I was probably a lesbian. "…a gay place. A safe…a *nice* one. I was upset when I saw Miss Pollard come in. It was bad enough that we were there, but the other couple were really Edward's friends and he wanted to impress them by providing whatever they wanted for the evening. But he didn't really want to go to a place like that. He doesn't really like..."

I filled in this hesitation. "Your husband is homophobic?" I was wondering how he could bring himself to entertain friends that way. I had to wonder at his real motives. Had he found out somehow that Darla might go there? Had his intention been to create a scene?

Her next words backed up my doubts. "If that means he doesn't like gay people, yes. He found out from Stacy that Miss Pollard was like that and tried to make Stacy quit her job."

I wondered if he had known about his wife's gay affair before their marriage. The whiteness at the corners of her deeply lipsticked mouth made me think so.

"What was your daughter's response?"

"It was the first time she ever stood her ground with him. Said she would leave home if he made her quit. But she didn't mean it."

Thinking back to my notes I had reviewed this morning, I doubted that. "Your husband seems to have carried his...displeasure with Darla Pollard beyond your daughter's death. Why was that?"

Gloria Driscoll sat up and tapped her shoeless feet on the floor. "Stacy has been gone only two months. We still...still grieve very strongly." She pressed her hands to her temples. "I don't know why it happened. I'll never believe Stacy committed suicide. But Edward does. And he blamed that woman. He thought maybe she had...had forced herself on Stacy, and confused her."

I took a chance. "Is that why he went after her at The Cat?"

She jerked her head up from her hands which then fluttered in front of her. "He didn't catch up with her. I..." She closed her mouth.

I spoke softly but firmly, "Don't stop. I know you talked a little with Marilyn Neff the next night. I think you need to talk some more. Try me."

She stopped all the extraneous movement and seemed to be looking inward. She inhaled and exhaled a long breath. Then spoke quietly, "For weeks after Stacy's death, Edward accused Miss Pollard of being involved. He would call her, go to her office. I was afraid she would call the police on him, but we never heard from anyone. I don't know what he wanted from her. What he wanted to happen. Stacy was gone. Nothing could change that. It was like he wanted to punish someone. Wanted revenge. What good would that be?"

"He went to Pollard's office that Friday afternoon."

She began the jittery movements again. "I didn't know that. I was petrified when I saw her come in the bar. I don't think she saw us. I thought being with friends would keep Edward calm, but he made some remarks and he kept watching the doorway where she went." She looked at me with weak, pale brown eyes. "I got scared there would be a public display when she came out, so I went back to warn her."

I could feel my heart rate increase. "Who did you see back there?"

Her eyes widened. "I didn't see anybody. I started to go in the restroom thinking she might be there, but then I heard her voice coming from behind a door further down. I stood in front of it trying to get up the courage to knock. By that time I realized there was an argument going on inside. I figured it was the owner who had taken her back that way. So I gave up. Then I saw Edward just starting down the hall, and I rushed to stop him. I made a lot out of how we were with his friends and begged him please to give up on her for the night. We left right after that."

"What about the woman who walked between the two of you in the doorway? She had come out of the restroom."

"I told you I didn't see anyone. Oh, yes, there *was* someone who had to get by. That helped make Edward realize we were in a very public place."

"And she had come out of the restroom?" I was angry at my own insistence.

"I don't know where she came from. I just wanted to get my husband out of there."

I changed my line of questioning. "Did your daughter and your husband not get along very well?"

"Oh, they did. They never even argued…except about her working for Miss Pollard."

"You said earlier that was the first time she stood up to him. That implies there were other times she needed to."

Gloria Driscoll's eyes darted around the room like those of an animal caught in a trap. "Edward's not her real father. But he's always been good to her. He even wanted to adopt her. But she loved her father and wanted to honor him by keeping his name. I understand that."

"Did Edward?"

"It…hurt him, but he accepted it. And he was better than ever to her. They really got along." She paused, then continued as though expressing something long on her mind. "Maybe it was because he never had any children of his own in his first marriage, but he didn't seem to understand her wanting to be by herself sometimes. He wanted her with us all the time. And go everywhere with us. It's as hard for him now, with her gone, as it is for me."

I was beginning to have an icy feeling about Edward Driscoll and his stepdaughter. I hoped I was wrong.

Mrs. Driscoll began putting on her shoes. "I have to go."

"Just one more question. Was it a man or woman arguing with Darla Pollard?"

She stood up and adjusted her clothes. "Oh, I have no idea. I only knew her voice because I'd heard it loud like that once when my husband accused her of…made those accusations." She moved rapidly toward the door, then stopped and turned so suddenly I nearly bumped into her. She said, almost plaintively, "Do you really think the skinheads killed her?"

"They've been involved in some hate crimes lately." I didn't tell her those crimes were presently classed as misdemeanors.

Without comment, she was out the door. I held onto the doorknob and watched her skitter down the corridor and turn out of my sight. I wasn't clear enough on a timeline to know if Edward Driscoll could have gone back later to accost, or kill, Darla Pollard. For all I knew, I had seen him arguing in the doorway with his wife after he had been in the office. Gloria Driscoll was jittery about something. Her calls and talking to Marilyn pointed to that. Or was she cleverer than she appeared, and had it all been a scheme to make it look like she didn't know Darla was dead?

The lounge door was still open by a couple of inches. I tugged it closed but held the knob. I mulled over what I did and didn't know about the death of Darla Pollard.

I thought of Oedipus in *Oedipus Rex* by Sophocles who found out how terrible knowledge of the truth could be. If I discovered who killed her, would it be a terrible truth I wished I did not know?

Outside the huge furniture store, I stood and watched the clouds in the darkening sky race east to west. Looked like the weather forecasters were on target this time. The temperature had dropped a possible fifteen degrees while I was talking with Gloria Driscoll. It would seem a lot colder when the high winds shoving the clouds, slanted earthward. Vacationers on early spring break were in for wind-driven sand and an ocean chop too rough for swimming.

I retrieved my windbreaker from the back seat of my car and settled behind the wheel. I also retrieved the Iron Maiden's note from my pants pocket, wondering both about the note itself and the nature of The Billet. A restaurant? A store? I had read enough war novels to know it meant off-base sleeping quarters for military personnel. But I couldn't envision Barbara MacFadden inviting me to meet her at a motel.

I laughed aloud and started the car. By the time I got to the area west of Kumquat Mall, it would be nearly six-thirty. Then I would have my ques-

142

tions answered, and my curiosity assuaged.

Due to long, rush hour traffic delays and rerouting, I almost missed my destination. A lumberyard evolved into a rectangular strip of concrete blocks housing some storage units, a pawnshop, and a used paperback book store. Above the door of the unit on the end was a faded sign proclaiming it 'The Billet.' All the front parking spaces were taken, but I let my car idle as I bent low to view the sign. I did not understand the meaning of the military insignia encircling the name.

I swung around to the side and parked. I sat for a moment, considering if my arrival at almost six-thirty on the dot would be admired or greeted with disdain. Outside the car, I shivered as a gust of wind snapped the collar of my jacket against my cheek.

I shrugged off the shivering, and walked around a metal door painted dull green. I entered, immediately experiencing the sensation of stepping onto a movie set. The room was warm with lighting of a yellow tinge. The left wall was a row of high-backed wooden booths, the right, a low bar with chairs like those I had seen in pictures of my grandparents' farm kitchen. In between were square tables and similar chairs widely spaced.

Instead of the expected mirror behind the bar, there were collages of snapshots, magazine glossies, and yellowed, brittle looking newspaper photos. All were of women in uniform. While most looked to be of World War II vintage, there was a smattering of newer ones, including women in astronaut gear. As I turned my head slowly and swept the room visually, I saw large wooden coat and hat racks. Draped over many of the branching, slender curves of wood were military jackets of varying blues, olive-green, khaki, brown, and white. Even in the soft light and at a distance, I could see the gleam of gold, silver, and brass insignia on collars and lapels, the fading colors of arm and shoulder patches, the stripes on lower sleeves. The hats were just as varied in color and brim styles.

There were perhaps twenty women scattered about the room. Though their heights and general builds varied, most sported short to medium hair styles, running the gamut from salt and pepper to astonishing white. A few darted quizzical glances my way as I left the doorway to approach the bar.

Before I could pull out a chair, the lean, craggy-faced bartender turned from an old wooden cash register to address me. "You must be Babs' reporter." Her full-lipped smile softened the harsh face.

"Babs?"

She waved toward the opposite wall. I turned to see the Iron Maiden in a booth directly across from us, drinking coffee with another woman. Feeling conspicuously young, I wended my way through tables to the booth.

Immediately the other woman, iron-gray locks framing a pleasant, chubby face, nodded to me and slid from the seat, taking her mug with her. "Don't forget, Babs, you're subbing for Shirley at Crestwood Lanes next week."

I took the vacated seat, and felt the body warmth emanating from the wood. As Barbara MacFadden lifted her mug, I said, "Babs?"

The quiet laughter was the first I had ever heard from her. "Barbara's my age were always nicknamed Babs. I preferred that to Mac." She speared me with that riveting gaze. "Possibly to the Iron Maiden."

I hoped the warmth of my face wasn't an apparent blush. I surveyed the room again, then asked, "Are these all ex-servicewomen?"

"Yes. Marlene, who just reminded me of an injudicious promise to sub in a bowling league, was a WAVE during the Korean War. Schooner, behind the bar—oh, beer only incidentally—was a WAC with me in Germany right after the war ended. She drove a jeep ferrying officers around. "

"Schooner? A last name or a nickname?" I asked.

A shadow passed over her face. "A nickname. It didn't take all that long for the German breweries to get going again. And she did love her beer, and drank from schooners only. Eventually she was drinking harder stuff…from schooners, too. Claims she never sobered up until a nephew came back from Vietnam minus a leg and an arm. Said she needed all her wits about her to get him moving again. She's been sober ever since."

I watched Schooner serve up frosted mugs of beer to two women at the bar. "But serves it to others?"

"But nothing harder. And never to anyone who doesn't need any more. And there's more than one woman in here drinking coffee due to Schooner's assistance." She drank from her own coffee mug again, and correctly judged the thought behind my eyes. She said with the thin-lipped grimness I knew well, "No. I'll be having a beer later."

I realized I was having my first real conversation with her, and was enjoying it. She had said more words to me in the last couple of minutes than I had ever heard from her at one time. And I was becoming aware of a watchful concern behind those piercing blue eyes that had deepened in the dim lighting of the room."

My own concern over the argument with Worthington washed over me. I said tentatively, "Miss MacFadden…"

"In here it's Babs."

I shook my head. "I don't think I could manage that. Will you accept Barbara?" At her nod, I went on, "I'm sorry about the problem with the files on American Health. I didn't mean—"

She interjected, "You and I have no problems. Mr. Worthington has one

144

with his conscience." She shifted, reaching down and coming up with a folder which she handed across to me. "Copies of what were removed from your desk."

Before I could react, she lifted a hand and motioned with her fingers. A woman with the first non-gray hair I had seen, and even younger than I, limped to our booth. A food-soiled apron was wrapped about a sturdy body. She had the same work-out look as Robbie Exline.

She saluted smartly with what I could tell was military precision. "What'll it be, Captain?"

Barbara MacFadden nodded a greeting to the young woman and said to me, "You basically have only two choices, Lexy. A hamburger and fries or broiled, skinless chicken with a salad. I'm having my beef fix for the week."

I responded, "I think I need to be good to my arteries for a change and have the chicken and salad."

As the young woman limped toward the door to the kitchen, Barbara said, "A bootcamp training accident. She was going to be a marine. Shirley, the one I'm going to sub for in bowling, noticed her drunk around the pool tables at the bowling alley time and again. Heard the talk about losing out on the career she wanted. She was scruffy and feisty like an alley cat. Shirley dragged her in here to Schooner. Really tested Schooner's patience. But I think you can see who won."

The next two hours passed pleasantly and speedily. We ate, concluding the meal with two mugs of dark beer. I talked of my family and teaching background and appreciated the fact that she was the first person not to challenge the wisdom of my leaving teaching. She spoke a bit about her military life. Often women paused at our booth and were introduced. Always Barbara would fill me in on their service records after they left us.

When the bill was dropped on the table, I reached, but her nimble fingers darted under mine to seize it. In the Iron Maiden voice I was more accustomed to, she said, "The first time as a guest, you are treated. If you are asked again, you pay your own way."

I thought about saying, "Yes, Captain," but knew instantaneously that it would not be acceptable or appreciated. I knew also that her reaching for the check was my cue to leave. After I told Schooner how much I had enjoyed the beer, she joined three women at a table where one was shuffling a deck of cards.

Back out in my car I turned on the heat against the dropping temperature and increasing wind. Waiting for the interior to warm, I switched on the overhead light and looked at the contents of the folder Barbara MacFadden had given me. Nothing seemed of any special significance, except that the references to charges against Pollard with regards to insurance policies still didn't jibe with Hal's reluctant praise of her advice to him concerning coverage. I supposed the problem could have been primarily with American Health.

I gunned the motor and spun gravel as I thought of American Health's current favored-advertiser status with *The Ledger*.

CHAPTER EIGHTEEN

"That's all I can tell you, Lexy. I didn't pay any more attention to them than I had to. The men were sneering and the women skittish. Their attitude was pissing me off. I can't stand it when straights come in here to ogle. That's when I'll usually flirt with the women just to scare them into thinking I'm definitely a big ol' nasty lesbian, and they don't know their asses from their elbows that I'm not. But they weren't any fun. I didn't like serving them, Lexy."

I thanked Alice and walked slowly to the bar, taking my regular stool to the far right. I waved away Melody, opening my notebook to what I had scribbled from my interview with Gloria Driscoll yesterday afternoon. There was little Alice could reinforce or refute.

One thing I was considering was the possibility that Gloria had been the other half of the argument behind the office door. She could have been lying about hearing voices herself. With her weak voice, she could easily have been the one Jodi couldn't distinguish when she went back that way to the restroom. Surely Jodi would have picked up on the deeper tones if it had been Edward Driscoll. If...if...if...

I slammed the notebook on the bar top, sending a napkin floating. The approaching Melody caught it in mid-air. She whipped a fresh one in front of me and raised an artistically shaped brow.

"Not yet, Melody. Someone will be joining me." I turned to avoid her expression of pleased interest. I didn't dare tell her that I was holding off on alcohol because I didn't want to dull the anticipation of seeing Wren Carlyle again.

Wren had called last night as I stepped from the shower, pleasantly immersed in thoughts of Barbara MacFadden and The Billet. Hurrying, I caught the phone on the fourth ring, still dripping but struggling into my terrycloth robe. When she asked if she had called at a bad time, I replied that I was only reading. I wanted nothing to disturb the delicate balance between us.

147

We talked politely…each distanced by a relationship not yet formed. I told her about my article in the coming Monday *Ledger*. She described a design logo accepted by a corn festival committee. We talked of the ever-changing March weather and how neither of us were looking forward to the spring rush of tourists. When our conversation lagged, and I sensed she was preparing to say good-night, I plunged. I asked her to join me for dinner on my turf at The Cat the next night. She accepted, saying she hadn't ever actually been there.

Then I stretched out on the bed, wallowing in my pleasure over the phone call. I patted my still wet neck with the wide collar of my robe. I trailed my fingers along side my breasts, over my ribs, pausing at my hip bones, then as far as I could down my thighs before drawing them back. I thought of a strangely soft line from e e cummings: 'your slightest look easily can unclose me.' I did not sleep well.

I swiveled further on my stool to watch the entrance of a group of city league soccer players in glossy, bright uniforms. Most of the women were of medium height, their arms and and legs attractively muscular. Only the goalie was different—nearly six feet with broad shoulders and powerful legs, and wearing a purple polo with multi-colored stripes. The butch cuts glistened while the damp strands and ringlets of longer hair clung to glowing faces.

Then I noticed a couple trailing in after, obviously not part of the soccer contingent. Casi Ziegler and her student nurse. I turned back fast so I could watch them in the mirror. The situation had the feel of a first-time excursion.

This time Casi's combat boots were black, and the harem pants as well. A loose apricot blouse was anchored by a black vest. The short blond spikes in her brown hair gleamed in the colored bar lights. Her girlfriend stood a fraction behind Casi. She wore her long blue shirt over cobalt slacks. Carefully styled curls softened the heart-shaped face.

At a word from Casi, they took stools a few down from me. I saw Melody's eyes register the likelihood of their being under age. That meant she would offer them virgin cocktails, and suggest they drink them at a table. I slid off my stool, scooped up my notebook, passed behind them, and took a seat left of Casi just as Melody reached them.

I said, "We'll all have soda water with lime. My treat." I ignored the sudden smoldering of Casi's walnut-brown eyes and smiled across her at the student nurse. "I didn't get your name at Brenda's party. I'm Lexy Hyatt."

We were both conscious of Casi stiffening, but she offered a tentative smile. "Stephanie Talbot. This is Casi Ziegler."

148

"We've half met, Stef. She knows my dad." The deep voice bordered on huskiness. "He's meeting us here soon." The jaw was set and the eyes steady.

I turned my attention to the drink Melody placed in front of me, pushing the slice of lime off the edge and into the glass. It appeared that Ziegler had acted quickly on my suggestion—he had asked Casi and her lover out to dinner. I was just as positive that his daughter had dictated the locale, probably to be assertive and challenging. Glen was in for a long evening. Before Melody moved away, I made introductions. I was careful to use Stephanie's full name, but she offered a hand to Melody and gave the shortened version.

Melody smiled benignly and said, "No," as she turned away to fill a drink order. Stephanie looked inquiringly at me. I explained about Melody and names. As I did so, something nibbled at the corner of my mind but wouldn't take shape.

I mentally shrugged it away in time to hear Casi say in a light manner, "Good thing she doesn't know my dad's first name is actually Zacharias, not Glen."

I laughed. "Zacharias Ziegler. Sounds like the minor comic-relief character in a nineteenth-century melodrama."

"Oh, you think so?" Ziegler stood behind us stiffly in a gray suit and a dark tie. Ill-suited to his formality was the orange notebook clasped in one hand.

Stephanie slipped from the stool as Casi introduced her to her father. She extended her hand, and I noted his discomfort at the forthright gesture. I could tell he was torn between being ultra-casual and really examining the young woman.

Melody appeared. "Something for you, Detective?"

"Ah, two things. A whiskey sour and a word with Hal if he's around."

Turning gracefully and lifting a glass from a rack, she said, "Harold will be in soon. I'll send him your way."

Stef flashed a half smile my way. "Guess I'll have to get used to Stephanie if we come here often."

Ziegler said, almost too quickly, "It's a pretty name."

She trilled a laugh, but when she spoke her tone was mildly caustic, "Pretty name for a pretty girl—that's what I grew up hearing all the time. And I was supposed to do pretty things. Play with dolls, pose for pictures, be a cheerleader, go to the prom…No one was very happy when I ran hurdles in high school. My mother and aunt thought the uniforms were obscene, especially when I was drenched in sweat and they clung so revealingly."

"Sorry I didn't know you in high school." Casi's suggestive comment jolted her father into dropping his notebook. I gave her a stern but also amused look and tapped the notebook now back in Ziegler's hand. "Planning to go over something with Hal?"

"Yes." He was relieved to change the subject. "Want to see if I can pin down some wheres and whens."

I lifted my elbow and tapped it down on my own. "Brought mine with me, too. Maybe we could compare notes later."

Before he could respond, Casi said, "Why don't you do it now? Stef and I would like to dance before dinner."

I shifted down to the end of the bar while Ziegler stood and watched uncomfortably as his daughter led Stef onto the dance floor. He took his drink from Melody, nodding once to her comment. Then he joined me.

I asked, "What did Melody say?"

He visibly shed some tension as he settled on the stool and answered, "Nice girls. I think she was telling me to relax." He took a healthy swallow of his whiskey sour. "Why'd she make me come *here* with them, Lexy?"

"I'd say she's testing you. Wants to see if you really mean it about being accepting. So, Daddy, what do you think of your girl's girl?" I had to laugh at the panic in his eyes but took pity on him. "Okay, okay. Let's talk about the case for awhile." I touched my notebook to his.

"And when did you join the force, Miss Hyatt? Just yesterday morning you were hitting on Robbie Exline." Panic in his eyes again as he realized his unintentional double entendre. This time my laughter was loud and wholehearted.

"Going to share the joke?" Marilyn stood behind us.

I toyed with saying, "Here's the lady who is really hitting on Exline," but thought better of it. I said instead, "Better left till later, Marilyn."

She shrugged and said, "Spiffy suit, Detective. Who's your date? I don't believe it's Lexy here. Or anyone else I see."

Ziegler flushed and I took pity again. "Go easy on him, Admiral. He's having a bit of a rough time. The truth is he's having dinner here with his daughter and her date." I nodded beyond the bar. "The harem pants dancing with the blue blouse."

Marilyn's 'oh my' said it all and I knew that she now understood our usurping her office for private conversation the other night.

At that moment, Hal appeared across the bar from us. "You wanted to see me?" There were circles under his eyes and I could see the concern on Marilyn's face.

Relieved to turn from us women, Ziegler nodded and reached for his

150

notebook. I slid from my stool and moved a couple of steps toward Marilyn to grant them a semblance of privacy. I asked her in a low voice about Hal, and she admitted to increasing pain. She added that he stretched the time between medication as far as possible to avoid becoming overly dependent. While I listened to her with one ear, I kept the other cocked toward the two men.

I heard Ziegler say, "And you can't place the whereabouts of Jodi Fleming when you heard the side door slam shut? But your sister was here at the bar with you. Right? And just how long were you out there checking?"

Hal replied, "Not even a minute. I opened the door, stuck my head out to check the alley, and closed the door again. That's it."

A couple more questions and Ziegler turned back to us as Casi and Stef approached from one direction and Jodi from the front door. There was a flurry of introductions and handshakes. I could tell that both young women admired Jodi's casual sensuality. She was wearing a deep salmon body suit, tiny loops of gold in her ears matching larger circles on both forearms.

Jodi toed my foot. "New boots. Match your hair. Nice."

I smiled at her compliment, then caught Casi's bold glance. I answered her questioning expression with a nearly imperceptible negative shake. Her wry smile spoke doubt.

In a general shifting, I had ended up with my back to the entrance while Marilyn's was to the bar. As Ziegler was suggesting his group go in to dinner, Marilyn's eyes widened and focused behind me. I turned and was stunned by the quiet beauty of Wren Carlyle standing a few steps back. She locked eyes with Jodi, then stepped forward, touching a hand to my shoulder and said, "I hope I'm not late." Her green eyes were cool and she held herself commandingly erect.

Again the flurry of introductions. Openly Jodi surveyed Wren from her hair, a tawny gold under the lights, over the pink silk shirt tucked neatly into tight-fitting terra-cotta pants, down to the mahogany boots.

Suddenly everyone moved. Ziegler, Casi, and Stef to the dining room, Jodi to a table of friends, Marilyn down the corridor to her office. Wren's hand was still on my shoulder. We smiled at one another.

I asked, "The bar? Or a table?"

She chose the bar. Melody approached us, her expression carefully pleasant and noncommittal. I requested my usual, and Wren ordered a scotch on the rocks. Then she eyed the bar and lounge areas. She said, "Seems like a nice place."

"You've really never been here?" As I said it, I knew she couldn't have been. I would have noticed her.

151

Wren shook her head, looking back at me. "No. Someone I was with, long ago and far away, was or became an alcoholic. I never did know which. So I avoided the bar scene, trying to save...us. Didn't work. I lost her to the drinking and to an older women who thrived on co-dependency. I never got back into the routine of going to bars."

I wondered how thoroughly she had gotten back into the routine of other women.

She appeared to read my mind. "I've been very cautious since then."

She held my eyes, releasing them only to thank Melody as our drinks arrived. Anxious to regain my composure, I introduced them, enjoying Melody's quizzical repetition of Wren's name.

I grinned. "Tell her what it's short for, Wren." I sipped my bourbon, relishing the recitation.

Melody was delighted. "You join Lexy in the exception category. I always thought I should be calling her Alexandra and meanwhile she was Alexis all the time. So she won and made me go with Lexy. So do you. Even I can't go around calling someone William, Rachel, Eliot, Norma." She danced away chuckling, her bulk floating above quick feet.

For the second time that evening, I explained Melody's quirk with names. I continued with an explanation of the Admiral and Hal, Alice, Ziegler and the two young women.

When I paused, Wren said, "And the tall beauty with the feline grace?" The moss-green eyes were unreadable but her lips toyed with a knowing smile.

I said only, "Long ago and far away."

We saluted each other with our drinks. Then Marilyn rejoined us, and talked to Wren, after first giving me a look behind her back that said "Stay calm, kid. Just a little friendly checking going on here."

Squaring myself to the bar, I discovered that both my and Ziegler's notebooks were stacked one atop the other. His had the cleaner cover, and I started to lift it toward Melody to hold for him. But she was busy and an imp whispered in my ear temptingly. I opened it randomly and thumbed a few pages. I started reading underlined data. As I read, I considered the possibility that he had placed it with mine deliberately. Leaking it to the reporter? Or saying thank you for family aid? Or had he been so nervous about meeting Casi and Stef there that he had actually been distracted enough to be careless?

Ziegler had underlined that Marilyn and Hal were related, a reference by Melody to Hal being gone several minutes to check on the side door noise, and missing fingerprints from the broom in the alley, as well as Hal going to see Pollard and admitting worry over Marilyn's past connection with her. Ziegler had placed a question mark over the word 'past.'

Occasionally information would have an 'X' in the margin. I assumed that came from comparing notes with Robbie Exline. One such note placed Jodi in the hallway to Marilyn's office. Also, Ziegler had added in later: 'affair with DP' and 'karate.' Another was a description of Marilyn's bruised hand. Obviously Exline didn't let her attraction to the Admiral interfere with her detecting.

Stacy Driscoll's name had question marks following it, as did later recordings of the names of her mother and stepfather. Also included was a reference to her real name of Garrison. Almost every notation on Janel was heavily underlined, as well as those on sounds of arguing coming from the office. More and more I believed that the second voice belonged to Darla Pollard's murderer. Nothing on Chrissy was emphasized, but I felt a twinge of guilt, realizing Ziegler didn't know she had been outside The Cat the night Pollard was killed.

I turned a page and read, "Lexy Hyatt doesn't lie—but doesn't always tell all." Now I believed for certain that he had left his notebook with mine on purpose, and was probably sitting in the dining room smiling to himself, thinking about my reading that statement.

Because I often wrote information of a special sort in the back of a notebook, I flipped past blank pages of Ziegler's to see if he did the same. The last page was a list of names, most of which I recognized as part of the murder investigation.

Curious about the ones I didn't recognize, I asked the Admiral for a pen. She plucked one from a deep vest pocket and slid it down to me. I realized Wren was watching me quizzically as I copied the unfamiliar names into my own notebook. I squinted intensely at a couple of the names, knowing I had seen them someplace else.

I caught Alice's eye and motioned her to me. I handed her Ziegler's notebook, asking her to give it to him in the dining room. I started to describe him but she stopped me saying, "He's going to be the only man in there."

Before I relinquished my hold on the orange pad, I said, "Tell him Melody gave it to you." I thought to myself that it wouldn't hurt to let him wonder if I had availed myself of his 'gift.' She shrugged an okay. I thrust my own notebook deep into my inner jacket pocket. The last thing I could bear was someone in The Cat looking through it, even by accident.

Marilyn came off her stool and stood behind Wren and me, a hand on each of us. She looked at our reflections in the mirror. "Feed this woman,

Lexy. That's what Hal and I did as kids whenever we found something we wanted to keep. Though they were generally of the four-legged variety." She squeezed my shoulder and moved off to check operations throughout The Cat.

Still looking in the mirror, Wren said, "Do you want to keep me, Lexy Hyatt?"

I answered her reflection, "I do believe I do, Wren Carlyle. I brought you to meet the family didn't I?"

"Then feed this biped."

We walked side by side toward the beaded entrance to the dining room under Melody's smiling approval.

CHAPTER NINETEEN

Wren and I lingered over dinner, sharing anecdotes, thoughts and attitudes, observations and discoveries. She would catch me following the movement of her hands, and give me a whisper of a smile. I would see the slide of her eyes over my throat and down the opening of my chambray shirt. I knew the Admiral passed near us occasionally. I was aware of curious glances from Casi Ziegler. I registered Jodi taking a table with one of the soccer players. But I responded only to Wren.

At the conclusion of dinner, we sauntered back into the lounge. With a light touch in the small of my back, Wren turned me toward the dance floor. Though I often led with other partners, it was amazingly natural to ease into her arms and accept her guidance. At first she held me slightly away from her, gazing into my eyes. Again I experienced the sensation of wanting to dive into the tempting green and let the smooth lids close over me.

I shut my eyes to escape the allure, only to feel her arm move up my back and her fingers gently force my head close to hers. I breathed her scent, and sighed. Her hand returned to the small of my back as she intensified the pressure of her firm thigh. Tiny shock waves coursed down my legs, and I broke rhythm. I tightened into her, thrilled by the brief nip of her teeth at my ear lobe.

The music stopped, but I was reluctant to step out of her embrace. Her warm breath stirred my hair. "Another dance?"

I had to swallow to regain my own voice. "I don't think I could stand it."

"Neither do I."

We left the dance floor and I was so wrapped in enchantment that I brushed by Janel without seeing her until she grabbed at my elbow, saying angrily, "Hey!"

I recognized the dark anger in her eyes. Even though I had no idea of the source, spoke placatingly, "Sorry, Janel. Didn't see you. "

"Well, I want to *see* you."

I was aware of Wren stiffening immediately behind me, and the watchful attitude of Melody behind the bar. I said bluntly, "I'm on a date, Janel. Can't this wait?"

"You couldn't wait yesterday morning. You had to upset Christine on her way to work."

I looked at Wren, who nodded understandingly. To Janel I said, "End of the bar."

Janel and I took the two stools at the end nearest the restroom hallway. Wren seated herself at the other end, and I saw the Admiral join her. I was still encased in the essence of Wren and did not hear the first part of Janel's statement, "...threatening Christine!"

I jerked into full attention. "What? I never threatened Chrissy. All I—"

Janel interrupted. "Not you. That bastard Driscoll. He was waiting outside her apartment when she got home from work this afternoon. Said a bitch reporter was bothering his wife and him about Darla Pollard. Blamed Christine. Wanted to know who else she had set up to attack his family."

I knew I hadn't told Gloria Driscoll I was a reporter, but I had given my name. "Look, Janel. I talked with his wife, but it had nothing to do with Chrissy. Sounds like he's afraid she knows something special on him to tell. What is it?"

She stared at herself in the bar mirror, struggling with how far to trust me. She caught my eye in the mirror. "How'd you find out she was outside here the night Darla was killed? Bet you've already told. You sure couldn't wait to tell those detectives I was here."

I strained to keep my voice calm and even. "They got it from other people here who saw you. I had forgotten about it. I didn't even know you then. And I'll be damned if I know why, but I haven't told anyone about Chrissy being outside in your truck. Hal saw her and mentioned it to me by chance."

Janel appeared to pull back a fraction. "All right. Look, there's something really wrong with Driscoll. He really scared Christine. And he was scaring Darla that time Christine heard them fighting."

"She heard things they said, didn't she?" I was making a statement more than asking a question.

"Yeah! She just told me a little while ago. It's stuff the police probably ought to know but I don't want them pounding on Christine to get it."

"Ziegler and Exline don't pound on people." As I said his name, I saw the detective take a seat next to Wren. I twirled Janel's stool so that she faced me squarely, her back to Ziegler. "Quickly, quietly, tell me what Chrissy heard. Maybe I can run some interference."

Her account left me disturbed and chilled. Mostly I was furious at the

156

harm done Stacy. The afternoon Chrissy had rushed back into the office to turn up the heater in the aquarium, she had heard Darla Pollard accusing Driscoll of an unnatural desire to keep his stepdaughter close to home, to him. She asked him if molesting would have been the next step if Stacy hadn't died. Told him she would spread it around if he didn't quit hounding her about Stacy's death. Driscoll had loudly and vigorously denied everything, and then retaliated with threats of damage to gay bars and restaurants Pollard insured.

Janel touched my knee. "Lexy, Christine wouldn't even repeat to me the filth that came out of his mouth about queers and deviates and perverts. It even hurt her to say those words. And it was plain that he blamed Darla for Stacy beginning to stand up to him and trying to leave home. Even accused Darla of being the one doing the molesting. Said he believed she pushed his daughter into suicide, and he was going to make her pay for it. Christine said he talked about Stacy like she was some kind of possession, not a person." Suddenly conscious that she was touching me, Janel withdrew her hand and clenched it into a fist. "Christine was about to cry over what she was hearing and wanted to get out before they heard her. But she made some noise and Darla came out and yelled at her and talked about maybe firing her. Darla was scared of Driscoll. Now Christine is, too."

I motioned to Melody to draw a draft beer for Janel, and I sat considering what I had heard. From articles and cases I had covered on child abuse and molestation for *The Ledger,* what little I knew about Stacy's situation didn't fit. Maybe Chrissy's perception was on target again. Maybe to her stepfather, Stacy was a prized possession. One he didn't want to share with her mother, let alone a Darla Pollard.

Driscoll could have stripped the girl of her budding self-esteem, and imprisoned her in doubts about functioning on her own. He would have led her to feel worthless and unable to get help. If she fell into the malignant pattern, Gloria Driscoll would have been unable to let herself see what her husband was doing to her own child. Probably rationalized it as protection and security on his part.

Faults or no, it looked as though Darla Pollard had been trying to draw Stacy from Driscoll's control. Had it led to her death?

I came out of my thoughts. "Ziegler's here now. Let me run all this by him." I tried to ward off potential objections. "I'll do my best to get him to check it out without starting with Chrissy."

She frowned but slipped a harsh, "Okay" through gritted teeth. "But I'm not talking to him either."

I touched her shoulder, unyieldingly tense, as I passed behind her on my way down bar to where Ziegler seemed to be in relaxed conversation with

Wren. The Admiral was off circulating. Wren watched my approach, and I was acutely conscious of every movement of my body. With difficulty I focused my attention on Ziegler and related Chrissy's story as I had received it from Janel.

I made a suggestion. "I know I'm out of line asking this, Glen, but if you have to check with Chrissy on this, could it be through Exline?"

He smiled agreeably. "That's not out of line, Lexy. Exline and I work well together." He glanced at his daughter expertly turning Stef to the beat of the music. "I guess my worries about that are pretty foolish compared to the real evils out there."

Melody checked to see if any of us needed anything, and Ziegler thanked her for sending his notebook to him in the dining room, but he did so looking at me. She read the lift of my head and the message in my eyes, and nodded vaguely to him.

I moved back to the end of the bar where I had left Janel, but she was gone. Then I caught sight of her entering a doorway far down the restroom hallway. I moved swiftly after her, and found myself at the door to the supply room. She hadn't closed the door firmly enough, so it swung open silently to my touch.

Janel was on her hands and knees feeling under shelving that was no more than two inches off the floor. She withdrew her hand, shaking dust and cobwebs from her fingers, then shifted into a squat and checked the lower shelves. Rising slowly and turning her head to survey each shelf, she froze at the sight of me.

"What the hell!" She straightened her small frame, moving toward me so quickly that I lifted an arm to ward off an expected blow. She stopped inches from me, and I could see an uncharacteristic trembling.

"What are you looking for Janel?"

"None of your business." There was a tremor in her voice, too.

The words came out of my mouth almost unbidden. "Something you dropped in here with Darla Pollard?"

"I wasn't in here with her. We were in…" She grunted as though hit in the gut, and compressed her lips.

I was relentless. "You were in Marilyn's office with her?"

"What if I was. I wanted her to lay off Christine. I didn't want her dead! We yelled at each other. Finally she said she'd make things all right with Christine as soon as she got some other things out of the way." Her bravado increased. "Maybe that two-bit woman who slunk in when I was leaving killed her. "

"Damn it, Janel! Why can't we just keep on track? What woman?" I

158

realized I was still holding the door open and closed it. I seated myself on a short stepladder, bracing my hands on my knees.

Janel backed into the shelves and slid down to sit on the floor, her knees almost to her chin. She eyed me warily and the leather fringe of her vest quivered with her heavy breathing. Finally she spoke. "I don't know who the woman was. I already had my hand on the doorknob when she knocked. Figured it was someone who worked in this place. So I just opened the door and slipped around her and went on."

"You had to see something of her. What did she look like?"

Janel snorted her irritation. "Taller than me but only because she had on those dumb high heels. Kind of frizzy blond hair."

I was excited. "Had to be Gloria Driscoll. You didn't recognize her?"

She gave it real thought. "I saw Mrs. Driscoll only once. At Stacy's funeral. But she had on a black scarf-like hat and dark glasses. I guess the height was right though."

I was sure the woman was Gloria Driscoll. So she had talked to Darla Pollard that night. And lied about it. I asked Janel, "Did you hear anything they said?"

"No. I just wanted to get back to Christine."

I closed my eyes and reviewed what I could remember of the night Pollard was killed. I hissed in frustration, and left the stepladder to tower over Janel. "You're still hiding things! It had to be a long time between your leaving the Admiral's office and my bumping into you coming out of the restroom. And Pollard died somewhere in between." I reached down as though to seize her, but she leaped up and dodged past me.

She was down the hallway and out of The Cat before I reached the bar area. Wren was alone, her eyes questioning. I knew what the phrase 'emotional roller coaster' meant. And seesawing. And being pulled in two directions at once.

"Sorry, Wren."

Humor and acceptance tinged her voice. "Life around you is not at all orderly. Any chance the rest of the night is mine? Or should I plan on more disorder?" Without giving me a chance to respond, she spoke a warm 'thank you and good night' to Melody.

I nodded to Melody and said to Wren, "The Ziegler party gone?"

She answered, "Scarcely a minute ago. Your speeding butch nearly knocked them down getting out the door. Should I not ask questions?"

We moved toward the exit and I said, "Any you want. But maybe they could wait awhile. I want our evening back."

She smiled the smile that took my breath.

Outside the air was damp and heavy with the smell of car exhaust. We rounded the corner of the building into the small parking lot, and halted at Wren's car. She took charge with the assumption, correct, that I would follow her to her place. She gave me simple directions in case we became separated in traffic, and I hurried toward my car.

What happened next I experienced almost as though I were an uninvolved observer in a dream featuring myself. A forceful shove from behind sent me stumbling into the hood of a car. I couldn't lift myself away or yell because the breath had been knocked from me. I felt disassociated from my body, unable to breathe. My assailant cursed vehemently as he failed to grip the short hair at the back of my head. Then he seized my collar and yanked viciously. I heard the double ping of two buttons striking the metal of the car, but I thought of skinheads and air rifles.

Next I was thrust on hands and knees into the gravel, stinging my palms and stirring dust. As though from a distance, I could hear my own strangled, wheezing gasp as I struggled for air. Trying to concentrate outside myself to gain equilibrium, I noted that the shoes appearing beneath my face were a polished dark brown, partially hidden by neat cuffs of olive green. Ridiculously, I thought to myself that the skinheads were dressing better. The shoes and cuffs disappeared and an unseen leg brutally tumbled me onto my back. My head banged against the hard rubber of a tire.

Suddenly, I focused enough to see Edward Driscoll standing over me. Before I could translate my thought of a foot to his crotch into action, he seized the sides of my open shirt and hefted me against the car. He snarled, "Let's see how much the tough dyke can take. I'll teach you to mess in my life."

I saw the fist coming at me as I was closing my eyes and turning my head protectively. The savage blow impacted high on my cheekbone. Cacophonous sounds and searing lights rattled my brain.

But there were other sounds, too. From somewhere there were car doors slamming. From somewhere there was the anxious voice of Wren shouting, "Lexy!" From somewhere there was the crunch of gravel under hurrying feet. I opened my eyes and saw a fierce Ziegler strong-arm Driscoll to the ground.

Unsteadily I leaned into Wren's embrace, and said in a ragged whisper, "*This* is where I was supposed to be going." Wren's tight clutch hurt, but it was welcome pain.

CHAPTER TWENTY

After soaking in a bath scented with soothing bath oil and nearly hotter than I could stand, I struggled painfully into a loose white and orange striped nightshirt that Wren laid out for me. She was sitting on the side of a queen size bed in the dimly lit room wearing pajamas of deep forest green. My mouth felt dry at the sight of her against the background of smooth, antique-white sheets and plump pillows, her blonde hair enticingly tousled.

I followed her to the kitchen where she prepared cups of steaming hot chocolate. After a few careful sips of the rich liquid, I met the determined gaze of Wren's intense green eyes, knowing what was coming as she said, "Now, start talking. I want to know exactly what was going on back there. Everything, Lexy."

And I told her everything. I told her the facts I knew and the concerns I had. I told her of my worries about the threads that tied Marilyn, Hal, and Jodi to the living Darla Pollard, how curious it was that I liked Janel and her fiercely protective stance with Chrissy, of the dysfunctional Driscolls. Not once did she interrupt me.

When I concluded, she made no comment, but I felt she had absorbed the information, and knew there would be real dialogue later. I watched Wren rinse the cups of their chocolate residue in a comfortable silence.

Back in the bedroom, we slid between sheets I was certain had been put on the bed while I soaked in the bath. Wren pulled a light thermal blanket over us and her warm lips brushed over mine. As I sought to deepen the kiss, she pulled back. Her quiet but firm, "Not yet," elicited an exasperated inward-drawn hiss from me. Pain prevented my turning my back to her so I stiffened my body and shut my eyes. But I couldn't resist the relaxing stroke of her fingers along my hairline and down my arm to entwine in my own fingers. I fell asleep holding her hand.

I woke up and lay very still. Without opening my eyes, I knew that things were out of kilter. I was lying on my back and could feel the softness of an eggshell foam pad beneath the sheet. I stretched in preparation to turn on my side and was stunned by a breath-stopping soreness. My eyes flew open and I was confused by the unfamiliar pattern of moonlight in the room. I turned my head to the left and was jolted simultaneously by a throbbing pain in my face and the sight of a figure huddled, back to me, along the edge of the bed.

Suddenly I remembered the attack by Edward Driscoll in The Cat's parking lot. Ziegler had called for a squad car and followed them away. Wren had compromised with my refusal to go to the hospital by taking me home with her in her car.

Now I knew she had been right to insist on sleep. The only violence I had ever experienced to my own body had been in mundane sports' mishaps. Driscoll's unexpected assault had robbed me of mental peace as well as violating me physically. Somehow running mindlessly from that into her arms would have soiled our first encounter.

Gingerly I turned on my side and matched my breathing to the rise and fall of her back. I considered the implications of Driscoll's attack. In one sense he was behaving consistently. His obsession with his stepdaughter, even beyond her death, had driven him to confront Darla in her office, Chrissy outside her apartment, and tonight me in the parking lot. But did any of that mean he could be guilty of murder?

I lifted myself to look over Wren's shoulder to the soft red glow of her digital clock. It was three-thirty in the morning. Wren shifted her weight more onto her back; my heart leapt at her soft moan. I traced the line of her shoulder blade, then detoured to the rounder flow of her hip. My elbow digging into the pillow, I rested my head on my hand, and watched her settle fully on her back. Even in the darkness, lessened very little by moonlight through the vertical blinds, I saw her eyes flutter open.

The drowsy invitation in the huskily whispered, "Lexy…," brought my body to the length of hers. This time she did not retreat from my kiss. Her breasts seemed to swell into mine as I took the measure of her face, my mouth coming back again and again to lips that soon parted for the eager exploration of my tongue. Her mouth tasted fleetingly of chocolate, the hollow of her throat infinitesimally of vanilla.

Wren chuckled at my mumbled impatience over difficulty with the buttons of her pajama top. "They're new. Let me."

I nibbled her ear. "Couldn't you have worn something old I could tear?"

"Why, Lexy Hyatt, I do believe there is a bit of the cavewoman in you." The mocking timbre of her voice challenged me. I whipped open the now unbuttoned top, seizing one breast with my right hand, sucking the nipple of the other full and hard into my hungry mouth. I was rewarded with a low

162

vibrating moan.

I rubbed my cheeks against the smooth twin mounds, oblivious to the soreness on the left side of my face. Wren's fingers plowed furrows in my hair, and forced me back to her nipples. I would suck one, then tongue the other, delighting in the inflectional changes of her cries.

As I began to tug the pajama bottoms, a quiver raced the length of her body, and she lifted her hips to assist me. When I had them nearly to her knees, I used my foot to push them further. Wren shook them from her feet, sighing deeply as I drew designs with my fingertips on the responsive flesh of her thighs.

I rested my head just below her breast, and traced the triangle of luxuriant hair. My breathing deepened as her thighs opened. I couldn't quell my own gasp as I furrowed fingers into her moistness. At her pleading, "Yes, Lexy, yes," I sought the satiny opening and held my breath as she widened to receive me.

I lifted my head, slipping further down her body to better control the rhythm of my welcomed invasions. Wren gripped the side of the bed with one hand and clutched at my head with the other. Her cries increased with the intensity of my thrusts until, with a shriek, she grabbed my hand and forced it hard against her as she arched away. I almost cried out myself as her thighs imprisoned my hand, and I felt her thick cream coat my embedded fingers. A weak sigh accompanied the removal of my hand. I pushed myself up, even with her, and gathered her into my arms. Except for the rapid beating of her heart, there was a delicious slackness about her. I kissed her closed eyelids and murmured, "Sweet Wren."

After a few still moments, she plucked at my flannel nightshirt. "Off," she ordered.

I sat up, and we both pulled it over my head. Wren returned to my arms, but began stroking me everywhere she could reach. I tried to stay silent but she drew whimpers of pleasure from me. The feathery touch of her fingertips following the curves of my breasts was maddeningly hypnotic. Carefully she avoided the nipples swollen with need until I begged through clenched teeth. I tilted my head as far back as possible at the slow suction, the flick of her tongue. When her hand began to play between my legs, she initiated an insistent rocking.

"Talk to me, Lexy," she whispered huskily.

"How can I? You've stolen my breath." I pulled up my legs, flattening my feet on the bed. I lifted myself with a tortured groan, trying to catch her hand where I so wanted it, but she only teased me with the swirl of her palm in my dampened hair. "Oh, I know what you want, my bold Lexy. But I'm going to take what I want."

"Then do it. Stop tormenting me."

With cool authority, she lowered my leg closest to her and with a fluid movement, mounted me, shedding her open top at the same time. She jerked my hands out of her hair. Then shoved my arms toward my own head.

"Wren?"

"Grab the railing of the headboard. And don't let go."

Her blunt command thrilled me. I reached for the square railing beyond my head. Inner tongues of fire made me twitch and moan as she moved slowly down my body. She blew hot breath into my hair, and I drew both knees higher. An eternity passed before I felt her tongue part me in a slow stroke of ecstasy until, at last, it reached my throbbing core.

I gripped the headboard tighter, and lifted myself more firmly to her mouth. She hissed a long sibilant, "Yessss," and placed her arms around my straining thighs to control my movement. I floated in pure sensation, hearing only our breathing until I began to tense with that passionate stirring, rising toward explosion. Then I split the early morning stillness with her name, drawing it out toward silence as my arms fell weakly away from the headboard. I touched her hair with powerless fingers. She rose toward me to cushion my face in her breasts.

We slept again.

CHAPTER TWENTY-ONE

I watched Wren pull out of The Cat's parking lot, and continued to stare after her even though the dark gold top had disappeared from sight. Our second awakening earlier had been accompanied by gentle embraces, soft kisses, and long looks into each other's eyes. She had fed me coffee and toasted bagels with cream cheese and jelly. Her body language had indicated disapproval of my intent to go to work, but she had not presumed to instruct me.

Only a moment ago she had touched fingers lightly to the puffiness on the left side of my face and said, "Learn to bob and weave...or run like hell." There followed the smile that spilled over into her eyes. "But I did enjoy taking care of you."

"Oh, you did take care of me, Wren Carlyle! You did indeed take care of me." I fingered the decorative pin with which she had closed my shirt.

"May I call you about going out tomorrow night?"

"Yes." I closed my eyes as the backs of her fingers traced my jawline. When I opened them, she was already climbing back into her car, and I was left with a deep wanting.

I eased into the my car carefully, my bruised ribs complaining. Resolutely I shook off the feeling and considered my day. I wasn't due at *The Ledger* until ten o'clock and an undemanding day stretched before me. I tossed my notebook into the passenger seat and tilted the rearview mirror my way.

No wonder Wren had raised an eyebrow when I sat down at the table in the early morning sunlight. My cheek was a ruddy red, my eye swollen half shut and ringed with the blue discoloration that was going to turn purple— a major shiner. I was not looking forward to the stares and comments I would have to endure for several days.

With a disgruntled sigh I repositioned the mirror and reached to close the door, but stopped when I saw Melody's flashy red Grand Am zip into the parking lot. Victoria got out, chattering excitedly, her hands rapidly checking her clothing and jewelry. She started to close the door, then dove back in to retrieve her clarinet case.

Melody rose majestically from the driver's side and waved. She greeted the other members of Victoria's combo and then proceeded on to my car. I lifted my face, steeling myself for her reaction.

Melody's mouth formed an 'oh' of surprise, her features becoming serious. "We didn't hear a thing inside till Detective Ziegler sent Casi running in to call a patrol car. She told us how you were assaulted. What a shock. The Admiral ran right out to see you, yelling at Hal to call an ambulance, but you had already been whisked away by your date. Ziegler said you were mostly shook up, and that your car would be in the lot overnight. We all got to see that creepy Mr. Driscoll carted off though. What a scene! Blue lights all over again. When will it stop? Anyway, I'm glad to see you're not in worse shape. That black eye looks bad enough."

I cut my smile short because it hurt. "I've got some complaining ribs too. But I'm all right."

"Well, you had better get in The Cat and call the Admiral. She was fit to be tied, worried about you until I convinced her you had to be safely ensconced in the arms of that duchess of a woman."

Despite the pain, I smiled at Melody's assessment of Wren. "Ensconced?"

"That's right. I recognize that air of I-will-protect-what's-mine when I see it. Your lady of many names may be just what you've needed, Miss Lexy. Don't fight her too hard."

That assessment made me uncomfortable, and I changed the subject. I waved toward the others. "What's going on?"

Melody explained that Victoria and the others were going to use The Cat for a practice session. She extended a steadying arm as I grimaced at my effort to rise from the car. By this time the others were gathered, and Victoria's dancing feet scuffed and scraped gravel as she fussed over me while Melody scooped me along with her toward the entrance of The Cat.

Once inside she asked how many voted for coffee. All but Victoria raised their hands, and I meekly wiggled my fingers at her. I said to Victoria, "Live music with my coffee will be a treat. Is it going to be something modern?"

Ingenuously she responded, "Of course."

Melody's musical laugh trilled through the unnatural morning quiet that settled over nighttime places. "Be warned, Lexy. Victoria thinks that modern music is everything after Gregorian chants."

I followed Melody behind the bar, watching her measure coffee into a

166

pleated brown filter as I punched in the Admiral's phone number. Her voice when she answered was gravelly, and I apologized for waking her up.

I held the receiver slightly away from my ear as she barked, "What makes you think I've been asleep! I've been worried sick about you, kid. I'm going to scuttle your vessel and anchor you to me if I don't like your report. What's happening to my patrons? This simply can't go on."

I made a face and Melody flashed me an I-told-you-so glance. I gave Marilyn a complete description of Driscoll's attack as I remembered it, but could answer few of her other questions. I completed the call with, "I'm going to find out from Ziegler what I can, and I'll pass it on to you... Yes, I'll be careful... Come on, Marilyn, I had no way of seeing it coming... Ziegler was there to take care of Driscoll and Wren took care of me." To her blunt questions concerning Wren's method of taking care of me, I choked out, "Things to do, Admiral. Bye."

Concentrating on filling the large metal urn with water, Melody remarked, "Gave you the third degree from stem to stern, didn't she?"

I nodded, giving most of my attention to the music surging from beyond the dance floor. Even my untutored ear recognized Duke Ellington. I listened appreciatively until Victoria silenced the group with a slash of her hand.

Melody said, "'Fraid you're in for a lot of that, Lexy. This is a work session. If you want to hear something all the way through, I suggest you go to Tempo tomorrow night." She named a currently popular jazz bar in the old downtown district.

"May do that. If Wren likes jazz. Is the place gay-friendly?"

She smiled wryly. "Would Victoria be playing there if it wasn't? Besides jazz nuts don't notice anything but the music. Coffee'll be ready soon."

"I'll make a quick trip first." I headed toward the restroom.

As I came out, still drying my hands on the rough paper towel, I glanced toward the supply room. Remembering Janel on her hands and knees searching for something, I opened the door and surveyed the floor area. I couldn't see how anything unusual could have escaped the police. I shifted some boxes and cleaning supplies to look behind them. Then with my foot, I shifted a brand new metal mop pail, a couple of replacement mopheads resting on the drain clamps. There was a tinkling sound.

I groaned as I squatted on my heels to look inside the pail. I saw nothing. But when I disturbed the stringy mop strands, I heard the tinkling sound of metal on metal again. I parted some of the twisted strands, and plucked out a gold bracelet.

I closed my eyes and watched a scene play out across my eyelids. I was back in Chrissy's apartment the night Janel and I carried the aquarium up the stairs. Janel asked about bracelets and Chrissy removed two from a large pocket, saying that she must have misplaced one. I was holding it in my hand. It was what Janel kept coming back to The Cat to find.

I got up and kicked at the mop pail. I even thought about putting the bracelet back in the grayish strands, but I knew I wouldn't.

Behind the bar, I stood by the phone and hissed at my reflection. Melody noted my sudden black mood, and pointed to a nearby mug of coffee before moving away. I sipped the coffee while considering my options. Reaching a decision, I called *The Ledger* and notified Worthington I would be late. Something crucial had finally come up on my story. I held while he checked schedules. When he admitted there wasn't anything that couldn't be covered by someone else, I said I'd put in weekend time to balance out today.

"Better be damn good, Lexy." He signed off.

Next, I pulled a small leather case from my back pocket. With Exline's card in my hand, I called the station number. As soon as I was put through to her, I asked for the name of Chrissy's new workplace. When she hesitated, I said, "Robbie, I *need* it. And I'm in no mood to be put off."

She said, "I would think you'd have questions about Driscoll. Ziegler's out in the hall. Said he was going to catch you at your office this morning. Want me to get him?"

"No." I knew I was speaking abruptly and tried to soften my voice. "Please, Robbie. Be nice to the beat-up broad."

"You hardly qualify as a broad, Lexy." I could hear the slide of her teeth against each other. "Okay. Let me check Shoemaker's file." A moment later she read the address to me.

I cut off her warnings with a quick 'thank you' and hung up the phone. I ignored Melody's puzzled eyes, downing most of my coffee. Then I mouthed a 'goodbye' to her over a thunderous passage from Victoria's group. The music followed me out the door as I tapped my fingers on the bracelet nesting in my pocket.

It took twenty minutes of fighting Friday morning traffic to arrive at Chrissy's work place. Having an entire building of its own placed this agency several levels above Pollard's business. I hoped that meant enough people and anonymity inside for me to locate and corral Chrissy without interference.

There was a cold efficiency to the place that reminded me of an expensive medical clinic. I resolved to make certain I never purchased any insurance from them. I approached the receptionist seated behind protective glass; she opened a sliding window with barely enough space for the exchange of papers.

"How may I assist you?" There was a bite to her voice that said I had better need assistance or I was wasting her time.

I tried to imitate her tone. "I wish to see Miss Shoemaker. I had coverage with the Pollard Agency." I kept my black eye tilted away from her.

She pointed down a wide corridor. "Third door on your left."

It was a small office—a desk, a couple of chairs, a file cabinet, a narrow table. Chrissy had warmed the room with some of her cross-stitch work on the walls and healthy plants spilling over the rims of attractive pots. I observed her unnoticed as she perused a computer screen, noting that she seemed more mature in this setting. Perhaps she was more secure.

I spoke her name. She looked up with a quick smile, her blue eyes wide and pleasant, but the eyes clouded at the sight of me and the smile froze. Then her mouth opened as she registered my black eye.

"May I close the door and sit down, Chrissy? And can we say I ran into the proverbial doorknob?"

She struggled with agitation. "Don't close it all the way." She fluttered her fingers toward a chair at the corner of her desk where a delicate fern cascaded to the floor.

I lifted the chair away from the plant and sat down. She cocked her head questioningly at me, and I felt compelled to explain. "I'm not comfortable with plants."

"Why not?"

I jerked my lower jaw to the side and back, a sign friends and family would take as embarrassment. I said quietly, "They grow. "

"Of course they grow. And especially mine. I take good care of them."

I cut my eyes back and forth between her and the plants. "They grow inside. Out of things. Toward things. Day and night."

Chrissy brightened with understanding. "You're afraid of them!" She appeared delighted. Maybe I would seem less an enemy now. She lifted a soft lace-like strand. "How can you be afraid of something like this?"

I knew I was looking sheepish. "I think it was all the science-fiction stuff I used to read and watch. There were always monster vines sending out tendrils to wrap around ankles or necks."

"I guess you were afraid to play outside."

I laughed. "Not at all. Things were supposed to grow outside. That's natural. In fact as a little kid I loved to help a neighbor garden. At least she let me think I was helping. One of the neatest things I ever saw was her lined, sagging face turning into beauty and happiness one day. She was digging in the dirt, loosening it around some green stalks that would sprout amaryllis blooms in a few days. And there on one of the stalks was her wedding ring. The shoot had come right up through it and carried it up out of the dirt. She had lost it months before working in the flower beds and didn't know where."

"That's a nice story, Lexy." There was honest warmth in her voice.

My stomach lurched as I thought of the bracelet in my pocket. "Chrissy…"

"What?" She was apprehensive again. I pulled the bracelet from my pocket, but kept my eyes on her face. I wanted to catch any change in expression. There was only puzzlement as she said again, "What?"

I placed it near her on the desk, and said, "Is it yours?"

She picked it up. "No. Wish it was. It's a quality piece." She put it down on the desk and pushed it toward me. "Why did you think it was mine?"

"When I helped you and Janel move stuff from the office to your apartment, you seemed to have lost one. Thought this might be it."

I continued to watch her carefully. She frowned. Was she trying to remember or to formulate a lie? Then her face relaxed. "Oh, I remember. I found it later in one of the boxes we carried in that night."

"Did you show it to Janel?"

"I don't know. I don't think so. Why should I? What are you after me about this time?" She had moved forward on the edge of her chair.

"I'm not after you, Chrissy. I'm after some truth about Darla Pollard and what happened to her."

She leaned forward even more. "What good is the truth? Darla's dead. Stacy's dead. She didn't mean any harm—"

"She? Who? Damn it, Chrissy! You and Janel are the two most frustrating—" I threw my hands in the air and growled.

Chrissy moved back into her chair. "Look. If I tell you the last bit there is, will you leave me alone?" At my silent nod, she heaved a huge sigh and then spoke almost tonelessly. "I really thought Stacy committed suicide. And that Darla was torn up about it because she didn't help her enough. Or maybe not soon enough. When I heard her and Mr. Driscoll going at it, I could tell she was talking about him having sex with Stacy, and he was saying she caused Stacy's death. Then she caught me back in the office. And it was scary the way she talked to me. I tried to call Jodi when I got home. She was always better at handling Darla than anybody else. Maybe because she didn't care all that much."

Once again I was surprised and impressed by Chrissy's perceptiveness. She went on, "When my phone rang, I thought it was Jodi answering my message. But it was Darla. She told me again that I wasn't to tell anyone what I overheard, and that I probably ought to find another job. I could be braver on the phone than in front of her and I kind of came back at her. She was using the phone on my desk and I could hear the hum of the air-filter."

"Just like the night Stacy died." I said.

"Yes. And that's what I said to her. I just jumped right at her about it. She got real quiet. Then she told me what had happened."

It was a sad story. One where you couldn't place any blame. You could only hate it for happening. Darla was seeing clients late that night because that was the only time they could manage it. Stacy had come in again…only *truly* upset this time. Darla told her to wait in her car till the clients left, and Stacy said she'd park across the street. When the people left, Darla stepped outside, waving to get Stacy's attention to come into the office. When she couldn't get a response, Darla dashed across to see if Stacy was asleep.

Chrissy said, her voice tight with pain, "You know how cold it was in January. The car was running for heat and Stacy had her head down on her chest. Darla opened the door to wake her…but she was dead. I asked her how she could tell. She just said it was too clear. Then the gas ran out, and the car kind of shook and stopped. Darla said she slammed the door and that made Stacy fall over. She ran back over to the office to call 911. But before she could, she saw people gathering around Stacy's car. She got scared of being involved and that's when she called me, pretending to be out on the road in her car." Chrissy looked directly at me for the first time since she started the recitation. "Anyway, that Friday night when she called me Darla kept stopping. And her voice kept breaking. I wanted to tell her to go ahead and cry, but I didn't know how. I promised I wouldn't tell anyone about it. But I broke that promise right away."

"Janel?"

"No. I called Jodi again. And I got her. I thought maybe Darla needed to be with someone."

I couldn't stop the clutching sensation in my stomach. "Did Jodi go see her?"

"I don't know. After I talked to her, I broke down and cried. That's when Janel came in. I was feeling guilty about telling Jodi what I wasn't supposed to and afraid it was going to make more trouble for me, so I didn't tell Janel. I just told her about Darla being mean to me and about Driscoll and all that. Janel flew off to find Darla and I had to go with her. But I didn't want us to find her. I was glad when Janel finally came out of The Cat and said she didn't see her."

I held the bracelet in the thumbs and forefingers of both hands, and kept turning it, tracing the fine scrollwork on the narrow band with my eyes. Had I gotten complete truth from Chrissy? Why had Jodi lied about the phone calls, claiming they were just messages on her answering machine? Janel was obviously afraid Chrissy had come into The Cat and lost a bracelet there. Is that why she told her partner that she never saw Pollard? Were the Driscolls in The Cat that night by sheer accident?

Chrissy broke into my thoughts. "Lexy...does the bracelet belong to the murderer?"

I thought of the many times Jodi had put her hands to my face or in my hair and I had seen the slide of her many bracelets along her forearm. "I hope not."

CHAPTER TWENTY-TWO

I ran a gauntlet of stares and comments, some sympathetic and some teasing, getting from the parking lot to my *Ledger* desk. Right now I could live with the closed, secure nature of Chrissy's office. If one more person said, "What's the other guy look like?..." Of course, Roger Lowe had made a point of saying, "What's the other *girl* look like?" complete with appropriate smirk.

My ribs complained as I stretched for the monstrous phone book before remembering that Robbie Exline's card contained the number I wanted. I hoped to catch Ziegler still at the station. I was put on hold while he completed another call until, finally, there was the click of my call being put through. "Lexy?"

"In the bruised and battered flesh."

He kept his tone light but insisted on details concerning my injuries. I stressed that they were superficial and made him laugh with a description of my black eye and the reactions of friends and cohorts.

Then he turned serious. "Driscoll's going to be with us till Monday morning. You don't even have to sign a complaint since I saw it all. I'm doing a little paper manipulation to hold him that long.

"Why did he come after me, Glen?"

"He claims you were harassing his wife on the job. Made it sound like you were coming on to her...you know." I could hear the discomfort in his voice. "He's smart enough not to tell the truth. Doesn't want it spread around that he had been molesting his stepdaughter. Looks like he was trying to shut up people who might know."

"I'm not so sure it went that far. Isn't it possible that Darla Pollard only threw that at him, along with the threat of spreading it around, to get him off her back?"

Ziegler's voice in my ear was contemplative. "Of course it's possible. Not wise on her part, but possible."

"Does that mean you think he killed her?" I touched the outline of the

173

bracelet in my pocket.

"Let's just say that before he is released, I intend to make sure he under-stands that any more violence on his part, verbal or physical, will be con-strued as connecting him with Pollard's death."

I pushed, "But is he?"

Ziegler spoke with an official tone. "There's no hard evidence. He's a good prospect in theory. But no D.A. would charge him on the basis of that alone." He softened his tone. "Wanting him to be guilty won't get the job done, Lexy."

"And what about Stacy! Even if he never touched her, the kind of man he was pushed her into being where she was that night." I trusted that he knew the anger in my voice wasn't directed at him.

"But that isn't something a policeman...or the law can hold him accountable for. Even her own mother didn't. But then Gloria Driscoll doesn't strike me as the kind to face up to truth very well. We all have prob-lems with the truth sometimes."

I didn't like the sound of that and, a bit childishly I knew, sought to deflect it. "And how *are* things on your home front, Detective?"

He grunted a laugh. "Remarkably well due to you. I think my daughter and me owe you a good dinner."

I resisted my urge to correct the grammar. "Don't think I won't take you up on that."

I concluded the call and then punched in Chrissy's new agency number from a card I had palmed on my way out. When I was put through and iden-tified myself, I could tell by the forced politeness that someone else was in her office.

"I know I said I wouldn't bother you any more, Chrissy. But I have to talk to Janel. And she will want to hear what I have to say. Tell her to meet me at Leather Fever as soon as she gets off work."

Coldly Chrissy said she would pass on my message but that she could not guarantee anything.

My next call was to Jodi's answering machine. I left essentially the same message with her.

I had carried in what I was beginning to think of as my 'suspect' note-book. I scraped off some dirt with a fingernail, wishing that the whole busi-ness of Darla Pollard's death was over with and I could throw it away. But a tougher part of me, the reporter part maybe, wanted to be in on the con-clusion, the resolution, the determination of guilt.

I flipped pages and scrutinized the names I had copied from Ziegler's notebook. Something kept drawing me back to them. I rammed paper into the old manual typewriter I had kept from my high school days. I copied them out carefully onto a sheet of paper, making a list.

Barbara MacFadden had just risen from her chair, facing me as I entered her cubicle. Her deep blue eyes registered a minimal reaction to the condition of my face, but she voiced no comment. Nor did anything about her indicate any change in our *Ledger* relationship despite the pleasant evening at The Billet.

I handed her my list requesting a check of each name, similar to my previous requests. "Just bare bones information will do, Barbara." I backed away, wondering if I had overstepped my first name privilege since we were at work.

"I will be thorough as always."

I nodded docilely and turned to go.

"Lexy—"

I smiled with relief. "Yes?"

"Ice packs for the first twenty-four hours, followed by the application of warm, moist heat. If the blow was especially severe, the discoloration may spread to the other eye. Ice may deter that." She reseated herself and clicked on her computer.

Unsure whether or not she could see my reflection on her computer screen, I did my best to imitate the precision salutes I had seen at The Billet. Then, a bit afraid of her reaction, I turned tail and ran.

Out in my car, I checked the time and was surprised that it was barely past noon. I gripped the steering wheel and straight-armed myself back against the seat. I couldn't tell if I was trying to think or not think. Janel and Jodi would have to wait until late this afternoon. Driscoll was safely in jail.

Why not?—I started the car and headed for the furniture store employing Gloria Driscoll. There had to be more she could tell me—or reveal unwittingly.

I managed to get to the counter in the back without being intercepted by a salesperson. A clerk put her hand over the mouthpiece of the phone, and asked pleasantly how she could help me. She told me Gloria Driscoll was taking her lunch break in the back and would be on the floor in about fifteen minutes. I agreed to wander about looking at things until that time.

As soon as she was sufficiently engaged in her phone conversation again, I slipped down the cluttered hallway to the lounge. Without hesitation, I opened the door and entered. Shoes off, apparently as usual, Gloria was curled up in the pool chair looking immeasurably forlorn. I could have pitied her if I weren't so outraged at her failure to stand up for her daughter.

"Mrs. Driscoll…Gloria…we need to talk again." I took a corner of the

175

uncomfortable, plastic-covered sofa and leaned toward her. I couldn't tell if her consternation was at recognizing or not recognizing me, or a reaction to my black eye. "Your husband attacked me last night outside The Cat."

She buried her face in her hands, then shifted them away from her mouth and said, "I know. That woman detective Exline came to the house last night. I have to go see Detective Ziegler when I get off work." She removed her hands from her face and straightened in the chair. There was a listlessness about her. I almost missed the erratic movements.

I kept my voice low and even. "It might help if you went over things with me first. A private talk...not for anyone else. I've learned how your husband treated Stacy—"

She came forward to the edge of the chair and her stockinged feet slapped down hard on the floor. "He did not molest her! It wasn't at all like that." I thought she would hide her face again but she stared at me a long while. Then it all came spilling out...quietly, unemotionally.

"The night my daughter died in that old car of ours I was trying to help her. Not soon enough, I know. It was a small thing that brought it all out in the front. I was letting dinner get cold because Edward was late. Stacy objected, and then she went on to other things I did in his favor, and...and then all of a sudden she was telling me how she really felt about him. How restricted her life was. How she felt like he would never let her be who she was. Said she didn't even know who she was. That sometimes he drained everything out of her. That other times he tried to fill her with his way of seeing things."

Her voice was so thin that I thought a sound from me would shatter it. A slight hesitation and she continued, "I don't want to believe that I already knew, but there is a dark place inside of me. I don't want to go inside that darkness. I'm afraid I'll find a person there who was glad for the little freedom I had because of his concentrating so on Stacy." She slumped back into the chair. "Then she told me she was going to go live with someone else. I tried to reason with her."

That was too much for me. "Reason with her! Maybe your daughter wasn't being raped physically by your husband but she was being raped emotionally. She was his prisoner. Where were you?!"

Gloria Driscoll appeared to strengthen. "I know I failed her! After she ran out of the house and drove off, even the silence accused me. When Edward came home, I lied to protect her. I said I had sent her out to return some gifts from Christmas." Her face held a pleading look. "It was a first step."

Part of me wanted to grant her that. I tried to sound more compassionate. "I don't mean to judge you. And I know that Stacy's death is a pain that will never fade. But you still owe her something. Even if it's just facing the truth and acting on it." This was a path I hadn't meant to walk. Maybe it was those years of trying to help adolescents sort through the chaos.

"I know that, too. That nice Detective Exline is going to tell me some people to contact for help. She even said there were places I could go if I didn't want to stay with Edward. "

"That's good advice." I risked shifting the direction of our conversation. "Tell me about talking with Darla Pollard in The Cat."

I got the long look again from dull eyes that seemed to recede. She said, "Edward was obsessed with blaming her for Stacy's death. It went back to when the school let Stacy get involved with a special program that helped her get some on-the-job training." Gloria Driscoll drew her feet up under her again. "But he didn't make a bad fuss until Stacy started working part-time for Miss Pollard that summer and getting some pay for it. He didn't like her having money that didn't come from him. Said she was too young."

I bit my lip to stay silent. I knew that keeping Stacy financially dependent was part of Driscoll's needs. I was surprised he let his wife work. But, looking at her, I realized he would never fear her developing an independent streak.

Gloria continued, but almost as though she were talking to the floor, "It was going to that Chamber of Commerce banquet honoring businesses and teens that did it. After the meal and before the awards, Edward went to the restroom. When he came back, everyone was milling around, and Stacy was off talking to another teenager." She touched her left arm. "He grabbed me hard and whispered what he had heard in the restroom. Two men had been talking about Darla Pollard, and called her a bull-dyke business woman. And they named some of the homosexual places she had coverage on."

Finally she looked at me. "He wanted us all to leave right then, but things were getting started. And there were men he knew and who had congratulated him on Stacy being picked for an award. I was scared to death when all four of us had to go up front to get certificates."

I remembered the picture. Edward Driscoll's grim face and his grip on Stacy. I said, "How did Stacy manage to keep working for Pollard?"

"That picture being in the paper, I think. And people's compliments. And I think Stacy kind of dug her heels in. Or maybe she bargained with him. When I tried to get her to do some of the senior class things, she said she didn't want to, and Edward acted pleased about it."

I raged inside. I wanted another round with Driscoll, maybe with Janel as a backup. And I wanted to hit out at his wife, too. But I needed information more than satisfaction. I tried to direct the conversation again. "Was your husband in The Cat on purpose that night looking for Pollard?"

She stared at me so hard that I thought she was looking through me to other things. At last she said, "Stacy dying across the street from the office convinced Edward that it had to be that woman's fault. And I was afraid to tell him my part in it. I couldn't even say it to myself. I knew he called her, and I thought he went to her office, maybe even her home. He told me the things he said. They were terrible. I don't know why she didn't call the police."

I knew why. Gloria Driscoll went back to talking to the floor. "He nearly tore up Stacy's room trying to find something connected with Miss Pollard he could use for an attack. Then I came home from working into the evening not long ago and found him sitting in the dark. When I turned on a light and saw what was in his hand..." She rubbed her forehead with tense fingers. Thanks to Robbie Exline, I knew where this was going. "We have a couple of storage closets in the house. Edward uses one and I use the other. He had gone through mine and found some letters and...and books. I always knew I should destroy them, but they were special. They were from...from a woman who had been a really good friend to me once." She tried to look at me but couldn't. "Her letters were so gentle, and meant so much...so much *to me*."

The hot dryness of her eyes was worse than tears. "I'll never repeat to anyone what he said to me. And he said it so coldly. He even read from the books and the letters aloud. I wished I had left the lights off. He was angry, saying that I must have passed on a bad seed to Stacy. That I was probably as much to blame for her death as Darla Pollard."

Just as I was thinking I would never get answers to the questions I was asking, she said, "We were in The Cat that night because Edward was tormenting me by taking us around to places like that. And he did it with that other couple along so I couldn't show how I really felt. So that I had to smile and pretend and laugh with them. When she rushed by our table, Edward saw her. He started talking viciously. For a second I hated her for coming in there! I was afraid he was going to really lose control, and maybe start in on me again...but in front of other people this time. Then I got worried that he might do her real harm, even though he wasn't a violent man."

Her eyes flew to my face and she winced. "Suddenly I felt like I was coming out of a fog. I realized that woman had tried to help Stacy. Done what I should have. So I decided to try to talk to her. To warn her."

Gloria Driscoll seemed to draw into herself with the remembering, but there was a whispering inside me, cautioning me to remember that she had had years of practice adjusting her behavior to the demands of others. It was entirely possible that she saw me as another heavy to be appeased.

"Gloria…" I spoke more gently than I felt.

She stirred and continued, glancing at me now and then. "I knocked on the first door without a sign on it. Some strange looking girl opened it and kind of dodged around me. Miss Pollard was glaring after her and then looked upset to see me. But I went in and told her about Edward being out front. I told her I didn't feel the way he did. And we talked. We even cried together about Stacy. It wasn't so much that it helped, but I felt less alone."

She began talking faster. "She told me about Edward coming to her office late that afternoon and making threats. And that it was hard for her to deal with him because she was gay…even though that didn't have anything to do with her trying to help Stacy. I said I didn't know how to get him to stop." She brightened a little. "But I did stop him from going back there. And I got him to leave that place."

"Did you go home together? Is there any way he could have slipped back to The Cat to see Pollard on his own?" I could hear Ziegler cautioning me that wanting Driscoll guilty wouldn't make it so.

"We took the other couple home, then went home ourselves. I wanted to tell him what Miss Pollard said about why Stacy was sitting in the car so long with it running." Her whole body tensed. "But I was still too bothered by it myself." She plucked at her hair. "It was hard being with him and not knowing how not to be with him. I was glad when he turned on the television and didn't fuss when I said I was going to bed."

"And when did you find out Darla was dead?"

"The newspaper article about someone being found dead at The Cat. I was so worried. I wanted to know it wasn't her, couldn't be her, so I called the owner, Marilyn Neff." She looked at me plaintively. "For a second I was almost glad. Stacy wouldn't have died if she hadn't gone to see that woman and had to wait out in the cold."

I suppressed the retort I wanted to make. In less than a minute, she had cast Darla Pollard as both saint and sinner. Instead I shifted in readiness to get up, and managed to remove the bracelet from my pocket. I got up from the sofa, took two steps, then knelt down by her chair. I reached under from the side, then stood with the bracelet dangling from a finger. "You drop this?"

She darted a glance at it. "Oh, no. I never wear loose jewelry. It just gets in the way."

I said, "I'll give it to the woman out front." I paused at the door and turned back to her. "Let Exline channel you toward that help." Her weak nod made me wonder if she would.

CHAPTER TWENTY-THREE

I wanted to be at the Leather Fever before Jodi or Janel arrived and I knew that opening time was four. When I drove into the parking lot, it was empty. Slowly I drove past the front of the building, then parked and settled back in my seat to wait the few minutes until it opened.

When a figure blocked the sunlight, I looked up. I couldn't help admiring the serene features of C. K. Chen. Though I had gone home to change, her cool appraisal of me as I climbed out of the car made me wish I had done better than my favorite broadcloth and brushed denim.

The provocative Miss Chen could just have stepped off a pirate ship. All she needed was a knife between her teeth or a sabre at her side. Tight suede pants, a midnight blue, disappeared into the wide cuffs of zippered black boots. Her diaphanous mauve shirt was open at the throat.

Her eyes didn't even flicker at my bruised face as she said, "Lexy? Right? You're running early—business or pleasure?"

I opened my mouth but couldn't formulate an answer since neither was true. We walked together to the entrance. The dim interior was lit only by the glow of garish beer signs.

I took a seat at the bar while C. K. went behind it. I liked the feel of the big room, empty, waiting for the rush and crush of bodies.

"Bourbon," she said. "With Perrier…three cubes of ice."

"I thought you didn't—"

She interrupted. "I stock it now. Knew you'd be back. Zen…or maybe it's more a matter of *jen*."

I didn't know if I was being teased or not and made no response. Even though it was early, I appreciated the drink. The past twenty-four hours had been a shifting kaleidoscope of emotions. The still barroom was soothing. C. K. dropped out of sight. I heard the opening and closing of some kind of compartment door. She got up with a stiff, blue-gel ice pack in her hand. Without a word, she wrapped it in a thin towel and handed it to me.

I held it to my eye and face. "You been talking to the Iron Maiden?"

She cocked an eyebrow questioningly.

"Never mind. Thank you. This feels good."

The whiskey-voiced bartender came in wearing a red jumpsuit, gold sandals, and a woven leather headband. She nodded to me, then began checking her work area as she and C. K. talked shop.

I sipped my drink and applied the ice pack. After awhile I drifted toward a pool table. For about forty-five minutes I played games of eightball against myself, contentedly lost in the precise geometry of pocketing balls.

I walked back toward the bar with my empty glass and could tell C. K. was instructing her bartender how to prepare my drink. I put a ten on the bar and said, "For both." She placed four ones in front of me and I accepted three. I sat angled to watch the door and the slow gathering of early arrivals, occasionally holding the ice pack to my face. Eventually someone fed the jukebox and I could feel the steam of the evening beginning to rise.

At one point, after a general sweep of the room, I turned my attention back to the door, and discovered Janel standing just inside watching me. I swiveled around, crossing my arms on the smooth padding of the bar front and waited. I felt rather than saw her take the seat next to me.

She said, "Nothing," to the bartender's query. To me she said, "I'm not staying long." As I looked at her full face, her eyes widened. "Chrissy said you had a shiner. I told you to take up karate." Her tone hardened. "What do you want, Lexy?"

I placed the bracelet between us. "I found this in a mop pail where Darla was killed. Chrissy says this isn't hers."

Even in the din of the bar, I heard the long breath escaping her. Her voice broke as she said, "It's not. She always wears the ones I gave her. This isn't one of them."

Janel watched me replace the bracelet in my pocket. In a pitch almost too low for me to hear above the music and bombarding chatter, she said, "Jodi wears bracelets. Always made a big thing of taking them on and off at karate." My stiffening must have registered. "I'm sorry, Lexy. But she was back there. And more than once."

I grabbed her forearm and she made no move to shake me off. "Tell me the truth for once, Janel. And all of it."

She nodded. Picking up my drink, I released her arm and gulped down the last swallow. I shoved the glass away, but didn't turn toward her.

Janel turned and leaned toward me. "I followed Darla into The Cat and saw Jodi talking to you at the bar. I stayed behind people and just watched. When that woman you call the Admiral came back from wherever she took Darla, and Jodi went to dance, I went looking. Found her in that office with the ship models. And we talked like I already told you." I gave her a strong glare. "Okay. We argued. But I left and that other woman came in."

"That was Gloria Driscoll," I said. "Where did you go then?"

"I went to the restroom. I wanted to think before I went back out to Chrissy. Jodi was in the other stall, maybe the one with the broken toilet. The water was running and running."

"How do you know it was her?"

Impatience raised Janel's voice. "Because I recognized those fancy embossed boots she wears a lot. I didn't want her to see me, so I went in a stall to outwait her. And that took awhile. I think she was waiting for some reason, too. Finally she left. I stayed where I was trying to decide if I wanted another go at Darla. I was really pissed at the way she tore into Christine all the time. I wanted more from her." She stopped as though weighing the next information.

I spoke firmly, "No more lies, Janel."

"I'm not going to. The next bit isn't easy. I came out of the restroom, and went back to that office. I didn't knock or anything. Just opened the door and walked in. No one was there. Then I heard a heavy door shutting, and I rushed to that exit door going into the alley. Thought Darla might have gone out that way. But I heard someone coming from the bar, a man's voice, saying he'd check on the noise. So I opened the closest door to hide."

I gave her a hard look of disbelief.

"Come on, Lexy. I didn't fit in The Cat. Figured it wasn't a good idea to be caught in that hallway or going out the side door." She brought a hand up to her mouth. "I just about fell over somebody. It was Darla. I don't know what kept me from yelling. Even with nothing but a low-watt bulb in there, I knew she was dead."

"And you were scared that Chrissy was involved."

"Not right then. I was just worried about me being caught someplace I didn't belong. I didn't want to be found with *her* in there. Later I got to thinking about my truck being parked right at the end of the alley. And Chrissy seemed relieved when I said I didn't see Darla. And there was this feeling she wasn't telling me everything…" She ran a hand through her hair and gripped the shiny mane. "Then when one of her bracelets was missing, I got scared she had come in that side door looking for us…maybe run into Darla…dropped the bracelet…you can see…"

I could see. I knew how I felt every time something drew one of my friends closer to the whirlpool that was Darla Pollard's murder. "You said Jodi was back there more than once?"

"Yeah. I waited until the hallway got good and quiet again. Then I peeked out real careful. Saw Jodi. She just stood there a little while, and I could see her moving the toe of one boot just a tiny bit back and forth. When we used to have run-ins, that was the only sign I was getting her goat. So I knew something wasn't right with her."

I knew she was on the mark about the toe business, and hated it. "How did you end up in the restroom again?"

Janel bit her lip. "As soon as the hallway was clear again, I was going to try to slip out that side door. But I made the mistake of looking back at Darla. Those eyes were looking right at me. I could feel the vomit coming. So I bolted for the restroom. I was sitting in a stall trying to catch my breath when I heard somebody bring the plumber in. I lifted both my feet up and stayed quiet. Couple of people came in and checked on him while he worked. I stayed put. He didn't take long. After he left, I decided I had to get out of there no matter what. That's when I ran into you. I heard that big blonde bartender scream as I was going up the steps to get out the front."

Despite all the noise and commotion around us, we both sat wrapped in the silence of our own thoughts. Janel touched my shoulder lightly. "I want to get to Christine." She slid from the stool, then tapped my shoulder again. "Lexy…"

I looked at her and she tilted her head toward the door. Jodi had just entered. Janel moved toward the exit, passing her without speaking.

Jodi, rakishly attractive in a simple denim suit, took the stool just vacated by Janel. "She's not speaking to me, I see."

"She has things on her mind."

Jodi smiled with her lips but her eyes were cool, measuring. "And you, my friend, what's on your mind? I would have thought it would be Wren Carlyle." She reached out and touched three fingers to my lips as I jerked my head to face her. "Shhh…don't hiss at me. She's an impressive woman. The two of you were a nice fit when you were dancing. And I already know from the Admiral that she's not responsible for that—" And she skimmed my bruises with her fingertips.

The reds, oranges, and golds of the bar signs highlighted her hair and floated in her eyes. I didn't love her—maybe I never had—but I cared about her.

I responded, "No. Nothing's wrong there. In truth, Jodi, I want very much to pursue that relationship. But I need to close…close this Darla thing first."

"You didn't even know her, Lexy."

"But I know all the rest of you. Or I've come to know…like Janel and Chrissy." I curved my hand about her wrist. "Clean the slate for me, Jodi.

You were supposed to talk with Darla that night. Chrissy asked you to."

Jodi called to the bartender, "Vodka, on the rocks." Then, to me. "You're right. But I didn't really plan to. Oh, I told Chrissy I would. But the more I thought about the pathetic, accidental way Stacy Garrison died…if Darla had just let her wait in the office…" She gripped my wrist with the other hand. "Ah, Lex, you know thinking about death's never been my strong suit. I didn't want to see Darla…let alone talk to her."

"But you did see her."

"I couldn't believe it when she came tearing into The Cat. When I went to the restroom and heard the arguing coming from Marilyn's office, I wasn't planning on any contact. But I was curious about what was going on. I sat in that stall with the running toilet for awhile, trying to decide."

She removed her hand from my wrist and I relinquished hers. She blinked, and cleared her throat after a swallow of raw vodka.

I prompted, "And…?"

"And I decided to go about my business. I went back to dancing. But after a time I realized I wasn't going to be able to enjoy my own evening if I didn't get her off my mind." Chagrin coated her tone. "And I knew Chrissy would check. She's hard to let down. So I went back to the office. She wasn't there. There wasn't anyone anywhere."

I thought about Janel watching from the supply closet. "And the next morning with Chrissy at Darla's office?"

"I was just admitting that I hadn't gotten around to seeing Darla yet. Damn it, Lexy, I didn't even know she was dead." She was breathing heavily and her eyes were a hard cold brown.

I asked, "Why all that rigmarole you fed me?"

Everything about her seemed to soften…to relax. "Like I told you before. I didn't like the detour I had taken with Darla. I didn't want any of The Cat people knowing. An ego thing. You know about ego." I acknowledged the hit with a mock salute. She took another swallow of her drink and tossed money next to the half-full glass. "Got to go. Big date."

"Youthful soccer player?" I teased.

"Older soccer coach," she answered back with a grin.

"I saw you with a player last night."

The devilish grin expanded. "The way to the coach is through a player."

"Jodi!"

"Can't be tamed, Lex. You know that." She gripped my shoulder as she stood. "Let all this go, Lexy. Give your attention to the resolute Ms. Carlyle."

I drew the bracelet from my pocket onto the bar. "By the way—is this yours? Alice found it on a table the night of the soccer players. I thought it might be yours. I said I'd bring it to you."

"Thanks…" She fingered it. "No, it isn't mine. Too bad, it's pretty."

I averted my attention to the dance floor to keep from seeing her go. I turned back to the bar and C. K. standing there observing me quietly. "Another drink, Lexy?"

"No. It's time to clear my head and face some things. Thank you."

"You're welcome…here anytime." I nodded my understanding. I sat in my car without starting it, envying the couples and groups descending on Leather Fever while wondering what Wren was doing. The ice pack had helped, but the left side of my face was beginning to throb again. Perhaps it was time to try warm, moist heat. That made me think of the Iron Maiden and what she might have found on the list of names.

I sighed my second 'why not?' of the day and started the car. As I drove to *The Ledger*, twilight was being driven away by night and I appreciated the battle.

Soon I was shaking my head in awe at the efficiency of Barbara MacFadden. A neat stack of computer sheets were waiting for me. I began sorting through them. Most were bland references to business activities, selections to committees, community recognition. Two were accounts of claims filed against the Pollard Agency for a lack of full disclosure concerning insurance changes. One differed completely from all the others. I put that one in the center of my desk pad, and sought my folder on Pollard. I pulled out a sheet and set it next to the other. I kept staring at one of the names contained in both.

I swallowed, trying to ease a dry mouth. A coldness was spreading through me. I reached for the phone and called The Cat. Melody answered and responded to my question with a puzzled but affirmative answer. I asked another question and received another affirmative answer. I made a request to which she acceded.

Next I called Robbie Exline and caught her just preparing to leave for dinner. I could hear the constraint in my own voice as I said, "I can't explain now, Robbie, but I need you at The Cat. I need you just to blend in out of the way until…until some things are settled."

There was the silence of hesitation, and the formulation of questions. But at last she said simply, "All right, Lexy."

I folded the two sheets of paper and put them in the pocket still containing the bracelet. Quickly I pulled my fingers away from it. About to leave, I stopped and picked up the phone again. This time I called Wren, not sure if I wanted her to answer or not. She did.

"Wren."

"Lexy!" The pleasure in her voice lapped at my ear. I longed to put my head on her shoulder. "I've called you several times today. I was beginning to feel like a lovesick adolescent."

I smiled fleetingly at the incongruous image. "I need you to come to The Cat for me, Wren. To just be there while I…while I…" I could not finish.

The pleasure turned to concern. "I'll leave now."

I drove slowly but too soon pulled into a vacant spot in the front of The Cat. For the first time in my life, the strutting neon feline was not a welcome sight.

Inside it was a typical Friday night. On the dance floor a crowded jam of bodies gyrated beneath moving lights to the thud and twang of acoustic guitars and the rhythmic beat of drums. Among them was Jodi, her height and lithe form an interesting counterpoint to the athletic muscularity of her soccer-coach date. Our eyes ricocheted off each other.

Behind the bar, Hal and Melody skillfully navigated the narrow work space while throughout the lounge servers, trays hoisted high, cruised among the tables. Watching Alice drop off drinks, I saw her deposit one at a table to my left, in a darkened corner. Robbie Exline nodded a 'thank you' and then looked up to acknowledge the appearance of Marilyn, who remained standing, one hand at rest on the back of the detective's chair. I locked eyes with Robbie for an instant, but avoided meeting those of the Admiral.

My heart lurched at the sight of Wren sharing the corner of the bar with Rita Burgess. The windswept effect of Wren's hair contrasted with Rita's dark swirls. Their heads were nearly touching, and I was ambushed by a pang of jealousy at their easy camaraderie.

I approached the bar, and stood at the corner between the two women. I delighted in the slide of Wren's arm about my waist, and placed my left hand over hers to hold it there. Tension had made my hands cold and I felt her flinch at my touch. Would she flinch also at my desire to pursue and unravel Darla Pollard's murder? I saw the concern and confusion in her face in the mirror behind the bar.

Rita said, "Wren was just telling me about last night, Lexy. Are you all right?"

I answered, "What's the phrase? Bloody but unbowed. I'm a little stiff and sore, but all right. Biggest problem is staying nice to all the teasing."

Both women laughed their understanding. Melody started toward us but, at the imperceptible shake of my head and narrowed eyes, she detoured by us. Barely fifteen seconds later I caught Hal's eye and nodded to the empty bar in front of me.

Wren withdrew her arm and sipped her own drink. I felt the questioning below her silence.

There was a sheen of sweat on Hal's upper lip, and his jowls sagged, but his voice was steady as he said, "That all right, Lexy?"

I knew by the direction of his gaze that he was asking about Marilyn hovering over Robbie Exline in the far corner. I touched his fingers, still curved about the glass he had just placed before me. "I feel good about it, Hal. I believe there is a shared interest there."

Gruff emotion deepened his voice. "Never been able to look after her like I wanted. And now...I just want things to be right for her." He moved off.

Rita spoke softly with sadness. "I don't know if I can keep on coming here. I can't bear to watch him fade and falter."

Wren reached across me to touch Rita's hand, tightening around her wineglass, much as I had Hal's. "No, Rita. Don't retreat again. Along with the taking away, there are gifts."

I didn't dare look at Wren despite the risk of her misunderstanding. I felt the withdrawal of her arm.

Then there was the pressure of fingers trailing down my spine and the scent of Jodi. I looked at her in the mirror, uncomfortably aware that Wren was toying with her glass, and keeping her head down. I ached to cup Wren's chin in my hand and turn her face to me.

Jodi jerked her head back and to the side. "The Admiral is certainly being attentive. Do you suppose that cop is going to become a permanent fixture here?"

"That cop is Detective Roberta Exline, as you well know. And she's an okay person. "

"A bit touchy, aren't we, Lex?" Jodi's eyes went from mine in the mirror to Wren's hand touching my shoulder as Wren turned to look directly at the woman she knew to have been my former lover.

The assertive timbre of Wren's voice thrilled me as she said, "I'd call it a desirable sensitivity."

Still watching in the mirror, I saw Jodi's cold smile yield to a rakish grin. Challenging Wren with an unblinking stare, she tugged at the spot where my ducktail ought to have been—a gesture of old intimacy that Wren wasn't party to yet, and I heard the clink of her bracelets. She said lightly, "See you around, Lex."

Rita swirled the little wine left in her glass. "Strong vibrations tonight."

The tightness in my chest nearly immobilized me. It took painfully concentrated effort for me to remove the lovely bracelet from my pocket and place it next to Rita's wine glass. Then everything else ceased to be. There was only the gleam of the bracelet and the long, slow sigh escaping from Rita that seemed to sap her of all strength and resiliency.

She reached to touch it, and two others slid down her forearm to the wrist. "Where?" she asked in a voice bereft of emotion.

"In a mop pail in the supply room." I felt Wren's hand leave my shoulder and, despite the noise all around us, I could hear her gasp.

I unfolded the two pieces of paper and spread them out near the bracelet. Each contained the name Delores Newcome. My call earlier to Melody had confirmed that Dee, the only name by which I knew Rita's partner, was indeed Delores. And Melody had confirmed that Rita was at The Cat. I had asked her to keep her there if necessary.

"Lexy..." I could hear the pleading in Wren's tone. I steeled myself against it.

Rita touched the piece of paper describing claims against the Pollard Agency for insurance improprieties. She said in a voice swimming in pain, "She never notified Dee of changes in insurance regulations that permitted her carrier to refuse coverage for certain very expensive procedures. They might have meant several more years of a decent life for her...for us. It was decided that her failure was not criminal. She was merely reprimanded. Dee died."

She looked at me with dark eyes awash in unshed tears. Then she picked up the obituary that Barbara MacFadden had placed on my desk just this afternoon. "When Darla Pollard came in here two weeks ago, it was the anniversary of Dee's death. I was holding my own private wake. I couldn't be alone that night. But I couldn't be with anyone either."

I stepped back to the previous weekend—into Rita's booth at the craft fair. I heard her saying, "I have a thing about dates, celebrations, anniversaries..."

Her hand began to tremble, and I took the obituary from her, returning it to my pocket. She continued in a monotone. "Hal spilled my wine on me and I went back to wash it out. When I came out of the restroom, I heard arguing coming from Marilyn's office. All of a sudden I wanted to confront Darla, too. I knew there was no value in it. I just needed to do it. I didn't want to barge in on whoever was there, and Jodi Fleming had gone in the restroom as I came out...so I slipped in that supply room to wait."

Rita was silent for a moment, and Wren leaned her head against my arm. I reached for her hand and was grateful for the warmth of her grip. In a choked whisper, I said, "Rita—"

"Let me get this said, Lexy. Darla Pollard and I stepped out into the hall at the same time. She started to walk past me going to the side exit. I could tell she didn't recognize me. I stopped her and identified myself as Delores Newcome's friend. That didn't mean anything to her either. I said something about how could she share blame for someone's death and not even remember her? She flew into a rage. Pushed me back into the supply room and closed the door. She was shaking with fury. Said she was tired of everyone accusing her. That other people dying wasn't her problem. That the only dying she was going to worry about from now on was her own."

I took my hand from Wren's and turned toward Rita. I wanted to enfold her in my arms, but her stoicism was a chasm I didn't know how to cross.

Rita went on, "Something happened inside me. She turned to leave and I grabbed a broom and swung it against her neck with all the strength I had. She pulled it out of one hand. Probably that's when I lost the bracelet. But I got a new grip and pulled her tight against me with the broom handle under her chin while she struggled. It took an eternity but I just couldn't stop. Then she went limp...and I let her go. I had to step over her to get out. When I saw the broom still in my hand I realized what I had done. I cleaned my fingerprints off it with with a cleaning rag...as if that would undo—"

She choked and shook her head, but went on. "The hallway was clear so I went out the side door. Tossed the broom. Went home."

I felt as though Rita, Wren, and I were the only reality. The colorful tableau reflected in the bar mirror was a fabrication for someone else's amusement. Any second the figures would all wind down, the sounds would diminish, the scene fade.

Rita swept my face with a gentle glance, then stroked my cheek with a feather-soft touch. "It's all right, Lexy. I knew this was coming. And it's easier coming from you." She looked past me to Wren. "She'll need you tonight, Wren. Be there for her."

Wren's arm encircled my waist again, and I felt the dichotomy of bleeding anguish and breathing joy. I had closed Darla Pollard's dead eyes. I closed my own eyes against tears. In a moment I would motion to Robbie... Rita would go with her... Then I would the seek the healing comfort of Wren's body, daring to hope she would still give it to me.

Yes, I had my story. All I had to do was file it. Would I dare admit at what price? How painful a success?

OTHER MYSTERIES AVAILABLE FROM NEW VICTORIA

PO BOX 27, NORWICH, VT 05055 Phone/fax 1-800-326-5297

MURDER IN THE CASTRO A Lou Spencer Mystery— Elaine Beale
Lou Spencer finds a counselor for victims of gay bashings stabbed to death
in his office, and her co-worker is arrested for the murder. As the Castro
community reacts in outrage, Lou is left trying to hold the besieged agency
together while falling in love with a beautiful lesbian cop. $10.95

NO DAUGHTER OF THE SOUTH — Cynthia Webb
Laurie Coldwater returns to her Florida hometown and the white southern
roots she has soundly rejected. Her black lover, Samantha, has persuaded
Laurie to look into the truth surrounding her father's death. Her investigation
turns ugly when she finds herself confronting the local KKK. $10.95

CEMETERY MURDERS — Jean Marcy
Dyke PI, Meg Darcy has the hots for Sarah Lindstrom, a city detective. Their
paths cross at a St. Louis cemetery where a serial killer has left the bodies of
homeless women. Conflict and competition dominate their erotic entangle-
ment, as both Meg and Sarah strive to be the first to find the killer. $10.95

TWIST OF LIME A Lynn Evans Mystery — Claudia McKay
Lynn goes to coastal Belize to help on a Mayan archeological dig where a
volunteer dies mysteriously. Lynn probes for answers among drug dealers
and artifact thieves, while wondering if she can trust Ivette, the most seductive of Ann's supposed friends. $10.95

JUST A LITTLE LIE An Alison Kaine Mystery—Kate Allen
Cool characters, kinky sex and a neat little plot twist. Alison was a cop too
long to ignore the undercurrent of malice and deception under the bantering
and blatant sexuality of a Wildfire conference. Can she uncover old feuds
and secrets—or will someone go home as cargo? $12.95

TELL ME WHAT YOU LIKE An Alison Kaine Mystery—Kate Allen
Introducing Alison Kaine, lesbian cop, who enters the world of leather-
dykes after a woman is murdered at a Denver bar. In this fast-paced, yet
slyly humorous novel, Allen confronts the sensitive issues of S/M, queer-
bashers and women-identified sex workers. $9.95
Allen's well-written murder mystery sports a heart-pounding ending.—Booklist

TAKES ONE TO KNOW ONE An Alison Kaine Mystery—Kate Allen
Denver cop Alison Kaine and her delightfully eccentric circle of friends
travel to a women's spirituality retreat in New Mexico, where Alison dis-
covers the dead body of a lesbian "shaman" in the sweat lodge. $10.95

I KNEW YOU WOULD CALL A Marta Goicochea Mystery—Kate Allen
Phone psychic Marta investigates the murder of a client with the help of her
outrageous butch cousin Mary Clare. Marta, using her psychic insights,
struggles to get to the deeper truths surrounding the killing. $10.95

OUTSIDE IN — Nanisi Barrett D'Arnuk
A suspenseful prison thriller. Cop Cameron Andrew infiltrates a women's
prison to expose drug trafficking. During preparation, Cam meets Michael,
a seductive female trainer. $10.95

SEVEN STONER McTAVISH MYSTERIES BY SARAH DREHER

STONER McTAVISH

The first introduces us to travel agent Stoner McTavish. On a trip to the Tetons, Stoner meets and falls in love with her dream lover, Gwen, whom she must rescue from danger and almost certain death. $9.95

SOMETHING SHADY

Investigating the mysterious disappearance of a nurse at a suspicious rest home on the Maine coast, Stoner becomes an inmate, trapped in the clutches of the evil psychiatrist Dr. Milicent Tunes. Can Gwen and Aunt Hermione charge to the rescue before it's too late? $8.95

GRAY MAGIC

After telling Gwen's grandmother that they are lovers, Stoner and Gwen set off to Arizona to escape the fallout. But a peaceful vacation turns frightening when Stoner finds herself an unwitting combatant in a struggle between the Hopi spirits of Good and Evil. $9.95

A CAPTIVE IN TIME

Stoner is inexplicably transported to a small town in Colorado Territory, time 1871. There she encounters Dot, the saloon keeper, Blue Mary, a local witch/healer, and an enigmatic teenage runaway named Billy. $10.95

OTHERWORLD

All your favorite characters—business partner Marylou, eccentric Aunt Hermione, psychiatrist, Edith Kesselbaum, and of course, devoted lover, Gwen, on vacation at Disney World. In a case of mistaken identity, Marylou is kidnapped and held hostage in an underground tunnel. $10.95

BAD COMPANY

A Maine B&B resort, summer home to a feminist theatre troupe, experiences mysterious and ever more serious "accidents." An intricate, entertaining plot, with delightfully witty dialogue.　　paperback　　$10.95
　　　　　　　　　　　　　　　　　　　　　　　　　hardcover　　$19.95

SHAMAN'S MOON

In the sleepy little New Age town of Shelburne Falls, dark forces are afoot, hungry ghosts with Aunt Hermione as their prey. Stoner must stop them before it is too late. But how can you stop an enemy you can't find? Stoner faces her worst fears. $12.95

SOLITAIRE AND BRAHMS A Novel

The early '60s—Young career woman, Shelby Camden wonders why her engagement and impending marriage seem to constrict her to the point of depression and drink. She meets her new neighbor, the independent Fran Jarvis, with whom she finds she can share her innermost thoughts.This is a gritty, painstaking look at the struggle for lesbian identity before Stonewall. $12.95

Order from New Victoria Publishers,
PO Box 27 Norwich VT 05055
Or write for free Catalogue